THE CANNON AND THE QUILL

BOOK 3: TO BE A PROPER PYRATE

BY THE SAME AUTHOR

The Cannon and the Quill, Book One: We All be Jacobites Here*

The Cannon and the Quill, Book Two: Princes of the World*

Three Gothic Doctors and Their Sons*

Jester-Night (Book 1 of the Ambir Dragon Tales)

Minor Confessions of an Angel Falling Upward*

Watch Out For the Hallway: Our Two-Year Investigation of the Most Haunted Library in North Carolina (with Tonya Madia)

Roommates from Beyond: How to Live in a Haunted Home (with Tonya Madia)

*Part of the Stanton Chronicles

THE CANNON AND THE QUILL

BOOK 3: TO BE A PROPER PYRATE

PART OF THE STANTON CHRONICLES

JOEY MADIA

New Mystics Enterprises
Leavittsburg, Ohio

The Cannon and the Quill Book 3: To Be a Proper Pyrate

ACKNOWLEDGMENTS

Huzzah to Jonathan Edwards and Port City Tour Company/Beaufort Escape Rooms for commissioning the walking tour, stage show, and escape room on which I based this series.

Thanks to North Carolina Maritime Museum, Beaufort Historic Site, Japan's "Passage of Dreams," *North Carolina Travel*, Athens Chatauqua, Handley Regional Library, Ravenwood Faire, and other venues that invite Angus to tell his stories for their audiences.

Cheers to all the pirate re-enactors with whom I have worked. Ye are my true and trusted mates. Lots of rum and coin to ye all!

To Baylus Brooks, Captain Horatio Sinbad, and other historians whose diligence and passion have made it possible for me to steep this story in history while also making it a fantastical journey into the unknown—I offer you my deepest thanks and respect.

To illustrator extraordinaire, Chuck Regan.

To beta reader Richard Copeland, whose knowledge of History and Story made this book better.

Most of all, to my love, my lass, my real-life Ailish. Tonya—There's no one else I'd rather sail 'round the world (or be quarantined) with, especially in Times of Pox and Plague.

DEDICATION

To Eric Vasbinder, my real life Blackbeard.

We have told our stories in many different ways, in many different places.

Cheers and huzzah for the ones still to come.

PART ONE:

'TIS WORTH A BIT A' EFFORT

WINDWARD PASSAGE, MID-FEBRUARY 1717

"**A**re ye awake, Commodore? Ye best be comin' topside, sir! She's the one, sir! She's damn sure the very, very one!"

Am I awake? Samuel Bellamy, the Robin Hood of the Seas, thought. *When am I ever* not *awake...*

So it had been, in the months since he had been elected commodore over the fort at New Providence and, in theory if not quite in practice, of the whole of the considerable fleet in and around the Bahamas.

If he had known the position would come with unrelenting insomnia along with its myriad pressures and constant problems, he might not have agreed.

Not that he had had a choice.

The situation in the Bahamas had been deteriorating from the outset of former commodore Benjamin Hornigold's dream of a Republic of Pirates on the heels of the end of the War of Spanish Succession. Hornigold, who had given Sam opportunities, whom Sam had affectionately called Gran'pa along with the rest, could not bring the warring factions together. Early on, he lost the loyalty of Captains Vane and Jennings, whom Sam had also tussled with on more than one occasion.

The arrival of the strutting, conniving Olivier Levasseur—known in French as La Bouche or La Buse and in English as The Mouth or The Vulture—with whom Sam aligned in the name of a higher cause than the Republic—the reinstatement of James Stuart to the throne of Britain—had heated a simmering pot to a boil.

Levasseur was the one who had pushed for a vote. Who had put forth Sam for election. Who had been the cause of growing friction between Sam and Edward Thache.

And it was Levasseur who had shown Sam—from the moment that Sam had first met with the ancient and secretive Star Quorum in their stronghold on St. Croix—just how fully he could live up to his pair of unflattering nicknames.

Just as Edward had said.

It had begun when, leaving St. Croix, they had decided on Trellis Bay in the Virgin Islands as their winter-long base of operations. From two strategic points—Blanco Islet and Sprat Point—they could lie in wait, undetected, as Spanish galleons and a steady stream of fully loaded merchant ships made their way through the perfectly named Sir Francis Drake Channel.

Drake had been a Devonshire man, same as Sam.

With Trellis Bay offering natural protection for their fleet—which included the *Marianne*, captained by Sam's mentor, friend, and fellow Jacobite Paulsgrave Williams—and the favorable conditions in the channel, Bellamy and Levasseur were soon amassing considerable wealth. A good portion they sent on to St. Croix and to other agents of the rebellion. Another portion went to the fort at New Providence for upkeep and enhanced fortifications, but even so, the men who served beneath La Buse and the Robin Hood of the Seas were content, and their cumulative future was bright.

Then, one morning in late January, just a few weeks ago, Levasseur had come to his cabin and announced that he was taking his two ships, the *Postillion* and the *Oiseau de Proie*, and sailing for the Spanish Main.

He did not offer an explanation, nor did he ask permission, and Sam had not been inclined to press him for either.

In truth, he was relieved.

"I say again, sir! Are ye comin', Commodore? The clouds are gatherin' an' ye will be likely ta miss her iffin' ye delay. I swear ta ye 'tis worth a bit a' effort!"

Resisting the urge to shout back an unkind reply about what might be worth an effort, Sam rubbed his weary eyes and answered, "I shall be there directly, Mister Fletcher"—for he knew the voice of his quartermaster well—"And I have no doubt ye are correct... it will surely be worth the effort."

Ten minutes later, spyglass to his eye and his officers—John Fletcher, quartermaster; William Main, sailing master; and Jeremiah Burke, boatswain—arrayed anxiously around him, Sam let himself smile for the first time in weeks.

Worth the effort indeed.

Through the glass, no more than a few miles off, Sam studied the ship that he had tasked his officers with finding several weeks before.

Well, not this *particular* ship, but one needing to meet a lengthy list of specifications.

This beauty in his spyglass certainly fit the bill.

Not that his current flagship, the *Sultana*, was significantly lacking. Any captain or commodore would be lucky to have her beneath him. With twenty-one guns and a fine trim, the former plantation patrol ship he had captured near St. Croix in late November of the previous year was certainly capable.

Just not capable *enough*. Not for what he had in mind.

This beautiful sight in his spyglass, though. She was quite another matter.

"What say ye, Mister Main—is Mister Fletcher guilty of exaggeration in his praise of the vessel in view before us?"

"Naught a bit, Comm'dore," Mister Main answered, clapping Fletcher on the shoulder. "She is all ye'd want an' more! Plenty a' hold space. High, solid gunnels..."

"And what say ye on the matter, Mister Burke?" he asked his boatswain, enjoying the combined perspectives of his trio of officers.

"Why, sir—just look at 'er! She is every bit of a 'undred feet. Tree-'undred tonne that would make 'er. Capable a'—wit' a few alterations that won't take but a week—eleven knots undah the right conditions."

"An'," Mister Fletcher added, not wishing to be left out of the excitement, "I estimate her at eighteen guns. With our twenty-one, she would be damned near unbeatable."

"Well then," Sam answered, taking the spyglass at last from his eye. "Given her hold space, solid gunnels, length, weight, and speed, and damned near unbeatability... I say we pursue her with all good haste. Inform Captain Williams—we are undertaking the chase!"

QUARRY PEAK PSYCHIATRIC HOSPITAL, A DAY BEFORE THE PRESENT

Kirstine was slipping. Slipping on the ice.

I know I have to run, but I'm slipping on the ice. I think I'm falling through!

PF was right there in her ear, as he increasingly was in recent days. *Bullshit on that, kiddo*, he said, just like her old gymnastics coach when she got butterflies before her floor routine. *This would-be hero needs your help. Don't be dead weight.*

The ice is going to take me. I can't... I CAN'T...

The voice then changed. "Haxx... Shit. *Tino*. You have to help me. Her legs are going to jelly."

Kirstine knew the voice. Which meant that she was dead. Which meant it was her *corpse* that was slipping through the ice, to check into a room in the opposite of Heaven.

Yes... I have to be dead. I HAVE to be... Because Jake is, and I am with him. I'm with JAKE...

Then she heard the klaxons. The blaring horns of Hell.

As she began to fall, the icy waters grabbed her, dragging her into their depths.

It was a little over an hour earlier that Jake Givens—pressed into service by a special division of the FBI despite being the assistant manager of a tourist-trap seafood joint and little-known podcaster—had put on the hospital scrubs and fake ID provided by Tech Specialist Tino "Haxx" Alvarado and entered the highly secure Quarry Peak Psychiatric Hospital.

They were on a mission to rescue Kirstine MacGregor.

Jake's part in the operation was about Kirstine's trust of him. The plan was, he would keep her from freaking out and jeopardizing the mission.

So far, he was failing.

The events of recent weeks danced in Jake's buzzing mind, breaking apart and coalescing as they made their way down a little-used service hallway, the doors to which had been opened by a man they knew only as Abel—dressed in tactical gear and armed with an array of serious weaponry both in his hands and strapped to his torso.

A few days earlier, Abel had saved them from the two thugs who had once beaten Jake badly enough to put him into two hospitals and put him on the radar of the Domestic Threat Early Assessment Unit—

5   To Be a Proper Pyrate

known as DTEAU. Tino, being a friend of Kirstine's, had been the one to make first contact.

Since then, he had rarely left Jake's side.

As Abel proceeded half a hallway ahead of them, disabling cameras and keycode pads with a strange, just a little too long pen that produced a light blue beam of light he aimed at whatever he needed to deal with to keep their presence a secret until the last possible moment, Jake willed his heart to stop his pounding.

If you screw this up, he admonished himself, *Kirstine will never forgive you.*

He would rather die.

It was not until Abel reached a door marked DED37: RETINA SCAN REQUIRED that he stopped, waiting for Tino and Jake to close the gap before saying through a microphone in his helmet into the earbuds they both wore, which plugged into iPod-like devices at their waists, "Far as I go, guys. You are now on your own. According to the schedule procured this morning through Tino's magic keyboard, your gal should be in recovery, left alone for several minutes due to a shift change, second room on the right. I'll be waiting and thinking pleasant thoughts." Pointing his tech-pen at the scanner, he made a few adjustments on the back end of the device, which emitted a deep green beam until the retina scanner clicked off.

"Damn," Jake said, not able to help himself. "That is wicked cool."

"Cease unnecessary chatter," Abel ordered in his earbuds. "Eyes and minds on the mission."

Proceeding through the doors, Jake walked just behind Tino, afraid to make a single decision on his own. Reaching the second room on the right, Jake watched as Tino made the sign of the cross, kissed the crucifix hanging from his neck, and pushed open the door.

Kirstine was there, as she should be, but so was a nurse.

Kirstine also did not look like she was in recovery. Dozens of wires, pads, and needles hooked her arms, head, and chest into a machine like something out of a horror film.

The kind you watched through parted fingers, stifling your screams with your palm.

"Shit," Tino muttered, pulling a pistol from an ankle holster of which Jake hadn't been aware, and using the butt end to strike the nurse—whose face was a snarling howitzer readying to launch a barrage of deadly bullet questions straight at their hearts—square in the temple, causing her to fold upon herself and hit the floor. As she did so, her pale, clawlike hand hit a stainless steel tray of surgical instruments that followed dutifully after her in a cascade of faux Morse code, tapping out, to Tino's ears, "Intruder! Intruder! Something here ain't *right!*"

"Double, triple shit," Tino cursed. "Let's get Kirstine unhooked and get the hell out of here, pronto," he said, already taking hold of an IV in her arm as he spoke.

As alarms began to sound, they worked together—hurriedly but with care—to remove the myriad tubes, needles, and wires embedded in her body. As Tino pulled the last gelled-up pad from her temple, they heard Abel in their earbuds.

"Move it fellas! Another sixty seconds and this mission goes to shit!"

Lifting Kirstine from the chair, they dragged her to the door as she began to mumble about childhood memories to someone they could not see.

The moment Kirstine collapsed against him in the hallway, Jake had felt a wave of nausea hit him from the concussion he had suffered from the thugs. Willing a wave of bile to stay inside his stomach, he had nearly shouted in relief as he felt Tino take Kirstine into his arms.

"Nearly there, Jake," Tino said, shifting Kirstine's weight and breaking into a run. "Abel's just ahead. Keep up with me and we're good."

As if in contrarian answer, the double doors just behind them opened wide, revealing a bear of an orderly with a black billyclub swinging from his wrist who shouted at them with a truckload of pissed-off in his voice to stop. Behind him were three uniformed men with guns.

"Keep moving!" Abel countered. "They aren't going to shoot you. They don't need the mess. And they know they won't survive it."

Wanting to argue, but hardly able to keep up as it was with Tino's pace as his head began to spin, Jake focused on the door where Abel waited, crouched and ready, automatic rifle on his shoulder and a look of determined evil in his eyes.

Past Abel and out the door they ran, climbing into the back of a waiting, already-running box truck, just as they had rehearsed.

As the door came down and the truck began to move, Jake crawled into a corner and let waves of scorching bile flow forth onto the floor.

Turning her eyes to the thick grey clouds above her, Ailish MacDonald willed Cailleach Bheur, the Blue Faced Crone, the bringer of winter storms, to send from the heavens a great gush of snow, that it might cleanse and protect her from the filth that lay panting and grinding upon her.

As had been her habit since the relocation of the clan families loyal to Rob Roy MacGregor from Balquidder to Glen Shira three months prior, she had been sitting in reflective silence beside Loch Fyne when the rank breath of Rob's eldest son, James, was hard upon her neck and his calloused, pink-scarred hands were clawing at her cloak.

"Ailish, mae lass," he had hissed, ripping open the front of her dress as he pushed her down into the hard, frozen ground, "thaer's nae tae protect ya noo. Baest tae lay back an' accept mae gift a' forgiveness. Take it as mae long-overdoo praeposal."

How many minutes had gone by she could not guess. Time stood still. Still as the clouds that held so hard and cold above her, refusing to yield their balm.

"Cailleach Bheur," Ailish screamed inside herself, grasping the frozen grass as an invasive pain began to spread throughout her stomach as James's numb, drunken fingers began to undo his trousers, "if ye wael nae send mae snoo, send mae deep oblivion. If ye haev ye any pity at all, let mae drift away."

Raising his hips to begin, James was, instead of descending, suddenly lifted up and back and Ailish's chest, released of the unwelcome pressure of his grinding bulk, began to heave, forcing needed air into her lungs and triggering her gag reflex. Turning on her side she began to heave up her breakfast as a welcome voice strained to pass the fortification of the pounding blood in her ears.

"Hang fast, mae lass. This filth shall trooble ye nae moor."

Duncan, her cousin and protector, was standing over James, who was pressing his hand to his temple, attempting to stem a steady flow of blood where Duncan had struck him with his fist.

"What did I tell ye, ya numpty roaster, noo moor than a week past? Eh? I raimember the words. Doo ye? 'I weel keel yoo, yoo bastard! Tooch hair again an' see if I jaest.' Doan ye recall? Or did ye think that was nae boot mince?"

Reaching for his claymore, James tried to stand, falling backward immediately, the injury to his head blurring his vision and throwing off his balance.

"I nae took ye serious, Dooncan MacDonald, fer ye air nae boot a *servant*. Mae da is yer *laird*. Lay anoother hand on mae an' I weel take it froom ye troo."

Kicking James's hand away from his claymore, Duncan placed his own upon James's neck, followed by his foot on the now trembling bully's chest.

"Yer da is many things, noot all a' them kind, boot hae weel not condone yer near rapin' a' this lass. Nae today, an' damn sure naever. Yer a damned wolf, ye are, an' by rights I oughta shoot ye. Ye baest bae away froom hair, baefore I keep mae promisin' tae ye of joost a week ago. Awa' an' bile yer heid, ye feartie gowk! Or a single clean shirt weel doo ye. An' doan bae clipin' tae yer da, or I weel make a report a' mae oon."

As James mustered enough strength and balance to stand and turn away—in the opposite direction from home—Duncan was at Ailish's side.

"This is all mae doin', lass. I should haev made a stronger point with James whaen last we maet. How bad bae yer wounds?"

Having managed to gather enough of her dress and cloak to cover herself while Duncan was dealing with James, Ailish leaned into her cousin's shoulder—the shoulder he had favored since his return from the Caribbean eight months earlier.

She was sure he kept a secret in the wound he also hid.

"I haev lost everythin', Dooncan," Ailish whispered, allowing her tears to flow. "Mae sense a' safety, mae honor, mae dignity, mae poor, poor Angus."

Taking her head in his sizable but gentle hands—so unlike James's—Duncan, at last preventing himself from telling another lie he would immediately regret, looked her in the eyes and said, "Nae lass. Ye haev lost nae a single one. *Nae a single one*."

"Doan speak mince tae mae, Dooncan," Ailish said, wiping her eyes with the heels of her hands. "Cailleach Bheur did nae answer mae pleas... She has abandoned mae in this, hair moonth, *Faoilleach*—the moonth a' the wolf—an' I doan baelieve in ghaists."

"Nor doo I, Ailish," Dooncan replied, forcing a smile despite the pit in his stomach at the revealing of what he had hidden for so long. "An' thair bae nae need a' it. Yer Angus is alive. An' I am heartfully soory at haevin' lied tae ye soo long aboot it."

APPLE-TREE TAVERN, CHARLES STREET, LONDON, MID-FEBRUARY 1717

L ord Andrew Colson, son of a ruthless tyrant from Exeter, stared into the eyeholes of the elaborately crafted and surprisingly heavy mask of Horus he was about to place upon his head.

Why the Grand Master, Anthony Sayer, head of the Free Masonic Grand Lodge, had chosen Andrew to portray the falcon-headed son of Osiris and Isis in the Mystery School ritual unfolding in the crowded room was just another minor mystery folded into the larger one. Horus was the protector of pharaohs. Not so long ago, Andrew had betrayed a modern pharaoh of sorts—Lord John Carteret—for whom he had served as second in both the very public Royal African Company and the equally secret Mammon Lodge of London.

Andrew's defection to the Freemasons had led to further betrayals of his former master—for that was what Carteret had been. Another ruthless tyrant like Andrew's father.

He was sick of tyrants. He was sick of darkness.

The Mammon Lodge swam in endless oceans of darkness.

Perhaps that was why Sayer had chosen him for Horus. The Egyptian falcon god was also the symbol of the power and protection of the son.

At the sound of a bull's horn, a door behind the specially designed two-pillared ritual area in this crowded back room of the Apple-Tree Tavern in Covent Garden opened with an auspicious creaking noise that nearly drowned out the horn. In the entrance stood a blindfolded young initiate with a noose—called a cable tow—draped around his neck. As all eyes turned upon him, he was led in and walked around the perimeter of the room by two senior members of the lodge—the former Lord Bolingbroke (who switched sides in the Jacobite rebellion as often as mood and matters suited) and George Payne, an official in the Exchequer.

Andrew knew what would happen next—the symbolism, the oaths, the necessary death and rebirth for those who have traveled from the Darkness and wish to enter the Light.

Tradition held that specially trained priests and their initiates had enacted these Mysteries without notable modification for thousands of years, numbering among their early members no less than Plato, Pythagoras, Iamblichus, Plutarch, and Herodotus.

Had one or more of them worn the Horus falcon head Andrew now placed upon his own? Andrew believed they had.

Even here, ego reared its terrible visage. He fought hard to suppress it.

Grasping a foot-long wooden ankh in his right hand, symbol of life and key to the Mysteries and their ultimate keeper of secrets, the thirty-thousand-year-old solar deity, the Sphinx, Andrew moved slowly toward the space between the two pillars, named Jachin and Boaz, exactly thirty-three feet ahead of him. His timing, which he had rehearsed for several days prior, was exquisite. He arrived between the pillars at the same moment as the blindfolded initiate, whose escorts guided him onto his knees, ready and willing for the Grand Master, who wore the hybrid-animal mask of Osiris's traitor brother Set, to cut him symbolically to pieces, as brother had done to brother in Set's bloody usurpation of the throne.

Sayer, whom the venerated Masonic leaders in Scotland had carefully chosen for his role, stared out through the almond-shaped eyeholes of his mask, a horned and horrific amalgamation of donkey, fox, jackal, aardvark, and giraffe.

As Sayer/Set raised a ritual, blunt-ended knife to usher the initiate into a welcome, wanted death of the soul and grand rebirth in Atlantean, all-engulfing Light, Andrew heard a commotion behind him as the entrance door to the room burst open despite the tavern owner's vigorous protestations directed toward those doing the bursting.

Not removing his mask, Andrew turned to see five well-armed men donning masks of their own—the jackal-headed god of the Underworld, Anubis—push their way through the crowd and join the participants between the pillars.

"Games!" the one in the middle said, pulling a knife from his belt. "If you wish to gather power, if you wish to hear the gods answer with the blood-scream that is their birthright, use a real knife and not that child's plaything!"

Noticing the bone handle of the knife the intruder held, Andrew felt his breath catch in his throat.

Known as the Abraham Blade, there was only one man in all of London—in all the world—who wielded it.

Lord John Carteret.

"You shame the god-king Solomon with these petty, empty displays," Carteret/Anubis continued, cutting the cable tow from around the initiate's neck—in the process nicking the soft skin beneath it uncomfortably close to the jugular, causing the now shaking young man to cry out.

"Shut up!" Carteret/Anubis hissed, kicking the initiate hard in the back so he fell forward, his blindfolded face striking Sayer/Set's boots with an ugly, cringe-inducing sound. Andrew heard the initiate attempt to stifle another cry.

"You shame the very memory of the murdered architect Hiram Abiff, instead of honoring it! How dare you call yourselves the Widow's Sons! Isis would not deign to piss upon your wounds were you to actually inflict them upon each other! Not one of you are worthy of the Underworld. Upon your empty deaths you will rot in shallow graves, for no god will be debased by claiming your souls."

"What is it you want, Anubis?" Sayer/Set asked in a far from fearful voice. "If we are so worthless, so devoid of power and purpose, why is it that you soil yourself by standing amongst us?"

Despite his fear—the fear of blood being spilled, the fear of being found out, Andrew allowed himself a smile behind the falcon's beak. *The venerable masters in Scotland have chosen well indeed.*

"I want your blood," Carteret/Anubis replied, raising the knife. "But more than that, I want the blood of the traitor Andrew Colson, who has—as do all spineless, wormy things—gone underground. Will you give him up to me? No? Of course not... you practice the silence of the Sphinx.

"But what if I told you," he continued, turning to face the huddled-together attendees of the ritual, non-masked and so all the more afraid, "that I will soon have something I can give you in return? The genuine article, symbol of this so-called third degree, instead of another false facsimile, like the skull you use to represent the Baptist?"

"Of what do you speak, Anubis?" Sayer/Set asked, a slight waver in his voice that had not been there before.

Without turning around, Carteret/Anubis laughed. "It is a honeycomb, brought to the temple of Solomon by the djinn-queen Sheba. How you Masons revere the blessed bee and its golden, medicinal honey. So like Menes, first of the pharaohs of Egypt, called The Beekeeper."

"You lie to us, false Anubis!" Sayer/Set challenged, the waver now gone. "The Sheba Comb is in better, cleaner hands than yours. There it shall remain. I swear before all assembled now before us, no member of the Mammon Lodge shall ever possess it!" Dropping the faux knife and producing a rather sharp, wicked-bladed one from the folds of his robes, Sayer/Set added, "Do you wish to see how serious our rites can be, *John Carteret?*"

Lowering the Abraham Blade, Carteret laughed through the snout of his mask. "I will get it, Sayer... Even now the Ravenskalds are tracking it down. I now declare that your united lodge shall *never* have it, so you shall never have the power you are all too unworthy to possess. As for Colson, do consider giving him up to me regardless. I wonder, Sayer, if he knows of my recent appointment as Lord Lieutenant of Devonshire? His father, I do believe, held that same position... Although, upon his death, it was not passed from father to son. It seems I have bested our Andrew yet again. "

His declaration made, Carteret jerked his head, indicating to his bullyboys that it was time for them to go. He exited the room without another word.

"Son of a whore!" Henry Bolingbroke yelled, helping the initiate to a standing position. "To defile our sacred rites..."

"He defiled nothing," Sayer/Set answered, putting away his real blade and retrieving the prop one. "If our initiate is willing to continue, he should retake his position that we may finish what was started."

In answer, the young man, defiantly letting both blood and tears flow down his face and neck, got upon his knees.

After George Payne had placed a new cable tow around the initiate's neck, Sayer/Set proceeded with the ritual.

As the rite unfolded, Andrew played his role fully and flawlessly, although his mind was also elsewhere.

By the end of the proceedings, as Sayer/Set removed the young man's blindfold once Andrew had placed the ankh upon each of the initiate's shoulders to trigger his rebirth, Lord Colson had made a decision. To prevent an all-out war between the lodges—a war that would rip London, Britain, and inevitably the entire world apart—he must go in search of a remedy.

A remedy he knew he could only secure on the Gold Coast of Africa.

He must seek the callers of the Jumbee.

Amidst the growing economic center that was Cadiz—owing to King Philip the Fifth's recent decision to move the House of Trade, the *Casa de Contratación*, to the port city from Seville—sat a nondescript two-story dwelling with a large back room. Large enough to serve as a planning center for the Catholic leaders of Cadiz to begin their talks with Spain's most talented architects about a new cathedral that would better pay homage to God in a manner worthy of the burgeoning city.

Today, however, there were no architects in attendance. Nor were there any priests. Instead, the room held Cardinal Giulio Alberoni—the most powerful Catholic in Spain—and two of his closest conspirators, Cardinal Filippo Antonio Gualterio, advisor to the exiled and rightful British king, James Francis Edward Stuart, and Cardinal André-Hercule de Fleury, former tutor of Louis the Fifth, too young to yet be crowned the king of France. It was his guardian, Philippe the Second, Duc d'Orleans and Regent of France, who had banished de Fleury from Louis's life.

As Philip met with his economic advisors elsewhere in the city, his wife and queen, Elisabeth Farnese—descended from nobility, cardinals, and a pope—stood to the side as the three cardinals prayed over a figure on a table around which they stood.

"Cardinal Alberoni… is the good friar awakened yet? It has been hours. The king will come for me eventually." She glanced toward the door, the nervousness in her voice not something to which either she or her confidante—the man responsible for arranging her marriage to the king upon the death of his first wife—were accustomed.

Not dropping his hands from their position of prayer, Alberoni whispered, "Any moment, Isobel. Patience, I pray thee."

It had been in this room, thirty hours earlier, that the trio of cardinals, assisted by the seventeen-year-old Franciscan friar, Guillermo Vincolaré, now asleep upon the table, had anointed Queen Elisabeth as their spiritual—in addition to political—leader. This young mother and wife was clearly the ultimate hope for the Catholic Church in Spain and France, as had been Isabel *la Católica*—from whom Elizabeth took her preferred name of Isobel—more than two centuries earlier.

Isobel had proven herself a worthy ally of the cardinals' powerful cabal, sending secret emissaries to lay the groundwork for an alliance with England while working through Cardinal Gualterio to see that James Stuart would take the British throne and destroy the aberration that was the Church of England.

Now her work would begin in earnest. Now that she had been further blessed.

Approaching the table, Isobel smiled as she heard the teenaged friar begin to stir. Her smile turned to laughter as she watched Guillermo raise and shake his tonsured head, and rapidly blink his eyes.

"How long was I asleep?" he asked, his voice a hoarse and barely audible whisper.

Before any of them could answer—although the answer was fifteen worrisome, interminable hours—the room's thick oaken door violently creaked open and the king of Spain stood before them, his eyes wide and a thick line of drool hanging precariously from his chin.

"Elisabeth!" he yelled, slamming the door closed behind him, nearly smashing the nose of one of his ministers. "I am losing all patience, wife! What is this conspiracy I find you amidst?" Brushing past both her and Cardinal Alberoni to grasp Guillermo's naked arm, he shot a hot stream of invective toward the ceiling. "Who is this? Eh? A lover, I have not any doubt! This is the devil's work—the fork-tongued *diablo* himself! And you... the mother of my children! How I hate you all! *Cerdos*! Pig-swine *bastardos*, all!"

Raising her hand slightly to keep the cardinals in their places and silent, Isobel turned and placed her hand upon her husband's shoulder. "This is Friar Vincolaré, My King," she whispered, taking a step forward to place her chin between Philip's shoulders. "He is assisting with the plans for the Cathedral. Do you not remember? We selected him for the purpose especially. You and I..."

Hearing his wife's tender words as birdsong, a calming salve in his ear, as he had heard them a hundred times before, Philip released the friar's arm and turned around to face her. "I... I do recall. Apologies, Friar," he said, not moving from his position. "You know my fears, my delicate flower... my dear, dear Elisabeth. There are those who wish to take what is rightfully, hereditarily mine. I shall not permit it, my darling. Not even by an angel such as you."

Philip—who was born Philippe, Duke of Anjou, the second son of Louis, the Grand Dauphin, son and heir of the Sun King himself, Louis the Fourteenth—was steeped in royal blood. It was the Sun King's marriage to Maria Teresa, daughter of Philip the Fourth of Spain, which had brought the question of the rightful heirs to the throne of Spain into its birthing. The matter proved even more complicated when Philip's father, who held the clearest claim to the throne held by his maternal uncle, King Charles the Second, was unable to ascend upon his uncle's death in 1700 due to his first position in the line of succession for the throne of France. Nor could his eldest son, Louis, Duke of Burgundy.

It therefore fell to the Duke of Anjou, who duly ascended as Philip the Fifth.

"I am sorry to have worried you, My King," Isobel said, stroking his face while deftly avoiding the drying line of drool. "We are committed to guiding the architects in designing a cathedral worthy of you, Cadiz, Spain, and the entire Catholic world. Poor Guillermo, whose ability in sacred arithmetic—as you well know, since you were the one to discover it months ago—is unsurpassed, was up all night figuring the dimensions of the altar. He had eaten nothing, drank nothing, in his fervor to serve you—yes you, My Beloved King—and so we found him, passed out upon this table, just before you entered."

Taking her hands in his, Philip smiled—and a bestial smile it was. "I have apologized to him, dear Elisabeth. Now I make my apologies to you. Though I demand that you leave this important work behind and come with me. Infante Charles, our child of barely thirteen months, is crying relentlessly for his mother. The other children, your step-sons—though they love you like a blood-mother—they are older… they understand your duty to country and king before them… but our precious Infante… he knows only the ache for your beautiful breasts."

Turning away so the pious men just beyond them would not see, Isobel leaned into Philip as his hands found the targets of his compliment.

Kissing the king's cheek, Isobel said, "You have a fierce internal fire, like your grandfather, *El Rey Sol*, Philip. You act sometimes as though the sun itself were sending a piercing ray to the very center of your being. You must go back to our apartments now, My King. Your special wine awaits you. I shall be their shortly. Now that our brilliant young friar is finally awake, the Cardinals and I must learn what he has discovered."

Giving her breasts a final, ungentle squeeze, Philip turned and left.

Waiting until he was safely out the room and the arguing voices of he and his ministers were comfortably distant, Isobel, dismissing the concerned looks of the trio of cardinals with a wave of her hand, took Guillermo's hands in her own as he sat up. "Tell us quickly, Friar— did you dream as we have hoped?"

Shaking his head regretfully, Guillermo, accepting a bowl of water from Cardinal Gualterio, which he emptied in a single swallow, said, "My dreams have ceased, Your Highness. Or, more pointedly, they are drowned out—*blocked*—by a chorus of dark voices… the beating wings and scratching claws of terrible, evil beings. Without the sleeping draughts you offer, I cannot close my eyes at all."

Showing the concern a mother would for her son, while hiding a growing fear, Isobel answered, "I shall make you another draft of *leche para dormir*—goat's milk and belladonna. You shall take it every evening until you regain your strength. You may not be the mathematician I need you to be in the king's inaccurate memories, but you are of greater value to us still."

As she gathered in her arms several rolls of plans the architects had left behind the day before—Philip would be expecting to see them—Isobel said to the cardinals, "The pathway is now clear. If Guillermo cannot dream the location of the Magdalene Balm and the Sheba Comb as we had hoped, then you must secure the mirror."

Nodding to the queen, Alberoni turned to de Fleury. "What do you make of the attacks against his dreams, André-Hercule?"

"It is the work of the Ravenskalds and their damnable Mammon lodges. The boy is in danger, my friends. As are we all."

"Then I shall take him with me to Saint Croix," Alberoni answered. "For that is where the wizard Abraxas Abriendo will eventually be found. It is he who holds and controls the mirror and within its obsidian depths, there the answers lie."

"I shall accompany you both," Cardinal Gualterio said. "I cannot bear to go back to France while James cowers in a corner in a castle where he is all too fast wearing out his welcome."

"As for me," De Fleury offered, helping Guillermo down from the table, "I must return to France—there are events afoot with Philippe and his finance ministers that I must make every effort to thwart. I will join you on Saint Croix as soon as I am able. It is time once again for the Star Quorum to convene our council in full. I shall send out the word to the others."

"May God bless you all," Isobel said as they all prepared to leave. "As you know, my hands are plenty occupied here."

"As are Philip's," Alberoni whispered to her as the others walked away. "Are you sure you are up to the tasks unfolding before you, Isobel? I fear he is actually going mad. If he were to harm you…"

"You chose me for a reason, Cardinal," Isobel answered, placing her arm in his as they headed for the door. "I am stronger than you know."

Some dreams a man is born with, taking a lifetime to achieve—if, that is, that man can gather the requisite amounts of preparation, discipline, and sheer dumb luck to even reach the *opportunity* of achieving them.

Other dreams are fleeting, come and gone in a moment, with no more investment than what the man can muster in the time the dream remains. This type of dream achievement finds its accomplishment in the proper turn of the card or roll of the dice at the gaming table, or brings a woman into his bed, or just the right wind to fill a vessel's sails.

Still other dreams—and some of the largest ones in history fall squarely under this particular reckoning—take precisely three days to bring into fruition.

Such was the case with the *Sultana*'s pursuit and capture—with naught a shot fired in anger nor in warning—of the three-masted slaver spoken of with such enthusiasm by Commodore Bellamy's officers—Misters Fletcher, Main, and Burke.

Watching with pride as this loyal trio of Jacobite pirates directed the men of the *Sultana* and her consort, the *Marianne*, as well as the officers and crew of the slaver, in the business of the transfer of power, Samuel Bellamy gave himself the rare permission to smile.

During the initial negotiations, Sam had learned that the impressive vessel's owner had named her *Whydah Gally*, after the kingdom and port on the western coast of Africa where the vessel procured her cargo of slaves.

"Whydah..." Sam repeated, motioning for an African member of his crew to leave the tallying of hogsheads with which Mister Fletcher had tasked him and join the commodore by the slaver captain's side.

As he did so, Sam asked, "Kikelomo. Ye speak Yoruba if I am correct, yes?"

"Aye sah."

"Excellent. What means this name Whydah?"

"'Tis the name of a native bird, sah. A paradise bird."

"Thank ye, Kikelomo. Ye may resume your task."

As the African man returned to the hogsheads, Sam took a step closer to the captain of the ship, a Dutchman called Lawrence Prince, looking him in the eye as a hawk might a field mouse before tearing off its head. "Paradise bird... Have ye no shame at all, Captain Prince? This vessel was a den of death, disease, and depredation.

What an effrontery to God as well as man you have ruled over! I have a mind—"

"Not my doing, sir," Prince answered, taking a step back. "As ye know well enough from a lifetime on the seas. Ah yes," he nodded as Sam's eyes widened, "I know who *you are*, sir, well enough. As I am sure ye know some facts about me. More alike than different we are."

Sam paused for an instant in thought. Prince had spoken truth—his name certainly was familiar. Well into his seventies—an age understandably rare for a man to be captaining a slaver working the Triangle Trade—Prince could boast of being a former buccaneer under the famous Sir Henry Morgan, who attacked Portobello and Panama in the sixteen seventies and eighties.

None of that mattered a bit to Sam right now.

All slavers were evil. That was his belief.

"Let us have a look at your quarters, Captain Prince," Sam suddenly said, motioning the old man toward a door at the stern of the vessel. "I have a feeling there are as yet treasures to be revealed."

Entering his former quarters just ahead of his captor, Prince let out a gasp. Several members of Bellamy's crew were dismantling the cabinets and shelves, boxing his books and papers, pulling down the heavy drapes and tapestries, and pushing all of the furniture into a corner.

Before Prince could speak he heard whooping, laughing, and an attempt at a dirty French ballad from behind him. Turning to meet this latest insult head on, he was astonished to see a boy of no more than ten or eleven dressed in the captain's best clothes, which dragged and snagged on the decking as the diminutive ruffian marched along, butchering the words of the off-key, ribald tune.

Seeing Commodore Bellamy as he reached the center of the room, the boy ceased his singing—just at the moment his horrible French would have revealed just what the mademoiselle who was the song's main subject did when she realized it was a monkey and not her young suitor that had climbed beneath her skirts.

"Mister King!" Bellamy yelled, giving his already powerful voice extra volume in order to make his point to Prince and anyone else that he was keen on law and order. "What is the meaning of this most obnoxious display?"

Knowing the commodore knew full well the ritual he and his co-conspirators were enacting—he had seen it half a dozen times in just the handful of months that John King had been aboard the *Sultana* since threatening to beat his mother if she did not let him join the commodore's crew—the boy thought better of saying so outright.

"Apologies, Cap'n," John said, pulling Prince's powdered wig from his head and giving his scalp a right and proper scratch. "Thought it might go well with the humblin' of the cap'n here's quarters to give his fineries a fling as well."

"Well fling them then, Mister King, and get on with your duties!" Bellamy answered, successfully hiding a smile. "And that length of ribbon 'round your waist... be sure it is surrendered for inventory."

As John King began to alleviate himself of Prince's clothes—handing the ten-foot length of white silk ribbon to a shipmate for cataloging with a huff—Bellamy turned his attention back to Captain Prince.

"Tell me about this vessel's owner, sir. And be quick about it. Or I shall ask young Mister King to sing another verse."

"She is..." Prince began, eager to prevent any such revival of the young man's lurid caterwauling, "rather, she *was*... owned by Sir Humphry Morice, Member of Parliament and director of the Bank of England. He commissioned her in 1715."

"Morice!" Bellamy echoed back, clasping his hands behind his back to prevent them from grabbling Prince by the throat. "The foremost villain in a trade full of demons! I am all the happier to strike this blow. I intend a full accounting of all ye have aboard, Captain Prince. When were ye last holding slaves?"

Pulling a logbook from the top of a box in the hands of a tattooed specimen Prince dare not look in the eye, he opened to the last written-upon page and handed it to his conqueror. "It is all there. Nearly five hundred slaves sold in Kingston, Jamaica."

"Five hundred lives," Bellamy said, leafing through the pages of the logbook. "Thousands sold overall and hundreds more dead due to the worst kinds of deprivations on your devilish trips, sir. Ye have much to answer for. And ye shall. Sit there, Captain Prince," the commodore whispered, pointing to an uncomfortable-looking stool in a far corner, "and say not a word, and this all might go smoothly for ye yet. After all, ye sailed with Morgan at Portobello. That must by needs account for something."

As Prince—after taking a moment to consider defiance—slunk into the corner as commanded, Bellamy was approached by Mister Fletcher. "Ah, my unparalleled quartermaster! What can I do for ye, sir?"

Motioning for the commodore to join him by a lantern sitting on the corner of the captain's table, Fletcher held something close to the light that gave off the glint of gold.

It was a ring.

"I took this offa one a' the officers," Fletcher said, his eyes widening as he watch the light reflect from its carved surface. "I was wonderin' what ye might wanna do with it…"

"Well," Bellamy said, holding out his hand, "let me have a look and we shall see." Carved in the center of the ring's rounded rectangle surface were the words TEYE BA. "Sengalese, if I am not mistaken." Turning it over and leaning into the light to inspect more easily what was carved there, Sam said, "And here… WFS. Perhaps for 'Western Fleet Station'… Might have belonged to a Royal Navy man. Well, Fletcher… 'tis a lovely piece. And, I believe, being that ye were the one who first spotted this vessel, that it is rightfully yours."

"Oh, sir!" Fletcher replied, taking the ring and slipping it on the middle finger of his left hand, "'Twas like ye read my mind! I shall wear it to my death in honor of this day, an' the liberation—nay—*transformation* of this former slaver into a vessel for right an' truth! As a matter a' fact… WFS is not at all for 'Western Fleet Station', sir! 'Tis for Whydah fightin' ship, for that is what she shall be!"

"Damned insubordinate..."
That makes seven. Three more to go.
"Caused failure in our mission..."
Two to go. You must not flinch nor scream.
"Cap'n Vane will nay stand fer such selfish—"
Missed that last part. Do not pass out. Let him see your eyes...
"Waste a' me effort ..."
There. That was not so terrible. Worth it, actually.
Julia would think it fitting.
"Do somethin' wit' 'im, someone."

Devon Ross, his chest heaving from the exertion of the ten lashes with the cat o' nine tails he had just inflicted upon Joseph Stanton's shoulders and back, was motioning with a few of the fingers resting on his left knee to a knot of men who had been forced to stand in service, bearing witness to the punishment.

"Ye two gawkin' bastahds—bring Stanton ta the surgeon's quartahs below decks. An' be quick about it!"

As Joseph felt his wrists freed from the rope that had kept him held tight to the mizzenmast, he glanced over at Ross. More specifically, to the cat o' nine tails as it trailed along the deck. Thick, bright blood covered the trio of knots on each of the nine twists of hemp.

Ross had done his work with vigor and intent. Joseph would be on his stomach for days.

Allowing the pair of men called into further duty to take him and his mincemeat back down to the surgeon's quarters, Joseph struggled against the part of him that wanted to pass out.

Do not give him the satisfaction. Not a moment of it.

Two weeks earlier, Captain Vane—now commodore of a handful of vessels of which the *Ranger* was the flagship—had given Ross and Stanton a clandestine command.

"I needs ye ta meet a man in Boston," Vane had said, as they sat in his quarters, away from prying eyes and ears. "Accordin' ta an unfortunate merchant cap'n I recently, uh... well... *interviewed*... 'e 'as intelligence on a map that could be a' service ta our cause. A map a' the north Atlantic islands that may be a' int'rst ta me. Map is not in Boston... only the infahmation. Retrieve it at this day an' time, at this locale..." He slid a slip of paper across his table, which Devon Ross pocketed without reading. "Any questions, Mistah Ross?"

"Only one, Cap'n. An' 'tis more a statement. I work best alone. Two men is double the logistics an' triple the risk. I would jus' as soon leave *'im*—"

"Joseph needs a test. As much as I value ye, Devon—yer a single man, an' we 'ave much ta do. The coin we clipped at Saint Croix is jus' the start. A means ta an end. Take 'im ye will an' teach 'im ye must. As Richard the Third, of which ye are so fond, tells us, 'An' thus I clothe me naked villainy with old odd ends stolen out a' holy writ; an' seem a saint, when most I play the devil.' No time left fer Stanton 'ere ta *play*. A devil 'e must be. An' who is better ta teach 'im? Return as soon as ye can."

A day later, Ross and Stanton had gotten on board a merchant vessel for the journey to Boston.

For the first several days, Ross kept to himself. Then, one night, as they were nearly through with supper, he said, not looking up from his plate, "Ye 'ave 'istory in Boston, lad. I know this. 'Tis where ye first broke ye bonds. First tasted freedom. An' that be all well an' good. But I furtha know yer sisters still reside there."

Pushing his plate aside, Joseph replied, his eyes afire, "How do ye know that? I just found out myself, not a week ago."

"Boy." Ross reached into his pocket, pulling out a pipe, which he slid inside the mouthpiece of the mask he always wore. "I 'ave tried ta teach ye. Been patient. Given ye ya 'ead like the unbroken horse ye fancy yerself ta be. But when will ye learn, ye exist at me pleasure. Break ye or make ye… I alone decide."

"I have no intention of trying to see them," Joseph said, wishing Vane had given Ross his way. "And they will certainly not see me. I will not fail ye on this mission, Mister Ross. An' I have learned every bit of what ye have taught me. Rest assured of that."

When he had spoken the words more than a week before, Joseph had meant them. But there was something about being back on the wharf in Boston, where Angus had coerced him into making a run for it more than a year and a half ago. A run for freedom, away from the hard years of servitude he would have to endure to pay his father's debt to a certain Captain Hubbard.

The scene played out in his mind… How Samuel Bellamy and Paulsgrave Williams had collected he and Angus—he would get that Scottish bastard yet—arranging to pay his father's debts with interest in return for Joseph pledging service to The Cause.

Made and kept his pledge he had. Although to a very different kind of captain than those idealistic Robin Hoods of the seas, as far too many simpletons were calling them.

He had more than proven himself. His reputation was fierce and growing. Everyone saw it, including Captain Vane.

All but one. *Faccia del Diavolo*. The demon Devon Ross.

Knowing they had another thirty-six hours to go before they were to meet their contact and retrieve the information about the map—they had arrived with several days to spare—Ross had thought it best they lay low in separate quarters, meeting only for their evening meals.

That gave Joseph a few precious days to track down and speak with his sisters—Julia, the eldest and Margaret, now fifteen.

All that was left of his family.

It had been an old friend of his father's who had given him the news that his mother and youngest sister were dead and Julia and Margaret, wasting away and taking the occasional beating in the back alleys of the East End, had managed passage to Massachusetts colony.

One sister dead and the other two whores.

One day soon, Joseph would find Angus—or Conall, or whatever the hell name he called himself—and kill him for what he had done.

It was on the morning of the day they were to meet their contact that Joseph had tracked his sisters down. As he had feared, they refused to engage in even the briefest of conversations with him. When, in his frustration and desperation for forgiveness—and well aware of the looming appointment he was duty bound to keep—Joseph had placed a restraining hand on Julia's shoulder in a final attempt to apologize, she had surprised him with the depth of her hatred by shouting for her pimp and a pair of his thugs. As they quickly descended upon him with fists and chains and bats, he cried out, "Julia! Margaret! Watch this, the both of ye! See how justice is served!"

Willing himself not to fight back—not yet—Joseph was yet again surprised when he felt the pimp pulled off him and heard—through a bleeding, aching ear—the flesh-peddler calling in a pained and high-pitched voice for his thugs to break it off and run.

As they departed, taking Julia and Margaret with them, Joseph looked up to see his savior.

Turned out to be the furthest thing from true.

Devon Ross, a bloody knife in hand, was pulling him up by the collar, his hat pulled low to cover both what remained of his face and his leather mask. "Damned fool! Damned, damned fool. Ye 'ave ruined it fer us good. An' that bloody imbecile Vane, thinkin' ye'd be *use*ful…"

Although Joseph did not understand it at the time, several hours later, as the appointed moment for the rendezvous came and went with their contact a no-show, it all became clear.

"The ruckus ya caused spooked 'im," Ross had whispered, as they boarded a ship prearranged for their return to the Caribbean in the late afternoon.

Captain Vane had said little upon their return. Hearing Ross's brief and pointed report, he had agreed with a nod to the flogging, to be administered by *Faccia del Diavolo* with all due haste and vigor.

As the two crewmen carried him below decks, Joseph put on his best face for Captain Vane, who was coming up the steps, no doubt on his way to talk with Ross. Only then did he permit the darkness of unconsciousness to match that of the passage they now entered.

Forgive me, Julia, he thought. *For I have paid a heavy price. Still not as heavy as yours.*

I am done with playing. Now an equal devil to Devon Ross shall I be.

FORT OF NASSAU, NEW PROVIDENCE, THE BAHAMAS, END OF FEBRUARY 1717

As Captain Benjamin Hornigold looked out upon the fortifications and anchored ships in the harbor of the fort on New Providence, he felt in his bones a change in the mood of the place. Although it remained a bustling beehive of activity—the foremost pirate outpost in the Caribbean—it had lost the sunshine of its promise, that of a true Republic of Pirates. Gone was the lightness to its work songs and the camaraderie of its gatherings. Ever since Hornigold had been replaced by popular vote by Samuel Bellamy, with the help of the Frenchman Levasseur, the spirit of New Providence had fallen into shadow. Although some of the fort's denizens still called him Gran'pa, it was not with the same respect and deference as when he was its commodore. And, of no surprise, Bellamy and Levasseur had rarely returned since the transfer of power nearly four months ago and New Providence, fallen under the nominal command of Captain Henry Jennings in their absence, was effectively leaderless.

"Sorry to bother ye, sir, but Abraxas Abriendo has requested immediate audience an' I cannot see a reason to deny him."

Knocking the bowl of his pipe on the parapet on which he leaned to empty it of its ashes—he had smoked it out many minutes before without noticing—Hornigold forced a smile. "How odd, Edward, the manner in which allegiances change in this increasingly forsaken place. Not so long ago ye would have thrown him out of the fort for being a fakir and a mountebank."

Edward Thache—still without a captaincy as he continued to serve as sailing master of Hornigold's sloop *Adventure*—shrugged his shoulders and put out his arms in a show of surrender. "I have no words to counter ye with, Cap'n. Allegiances indeed are changing. Who would have thought that Jennings and Vane would come to blows, putting Jennings on our side? *If*, that is, we can trust him..."

Hornigold, putting his pipe in his vest before quickly removing it and filling it with tobacco, said, "I believe we can, Edward. The things he has told me in confidence—about the true aims of Vane and his henchman Devon Ross—prevent him from ever returning to them. He may not fully wish to be here, aiding in our cause, but it is better than torture and a prolonged, nightmarish end to his life. Which is exactly what it would be."

Looking back out to sea as he lit his pipe, Hornigold said, "Let Abraxas come. Having to hear whatever he wishes to tell me will be payment for what I wish to know about the whereabouts and actions of Bellamy and Levasseur."

"Ye doan enter unless ye are allowed, ye scabby roaster! Oi!"

Hornigold and Thache turned as one to see Conall MacBlaquart—whose true identity, Angus MacGregor, was still a (mostly) well-kept secret—attempting to block a very determined Abraxas Abriendo from entering the rampart where the two men stood.

"Dammit, Abraxas!" Thache yelled, putting his considerable height and width in front of Abraxas to break his momentum as he successfully passed Conall. "I told ye I would seek ye an audience. Have some patience, man!"

Shaking his head and giving his long white beard a tug, Abraxas laughed. "Audience? You pretend this man is still the oil-annointed king of the pirates. He is not, Edward. He is not even a commodore, though I know it pains you more than most to know it, seeing as it means that you are *still* without a ship of your own. Am I correct?"

"Ye were never one for humility nor sense, ye damned, half-mad magician," Edward answered, taking Abriendo by the arm and pulling him to the side. "Why offer insults? If that is why ye have returned, ye can—"

"Don't be a fool, Edward." Abriendo made no attempt to remove his captor's hand. "I merely dislike false authority. One would think you would understand. Like it or not, we are equals. Your gran'pa here included. Now, if you are through with the needless brutality, I will say what I have come to."

Removing his hand from Abriendo's arm, Edward motioned for him to join Hornigold at the parapet while he took a step back to join Conall in the doorway.

"I am truly sorry, Maister Thache," Conall whispered. "Hae has always baen a slipp'ry fish."

"That he has, lad. From my net most of all. Now let us hush and take a listen to what he has to say."

"Captain Hornigold," Abriendo said, "I bring you news in the form of a child."

Before the former commodore could enquire as to the meaning of the words, Abriendo waved vigorously in the direction of the door in front of which Edward and Conall stood. Glancing over their shoulders, they saw an African boy of no more than eleven, dressed in the simple garments of a cabin boy, but sporting a gold hoop in each of his ears, emerge from the shadows.

"Excusing me please," he said, pushing his way gently between them. "My long-beard master summons me."

"By all means, young terror," Edward said, crossing his arms and smiling. This was most unexpected, although when it came to the tricks and maneuvers of Abraxas Abriendo, he had learned long ago never to be surprised.

"And who is this?" Hornigold asked, squatting down to look the African boy in the eyes.

"Cardinal Giulio Alberoni, chief advisor to the king and queen of Spain, with whom he traveled aboard the *Bonetta* for a time before arriving in St. Croix, has named him Caesar," Abriendo said, stepping aside to let Hornigold have a look at him.

"An ancient and noble name. Tell me, lad… Why did he choose to do so?" Hornigold asked.

"Because I have in me a proud, defiant de… de… de–meanor!" Caesar answered, puffing out his chest to prove it.

"Indeed, indeed you do," Abriendo said, clapping. "But that is not the only reason. Tell him, Caesar. Tell Gran'pa Hornigold who you *truly* are."

Leaning in so his nose and Hornigold's were nearly touching, and dropping his voice to a whisper, Caesar said, "My grandfather, Kwasi, is a powerful practitioner of Obeah. He was, until a few years ago, the chief advisor to Chief Dagaakutsu of the Ashanti. But he fell out of favor because he disagreed with the chief over a terrible conjuring trick…"

The boy dropped his head, unable to go on.

Amazed at the sudden change from puff-chested preening to abject fear, Hornigold placed his pointer finger gently beneath the frightened boy's chin. When he met no resistance, he raised the boy's head until they were again looking one another in the eye. "And what was this trick, Caesar? It is all right to tell Gran'pa Hornigold. I will not tell another soul."

His eyes widening as he spoke, Caesar said, "It was the conjuring of the Jumbee… The black dog of vengeance whose thirst cannot be quenched nor its mighty appetite sated once it has been woken."

Understanding now why Abraxas had brought the boy to him—he must have heard that Jennings had shared what he knew of the origins of the devil Devon Ross and the disfigured face he hid beneath a leather mask—Hornigold produced a bag of dried mango slices from beneath his coat and offered it to the boy. "Thank you for your trust. Help yourself, Caesar. Take the bag and seek some shade for your feast."

Glancing at Abriendo, who nodded his approval, Caesar took the bag with a laugh and ran back through the door, Edward and Conall parting to make a path as he went by.

"How did he come to be in the care of a Cardinal?" Hornigold asked, standing with a wince, and rubbing his right knee.

"After his grandfather's falling out with Dagaakutsu, the heartless chief of the Ashanti sold Caesar into slavery through traders of the Royal African Company. Reaching Port Royal, he was sold to then-governor Archibald Hamilton."

"Vane's benefactor..." Hornigold whispered.

"Exactly. Although Caesar quickly proved himself unmanageable to Hamilton's replacement, who was completing the papers to have him shipped to another sugar plantation on some other island or perhaps the Carolinas, where he would certainly be beaten and worked to death within a matter of months, when one of our agents rescued him."

"Why?"

Leaning in conspiratorially and dropping his voice as Caesar had done, Abraxas answered, "Because the boy has learned Obeah from his grandfather, and he is a powerful young practitioner. It is my task to train him, to protect him. Because they *will* come for him, Benjamin. Those who wish to see all of this—all of *us*, and the Jacobite revolution—obliterated once and for all. Mark my words on that." Then, turning to Edward, he added, "Training him I am suited for. Protecting him, however... That is why I am here. Will you help me, Edward? To protect him? No matter the ultimate cost?"

Stepping forward, Thache answered, "Aye, Abraxas. I shall."

"Mister Fletcher, sir. Have ye made ready a general accounting? I believe Captain Prince would like to hear it as well, before we go our separate ways."

For three days, Commodore Samuel Bellamy had been directing his trio of officers in the transfer of materials from his flagship the *Sultana* to the former slave ship *Whydah*, already noticeably altered by the carpenter's crew, which was nearing its completion of repurposing her for piracy. Upon her decks were added ten six-pound cannons, to bring her total to twenty-eight, with another dozen stored safely below. His new command quarters—far more modest than the rich appointments and luxuries enjoyed by Prince, the *Whydah*'s former captain—were abuzz with the comings and goings of his quartermaster, sailing master, and boatswain and his mentor and captain of the *Marianne*, Paulsgrave Williams, who now sat beside him.

"Aye, Commodore, I am ready an' willin' ta make a gen'ral accountin'," Quartermaster Fletcher responded, opening a thick ledger with his ink-stained fingers, one of which was adorned with the gold TEYE BA ring Bellamy had gifted him from the spoils of their conquest. Clearing his throat, he read with enthusiasm from his notes on the captured inventory. "Full an' particular accountin' a' tonnage an' hogsheads, sacks, an' bales ta be delivered at a later date in private audience, Commodore, as ye have prev'ously instructed. In general, however, considerable presence a' ivory, molasses, indigo dye, sugar, an' various an' sundry Akan jewelry—ornaments, pendants, an' beads. Considerable gold an' silver, sir. Considerable indeed."

Closing the ledger and preparing to depart, the quartermaster was surprised to hear the commodore ask, "Let us have the particulars of the silver and gold, Mister Fletcher, if ye please."

"As ye wish, sir," he replied, reopening the ledger and flipping to the page with the details requested. "Of gold an' silver, the final accountin' is as follows: 4,131 pieces a' eight, seventeen gold bars, an' 6,174 bits a' gold. All said an' done, twenty ta thirty thousand pounds, Commodore."

"Excellent work, Mister Fletcher," Bellamy replied. "Now, if ye would be so kind, portion out and log as having done so twenty pounds of silver and gold for Captain Prince, which I offer with my compliments along with the *Sultana* for his unwavering aid in our smooth transition."

Having a reason to smile for the first time in days, Captain Prince replied, "I thank ye, Commodore Bellamy. Ye truly are a prince amongst men."

"A prince the same as all these other men," Bellamy corrected him. "Now, if ye shall be so kind as to take what I offer and make sail as soon as ye are able, I would be much obliged."

When Prince had bowed and gone, Bellamy dipped a quill in a pot of ink and, working some figures on a piece of parchment, turned back to his quartermaster. "Listen well, Mister Fletcher. I have given it considerable thought, and I have chosen Misters Julian and Davis to assist ye in apportioning the treasure. Fifty pounds per man. See to it."

"Thomas Davis is a good man, true 'nuff.... But John Julian, sir?" Fletcher replied, gathering his papers beneath his arms. "He is but sixteen, an' a Miskito Indian at that..."

"Precisely why I selected him. Ye seem to forget, Mister Fletcher, when it comes to young master Julian, that every man is equal in this flotilla when it comes to his general background. Do not ruin your splendid reputation with such slips in your beliefs again. Am I understood?"

Watching Fletcher nod enthusiastically, Bellamy fixed his attention on Paulsgrave Williams, who sat with a look of subtle shock upon his face.

"And what is that gaze supposed to tell me, Captain Williams?" Bellamy asked, pouring three mugs of ale for himself, the captain, and the quartermaster.

"That ye have been more than generous with Captain Prince, my friend," Williams replied, taking a long draught from his mug. "Ye no doubt want him gone and away without delay. I must confess, I am curious as to why."

Suggesting that Mister Fletcher take his mug of ale topside to enjoy the sunshine and oversee the final transfer of items between the two ships, Bellamy dragged the barrel on which he sat closer to Paulsgrave Williams's knee. "Right ye are, good sir. While the bounty from the holds of this ship are greater than we could have imagined, there were other treasures found within her hull. Treasures that shall buy victories her gold, silver, and other assets could not."

"Do talk on."

Glancing around him to be certain no one was listening, Bellamy stood and made his way across the room to a locked chest Paulsgrave knew contained the commodore's private effects. Removing a key from around his neck, Bellamy opened the lock and threw back the lid. From beneath a pile of trousers and vests, he produced a pair of manuscripts, loosely bound in sheaths of leather and tied with string. Returning to his seat, he said, "These were found in a chest containing coconut matting and vials of mercury."

"Someone intended to hide them beneath the earth for a considerable amount of time," Williams remarked, running his fingers along the leading edge of the topmost sheaf of papers. "What do they contain?"

"See for yourself."

Unwrapping the yellowed, delicate pages with care, Williams found himself gasping aloud as he read their titles. "These are copies of Christopher Marlowe's *Jew of Malta* and *Doctor Faustus*! Such copies are exceedingly rare."

"Yes they are. *Copies* that is… But coded *originals*, Paulsgrave… and that is what these are—I stake my life upon it!—these are truly priceless. And invaluable to our cause."

Williams, now knowing what he held, resheathed and retied the manuscripts, placing them carefully on the desk, as if at any moment they could burst into flames. "Did the council on St. Croix speak to ye of these?"

"These and other items," Bellamy answered, returning them to his sea chest. "They were destined for an island in the north Atlantic, the fortifications, holding mechanisms, and booby traps of which are true marvels of engineering, centuries in the works. But we shall see them to another, even more secret and secure location, also in that vicinity. And we must head there without delay."

Williams shook his head. "The north Atlantic is no place for our flotilla in the height of winter, Samuel. This ship not only contains the ill-gotten gains from her recent sale of slaves—oh, do not look at me that way—I know their value to the cause. Ye have also arranged to be stored in her spacious hull the spoils from the well over forty ships we have taken this past year. She shall be slow and ponderous. I know ye realize this."

"I do indeed," Bellamy answered, taking a drink from his mug. "So we shall take our time getting there. There are riches and further means of funding the cause awaiting us in the mid-Atlantic shipping lanes. And, by the grace of God—who is wholly sympathetic to our mission— we now have this impressive specimen of a man of war with which to do it. The Royal Navy has not quite organized itself there as of yet. So our contacts tell me. Then, when we are well into April, I shall send ye to that island and I shall finally head home to Cape Cod to wed my precious Goody and see to the necessary task of refitting and resupply. We shall meet at a future-determined time, my friend, although I intend, in all honesty, to continue to contribute to the cause primarily from a house I plan on building on the Cape."

Raising his mug with a smile, Williams said, "A glorious plan indeed! Ye have far surpassed all my expectations, Samuel. And they were always exceedingly high."

"I am goan', Dooncan. An' ye cannae praevent mae!"

For what seemed like an eternity, although it had been all of five weeks, Duncan MacDonald had been steady at the task of dissuading his cousin Ailish from leaving Glen Shira to go in search of Angus, whom she had until recently believed to be dead.

To further sour the stew, Ailish had gone red with rage when Duncan had further shared with her that Angus's uncle Rob had ordered him to murder the boy, which he had actually attempted to do!

"Fer the love a' God, Dooncan!" she had screamed beside Loch Fyne as her older cousin—finally forced to confess after rescuing Ailish from the ill intent of Rob's eldest son James—vomited up the truth despite his best attempts to leave certain bits digested, in their secret, sullen hideout in his churning intestines. "Ye actually *tried*?"

"Aye lass," Duncan had further confessed, wishing she would hit him in his wounded shoulder, in exactly the spot where Samuel Bellamy had shot him in the fort on Nassau, preventing him from doing to Angus what Rob had so coldly commanded.

It would hurt him far less than the icy look in her heather green eyes.

"Ye naid tae listen tae mae, lass!" Duncan continued, taking her gently by the arms, all too aware of the way Ailish flinched when someone touched her, or even came close, since James had tried to have his way with her. "I pay ev'ry day fer mae actions. An' Angus took a bit a' extra blood froom mae shoulder tae put on his da's cloak. An' hair it bae, tae proov it."

Taking a bundle from behind the saddle of his horse, Duncan undid the buckles of the straps that held it together and handed the dark green cloak to Ailish. "I took this withoot Rob's knoowin'. Boot it rightfully baelongs tae Angus, an' soom day ye shall bae taegether again. Hold fast tae it 'til thaen."

As Ailish held the cloak tightly to her body, Duncan removed a ring from a pouch on his belt. "An' this is soomthin' I haev haeld in troost fer him fer many a year as weel."

Taking the ring in her hand, Ailish examined it closely, welcoming a diversion from her cousin's troubled face. Made for a man, it was worked silver in the shape of a dragon's scaly hand and claws grasping a pale blue rectangular stone.

"Whair doos this coom froom, Dooncan?" she whispered.

"'Tis a talisman a' the Lords a' the Isles, held in troost bae mae at the request a' Angus's ma Rowan, who gave it tae mae the night baefore she an' her hoosband wair killed. Rowan was a MacKinnon, as ye air weel aware, an' it wair the MacKinnons that hid Robert the Bruce whaen hae fled tae Carrick. They fought haird fer his victory at Bannockburn as weel, which is whaen hae gave thaem land on the Isle a' Skye. Tho' it was thair alliance wit' Saint Columba, founder a' the abbacy at Iona, that laed tae thair buildin' thair stronghold at Strathairdle, tho' they haid numerous castles throughout the Isles."

Ailish shook her head. "I nae knoo why ye knoo so mooch aboot the MacKinnons. An' I haev tae ask… Why give the ring tae you, Dooncan? Oor own history wit' the MacKinnons has nae baen always neat an' fain."

"This bae true as ye speak it, lass. Boot raemember—whaen it moost mattered, the MacKinnons an' MacDonalds weer fiercesome allies, as whaen wae fought the MacLeods. An', if it were nae fer the wavin' a' their silk faery flag, wae would haev baest 'em."

Ailish's eyes began to gleam as another question formed in her mind, dancing itself nimbly down to her tongue. "I still doan oonderstand. Nae fully. The MacKinnons air kin tae the MacGraegors, both bein' one a' the seven clans that descended froom Alpin, father a' Cináed mac Ailpín."

"Kenneth McAlpin, fairst a' the Scottish kings," Duncan said, nodding. "Good ye knoo yer his'try, lass. The answer is a simple one. Rowan nae troosted Rob. Noot wit' him haevin' sons a' his oon tae which hae'd bae fiercely loyal."

"Wise poor Rowan was," Ailish said, running the tip of her finger over the dragon's scales covering the side of the ring.

"Aye lass. An' she had great hopes fer yer Angus. An' right she should. The marriage a' Angus's da John an' Rowan MacKinnon was nae wee thing. Thair was great power in thair joinin'. Rob knoo it. An' perhaps even feared it. Especially after the namin' a' thair bairn. Do ye know the story a' his name, coosin?"

"All these years, I nae gave it a thought," Ailish answered, unconsciously slipping the dragon ring on and off her thumb as she gathered her thoughts. "Boot I haev haird the stories of Angus, the son a' Dagda, the troo an' good god. Angus was also known as Mac Oc, meanin' the young god, who played a harp a' gold tae please the faeries in thair palace."

"Ye make mae proud, Ailish," Duncan answered. "An' that ring thair was forged wit' the help a' the faeries a' the Western Isles within a sìth near the abbacy on Iona in thair quest tae protect the MacKinnons."

Grasping the ring tightly and draping the bloodstained cloak on her arm, Ailish cleared her throat and stood up from her familiar spot beside the lake. "I thank ye fer givin' these tae mae, Dooncan. I weel see that Angus receives them. Bae mae hand, if ye ken?"

"I lass, that I doo," Duncan said, pulling a map from his saddlebag. "An' since ye air so saet on goan', I am goan' tae help ye as mooch as I caen in reachin' yer destination in the Caribbean, while Rob Roy is nae tae bae found." Unrolling the map, he said, pointing, "Noo, haer's the port in England that weel take ye on tae Boston…"

"*Santa María Madre de Dios*! It is the *Ranger*, Satan's flagship, come from the boiling waters of the *infierno*, captained by that *cerdo*, that stinking piratical pig-swine, Vane! Pour the iron into them, *mis hombres fieles*! At long last, victory shall be ours!"

Nineteen frustrating months had passed since Capitan Amaro Rodríguez Felipe y Tejera Machado's initial encounter with Vane, when the pirate, still a member of the Republic founded by Hornigold, had the sheer audacity to storm the Spanish fort on the Florida coast, robbing it of the silver and gold thus far recovered from the Plate Fleet debacle of July 1715.

This affront to Spanish sovereignty was made all the worse because it was Capitan Machado's mentor, Capitan General Don Juan Esteban de Ubilla, of the flagship *Urca de Lima*, who had commanded the Plate Fleet of eleven treasure-laden ships bound for Spain. Capitan Ubilla had lost his life in the hurricane-fueled disaster.

Pacing the deck like a caged panther, Machado—called by many, friends and foes alike, Amaro Pargo—waved his rapier in the air as he continued to direct the firing of the cannon and chew on the past embarrassment of his second encounter with Captain Charles Vane.

On June 20, 1716, Vane had captured the *Señor San Miguel* off Port Royal, Jamaica. Pargo's ship, the frigate *Ave María y Las Ánimas*, arrived too late to take the stolen frigate back—it was already protected by Port Royal's formidable defenses.

What a sleepless and agonizing ten months it had been.

Then, first thing this morning, as the fog cleared and Pargo's crew had readied themselves for their daily cannon drills, the cry had come from the crow's nest that the lookout had spotted the *Ranger*, flying its formidable skull and crossbones flag. No hourglass, sword, or full-bodied skeleton. Just the damnable Jolly Roger.

Vane likes his business plain, I see, Pargo had thought, boring his eye into the flag through his spyglass. *I shall therefore deliver it direct and without adornment*.

For ninety minutes, the well-matched pair of ships—frigate and sloop—maneuvered and traded fire. Casualties had been minor on both sides, and neither captain seemed inclined to release their prey.

As Pargo encouraged a cannon crew to be quicker in their swabbing and reloading, he saw his second in command, Lieutenant Renaldo de Recalde, limping toward him.

"Capitan," Recalde said through clenched teeth, "What is the point of this engagement? We will destroy one another... I see no means to a clear victory by either of our ships. There is no shame in breaking off to fight another day."

Pargo shook his head. "But there is, *mi amigo*! There is. Because this is English pig-swine. The most *enfermo* pig-swine on the seas! He and his *pedazo de mierda cerdo* crew will pay for their insult to the memory of Capitan Ubilla and for the taking of the *Señor San Miguel.* In addition, Renaldo, there are whispers amongst the other captains that this Vane has come into another pile of ill-gotten coin from Saint Croix. Such a take would be just what I need to return to the good graces of our king and queen! This is what we need—a victory for España! And please, *viejo*, do not question me in front of the crew."

Changing his position to take pressure off his left leg, to which he sustained a serious wound during an encounter with Samuel Bellamy two months after the initial encounter with Vane, Lieutenant Recalde gestured to the growing mayhem around them. "Apologies, Capitan. I only speak this way because the men are exhausted. As good as they are, they cannot keep up the pace that you demand of them. I know you have been patient, Capitan, and to have him in our sights and not be able to end him is for you a torture beyond words, but—"

Recalde's words ceased as an incoming six-pound cannonball met its mark with breathtaking accuracy, leaving the lieutenant's headless torso pinned to the mizzenmast by a ghastly length of splintered wood that had been forcefully detached from the rail.

"*Bastardos!*" Pargo yelled, after wrapping what was left of his closest friend's head in a length of fallen sail and returning to the rail. "You will pay for this day and deed! *Pedazo de mierda cerdos!* Spawn of *el Diablo!* Back to *el infierno* with thee!" Wiping a hot stream of tears from his eyes, Pargo screamed at his men, "My *mis hombres fieles*! Fight with all your heart, for your fallen lieutenant, Renaldo de Recalde! Fight to the very last of your breath!"

"Well done, ye pirates from 'Ell! Our work 'ere is finished… fer now!" Putting aside his spyglass, Captain Vane applauded his crew. "Ye 'ave ended Marchado's second in command. Poor bloke lost 'is 'ead, 'e did! I think we 'ave made our point!"

"She be a fine vessel, sir," Devon Ross whispered, not wanting to call attention to his questioning of his captain's command. "An' her fish-faced captain cannot be at 'is best in the midst a' such a loss. Perhaps if we press…"

"We 'ave not got the time," Vane answered. "The delay the madman caused us is already a' concern ta me. 'E 'as been 'it. An' 'e 'as been shamed. We shall no doubt see 'im soon. In the meantime, we 'ave orders from our benefactors. We sail north wit' all 'aste. Pressin' concerns in the colonies. Make it so, Mistah Ross. An' quickly, sir, if ye wish ta keep ya position."

Transitioning the ninety men of the *Ranger* from fighters back to sailors, Devon Ross tried not to chew too hard on the hard, dry bone of Vane's less than forthcoming explanation.

I have ever-lessening interest in keeping my current position, he thought, coming down harder on the crew than he otherwise would as he did so.

I am better suited ta yours.

Cannon and the Quill   42

PART TWO:

SO CLOSE TO COMING HOME

Rob Roy MacGregor had always been good at completing multiple tasks at once.

At the moment, for instance, the Highlander chieftain was currently working on three separate things: (1) Surreptitiously undoing the leather straps that held his hands behind his back while a bullyboy in the employ of John Murray, first duke of Atholl, led the horse to which Rob was also strapped through the darkness between Loch Lomond and Ben Lomond. (2) Judging the best place to make his escape in this hilly, wooded terrain. (3) Trudging his memories through the tangled mess of circumstances that had led him into his current predicament.

It had all begun with his initial shifting of allegiance from the Duke of Montrose—a King George loyalist and Rob's former business partner—to John Erskine, now former earl of Mar, whose battlefield losses at Preston and Sheriffmuir in November 1715 had led to Rob's being caught between the equally powerful dukes Montrose and Argyll—Erskine's primary backer. Argyll, being fiercely loyal to the Old Pretender, James Frances Edward Stuart—for economic more than political reasons—had zero use for anyone loyal to George.

Then there were the Murrays. Although overwhelmingly loyal to the Jacobite cause, the Murrays had exchanged words and crossed claymores with Rob and his men more times than they could count. Fueled by his hatred of Montrose and all that called themselves Murray—David Murray, Fifth Viscount of Stormont most of all—Rob aligned himself and the clans who followed his every order more closely with the powerful Argyll than a man of his fierce independence might otherwise prefer in order to have the backing to continually act against his enemies.

Such forced allegiances had resulted in his sending Duncan MacDonald to the Caribbean to murder Rob's nephew Angus at the order of the Old Pretender, now back in France, hiding in shame. They had led to Rob's becoming the temporary jailer of Montrose's factor John Graham in the hopes of procuring a rich ransom—which Montrose declined to pay. And, most directly related to his current situation, his looking after the mad barber Finlay Fletcher—whose equally mad fiancé Rowan had been held captive and repeatedly raped by one of David Murray's nephews at Scone Palace until Rob and his closest compatriots had rescued her, taking a number of firearms from the Murrays while they were at it.

That particular action resulted in yet *another* of David Murray's nephews—newly arrived from Glasgow to learn the family business, according to one of Murray's men—bleeding out on Rob's boots outside his homestead in Glen Shira.

Rob did not believe for a moment that David Murray had sent his green-as-a-sapling nephew with an armed force to Rob's farm solely to take back the girl.

It was a pretext to an all-out war and land-grab.

Such were the cold machinations of the Murrays.

Machinations like Rob's recent kidnapping, which he was very close now to bringing to an end. Not content to keep his nemesis in just any old prison, John Murray, earlier that day, had ordered five of his men to move Rob to a more secure location.

That was his first mistake.

His second he made in choosing the five men for the transfer. Two of them—the two who were supposed to be riding behind Rob to watch his every move—had left the party an hour ago to ride ahead and secure lodging, a feast, and some wenches for after the remaining three had Rob secured in his new holding cell.

The one who held the reigns of Rob's horse, having begun sipping from a flask of ale shortly after they had set out, was by now more than a little inebriated. The other two, riding increasingly ahead, were talking loudly about what they intended to do to the lucky, lucky wenches their companions were in the midst of finding.

Sooch complicated games, Rob thought, freeing himself from the straps that bound his hands and turning his attention to the straps that held his thighs. *An' fer what? John Murray an' mae are moor alike than diff'rent. If noot fer his name, we might be fraends.*

Indeed, Murray was just as complicated and unpredictable a Highlander as the infamous outlaw he had kidnapped.

Yet enemies they were, which was at times more than sensible. After all, while Rob's father was fighting for the Catholic Stuarts—losing his life at Killiecrankie in '89 alongside Bonny Dundee—John Murray was fully in support of William and Mary during the Church of England's removal of James the Second—Mary's *father*—from the throne of Britain in the so-called Glorious Revolution of damned near three decades past.

Here is where it gets most complicated, as so much of the politics between the ill-tempered Highlanders were. Some of John Murray's allies—including some of his sons and the Murrays of Scone—had fought with the *Jacobites* during the action in '89. Furthermore, despite being made a Knight of the Thistle, an honor first bestowed upon his father, Murray was in and out of favor as the throne passed from William to Mary to Mary's sister Anne to the Hanoverian George, who—not trusting the vacillating first duke of Atholl a bit—had recently dismissed him from his position as privy councilor.

Which is why, in part, he had kidnapped Rob. John Murray no doubt felt that turning Rob over to Montrose and those loyal to King George would restore his reputation and his office.

The other part was far simpler. Rob had interfered with the personal and public affairs of Clan Murray and John, as head of the family, had to teach him a lesson.

Happy to deny the fruition of either to the first duke of Atholl, Rob now worked the straps that secured his thighs to the saddle all the harder. Then, as they crossed a bridge over a shallow stream, Rob went up and over the wooden rail, and into the chilly water below. If the drunkard holding the reigns of his horse was aware his captive had escaped him, he made no move to chase him down.

Most likely, his mind was on a tankard of ale and a sizable set of breasts, and anything that would delay his obtaining them was no longer his concern.

Wading through the water, Rob thought back to a visitor he had spoken with just prior to his transport. An agent of Argyll's, he had assured Rob that all he need do was slip his bonds and his captors on the journey and the duke would happily send someone to fetch him.

Pointing himself toward a pair of men on horseback holding torches half a mile ahead, Rob thanked his stars that the powerful men of the Highlands were as unpredictable as they were and that he could match wits and continue to win against them all.

"I need to find the bees… I need to *FIND* the *BEES!*"

Kirstine awoke with a start, relieved and for a second confused to find that she was no longer hooked up to Doctor Reinhardt's mirror-machine.

Focusing her eyes, she felt a hand in hers. Looking to the side she saw Jake Givens, looking like he badly needed a nap.

"Hey," he said, his glassy eyes brightening at the sight of her.

Kirstine felt tears begin to flow. "They told me you were dead," she whispered. "And it was *my fault…*"

Leaning into her, so she could put her face in his chest, Jake admonished himself for noticing the lavender smell of her recently shampooed hair.

"They lied to you," he whispered. "Another means of their control. That's what Haxx… uh, Tino… told me. The staff psychologists are a little concerned. You've been through a lot—mental conditioning, sleep- and dream-state manipulation, memory extraction… Tino's division seems to know quite a bit about it. We'll be briefed once you're feeling better. There's something else… someone you apparently dream about every time you sleep. Someone you call PF…"

Before Jake could continue, a young, attractive nurse came in with Kirstine's dinner. "Hi Jake," she said with a smile. "I would have thought you'd had enough of Johns Hopkins's trauma ward to last a couple of lifetimes."

"Funny how it all works out, Deva," Jake replied, feeling his cheeks start to flush. "Turns out all the best people come here for treatment."

Bringing the bed's food tray up and locking it in position, Deva placed Kirstine's meal—a bowl of chicken soup, a package of Saltines, a container of apple juice, and some rice pudding—down in front of her. "Make sure you eat and drink all of this, Doctor MacGregor," she said, the words more stern than her tone of voice. "You've been through quite an ordeal according to your chart and the quicker we get your strength back, the quicker your mind will heal." Making some notations on an app on her phone, Deva smiled again at Jake. "Good to see you again."

"You too," Jake said.

"You've got a fan club," Kirstine said, lifting a spoon from the tray and scooping up some soup. "I'm glad you got some benefit out of all this." Stopping the spoon a few inches from her mouth, she dropped it into the bowl. "I am so sorry, Jake. Sending you that hard drive was inappropriate... I hardly know you..."

Not knowing what to do or say as Kirstine brought her hands to her face to hide a fresh bout of tears, Jake stuttered out, "First of all, this... this is *my fault*... using that information my father passed on to me... to sabotage you... to get listens... sub*scri*bers, for fuck's sake... So, I think... under the circumstances of what we have been through... together... and apart... saying you hardly know me.... really isn't true. Or... more accurately... it... actually doesn't matter. Because getting to know each other will be easy, because we are both so very sorry and it maybe isn't even our fault." Reaching for the package of crackers and opening the plastic with a tug, he added, more confidently, "You really should eat. Deva's right, you've—"

"Been through a lot. I know," Kirstine answered, wiping her nose and eyes and taking the Saltine Jake was offering. "I remember a lot. And I haven't shared quite everything. PF, for instance... It is just completely crazy. Embarrassing. Probably a subconscious artifact of the trauma..."

Leaning in, Jake said, "Maybe not. Seems like it was real. Like a conversation with someone *actually there*, I mean. Someone who is trying to help you... protect you. Like I am..."

Eating some soup and sipping on the apple juice, Kirstine nodded. "I think so too. Okay, Jake... given our very odd, strangely deep yet admittedly fledgling relationship, I am going to be honest. I think... well... I think that PF is an *angel*. But not the white robes and halo kind. Something darker... Ancient. And very powerful. Tied up in all of this craziness about the pirates and the codes and whatever Reinhardt was trying to pull from my mind."

"Well," Jake said, taking her hand once again in his. "Next time he comes around, tell him I'm immensely grateful—we all are—but we can take it from here."

On an uncomfortable chair behind the stained oaken table in the modestly converted captain's cabin of the *Whydah Gally*—dubbed by Quartermaster Fletcher the *Whydah Fightin' Ship*, which had caught on with the crew—Commodore Samuel Bellamy poured over his carefully scribed logs from the past six weeks.

It was an incredible amount of information and adventure to absorb.

As the *Whydah* and *Marianne*—under the capable command of Paulsgrave Williams—had made their way up the mid-Atlantic Coast, the converted slave ship of twenty-eight guns and the battle-proven sloop of eight guns and their well-seasoned crews proved to be more than a match for the fourteen ships they had engaged. In just the previous two weeks, they had captured three notable prizes: First, the *Agnes*, fifteen miles off Cape Charles, Virginia, her hull filled to bursting with sugar, rum, and molasses. They then took a galley out of Glasgow called the *Mary Anne*, which they were currently using as a supply vessel under the command of Williams's quartermaster, Richard Noland, although it was Sam's plan to abandon her before the final phase of their operation. Then they encountered *The Endeavor*, a pink out of England, with a cargo—soiled though it was—that was truly unexpected.

While Captain Williams, Mister Fletcher, and the other officers inspected the captured vessel's goods, sheets, and cordage, Bellamy boarded her and began his interview of her captain and complement of officers. He had barely begun when an overdressed aristocrat came bursting forth from below decks, powder flying from his curled grey wig as he exclaimed, "What is the meaning of this intrusion!"

Drawing a pistol and his sword while indicating to the rest of his crew that they should not follow suit, but continue with their inspections, Commodore Bellamy said, "Ye have been fairly boarded, sir! No harm shall come to ye or these others, provided ye do not interfere, nor raise your voice to me again."

"And who are ye, sir, to make such threats to me?" the aristocrat replied, a hint of weakness creeping into his voice.

"I am Commodore Samuel Bellamy, of the New Providence Republic of Pirates. And who might ye be, ye prattling, squealing pup?"

The look of surprise upon the aristocrat's face gave Bellamy pause. He had to keep himself from lowering his pair of weapons even an inch.

"Samuel Bellamy, formerly of Hittisleigh, Devonshire?" the aristocrat asked, the tone of his voice signaling that the answer could possibly cost the man his life.

"The very same. And I ask thee again for your name, *sir*."

"I am Lord Andrew Colson, former deputy governor of the Royal African Company, due to rendezvous with a ship in three days' time and hence to journey to the western coast of Africa on a matter of extreme importance."

Now it was Bellamy who felt a wave of surprise washing over his mind, although he could not afford to show it. "Lord Andrew Colson… Son of Lord Richard Colson of Exeter, claimer of the common lands of Hittisleigh, and owner of a devilish cane brandished by a cowardly son many years ago? Lord Andrew Colson… trafficker of slaves, purveyor of human misery, and therefore not worthy to exist?"

Cursing the god who would bring those two frightened youth of so long ago together again under such unimaginable circumstances, Colson willed himself to show the strength he had until recently lacked.

"The very same. I have also heard of *your* exploits, Commodore Bellamy. I heartily congratulate ye for all ye have done for your righteous and rightful cause."

All of the men who had frozen in place around them—from all three crews—as this most extraordinary exchange unfolded now breathed a sigh of relief, as Bellamy sheathed his sword and stowed his pistol in his sash.

Asking the captain of *The Endeavor* for permission for the two men to use his quarters so that they may talk in private, Bellamy invited Colson to join him below decks. Emerging alone two hours later, the commodore received an update from his officers, made generous terms with the captain of the pink, and prepared to return to the *Whydah*. As he swung his leg over the starboard gunnel, he heard Colson's voice.

"May God look down upon and bless your mission with mercy, Commodore Bellamy," the traitor to the Mammon Lodge and King George offered, raising his hand in salute.

"And may He do the same for yours, sir," Bellamy answered, returning the gesture with a smile.

If anyone—Paulsgrave Williams included—wished to know in detail what had taken place, both on deck and below, between their commodore and Colson, something in Bellamy's eyes and the set of his jaw kept them from making the request.

Unless he was putting his crew at risk, a pirate captain's reasons for his actions were no one's business but his own.

Proceeding northward from Virginia, and well aware of the formidable presence of the ships of the line of the Royal Navy near the major northern ports, they planned to keep their trio of ships well clear of New York and Boston, instead heading for the smaller colonies beyond them.

A day into their journey, Bellamy and Williams took advantage of an approaching storm. Waiting until the fog settled good and thick, Mister Noland—who had relinquished command of the supply ship *Mary Anne* after all of her cargo had been split between the other two ships—had come over the gunnel of the *Whydah* from a longboat in which his captain waited. Meeting Bellamy in the deep shadows beneath the forecastle, Noland wordlessly received a carefully wrapped, secured package and crept away before anyone could see him.

Within hours, as dawn broke upon their vessels, the sea began to rage and the early spring Atlantic winds to blow both fierce and cold. As they weighed anchor and set about riding out the storm—leaving the scuttled *Mary Anne* to be taken by the sea—the *Marianne* "became separated from the *Whydah*," as the official story for several centuries would say.

In truth, Williams, the irreplaceable, invaluable package now in his hands, headed for Block Island, twelves miles off the coast of Rhode Island, where he would meet with one of the leaders of the Jacobite cause in America—a man whom Bellamy knew virtually nothing about.

Not even a name.

All had gone as planned, with the sole exception being the fact that the main mast of the former slave ship *Whydah* had sprung during the worst of the storm, necessitating immediate and careful repair. Despite this potentially catastrophic incident, a week later, off the coast of Rhode Island, the *Marianne* and *Whydah* made a joyous—and to all general accounts amongst the crews, happily *coincidental*—reunion before heading further north to Machias, Maine and Newfoundland, for reasons the pair of captains did not care to share.

Then, early this morning, as they were preparing to turn south for the Province of Massachusetts near the St. Lawrence River, a thirty-six gun French warship had appeared out of nowhere, taking the captains by surprise. After exchanging cannon fire for the better part of two hours, and the *Whydah* suffering heavy casualties, the wind rose in their favor and Bellamy and Williams were able to engineer—though barely—their escape.

"That ambush was no accident, Samuel!" Paulsgrave had said, pouring them each a mug of rum in his cabin several hours later. "They were after the Marlowe manuscripts—no doubt at the behest of Athelstan Ravenskald or one of his sons. How wise ye were to have me hide them. We are still, however, in danger. We must act quickly, with resolve."

"Tell me what to do, Paulsgrave, and I swear I shall obey," Bellamy said, his blood going cold at the name his mentor had finally said aloud.

"Ye must make it known that ye are done with pirating for now, and are returning to your one true love on Cape Cod. I shall return to Block Island for further council with our leader. He is proud of ye, Sam. Rest assured of that."

"Yet ye cannot tell me his name."

Placing his hand on Bellamy's shoulder, Williams whispered, "For the safety of ye both. Though one day, not very far in the future, ye shall be summoned from your happy life with Goody Halleck to Rhode Island so that ye two may finally meet."

Finishing his rum, Bellamy answered, his hand upon Williams's, "I shall hold ye to that. And as to your request for my announcement, I shall happily make it so."

"Why is it, my somber friends, that, instead of a joyful reunion, we are better suited, based on mood and visage, to be attending a funeral?"

Lifting a candle and bringing it close to his companions' faces to better gauge their answer in the dark, dank basement of the Constant Companion tavern, Colonel James Moore, newly arrived from South Carolina Colony, tried not to laugh.

"Honestly, James," Edward Moseley, head of the cooperative of landowners, military men, and provocateurs known as The Family, said, gently pushing the candlestick away. "While ye have met with continued success—extending our gains from the Tuscarora War here at home to the Yamasee War in South Carolina, Jeremiah and I have been brutalized by Absalom Ravenskald—who disappeared some months ago without a word, adding to our misery."

"Ye contradict yourself, Edward," Moore replied, pouring each of them a glass of claret. "If the damnable man is such a misery, are ye not better off without him?"

"One would think," Vail responded, draining his glass and leaning back in his chair, out of the way of the candle Moore still held. "Although his tentacles extend far and wide—into all of our varied businesses. Not one of our allies is free from his influence and opinion. And his opinion of The Family is rather low indeed."

Placing the candle on the table, Moore shook his head. "Not the Family—the two of ye. Oh yes... I have not been so busy with the Cherokee and Creek—and our new friends, Deputy Governor Daniell and the ambitious pirate turned loyalist, Colonel William Rhett—that I have not been able to keep current on the news from the Albemarle. Ye gave ground to this Ravenskald in February of last year, when you broke into Eden's office. He pegged ye as a pair of malleable cowards, and ye have lived up to it at every turn. So do not whine... Ye have put us well behind, and I have not the humor for it. Not as hard as my brother Maurice and I have been working in our stronger sister colony."

"Now see here, James," Vail replied. "We are still the primary agents of the Lords Proprietors Carteret and Craven here in the Carolinas, as well as Governor Spotswood in Virginia. We have not stopped filling our coffers, extending our holdings... So, if ye please... show some fucking respect."

Within the blink of an eye, Jeremiah found himself out of his chair, which remained tangled between his legs, and pinned against a wall dripping with a foul, musty liquid from some unseen clump of moss growing near the ceiling. Of greater concern was Moore's impressively sized knife tucked up tight against his throat.

"Respect, Jeremiah?" the colonel whispered, as Edward retreated to the corner to the right of the pair. "That's right, Edward. Ye just stay there, where I can see thee. Not that ye would come to this loud mouth's aid. How many sleepless nights have his snide remarks in this very room aimed at Absalom Ravenskald cost ye?"

"Ye know more than what ye have told us," Moseley said, careful and polite, causing Vail to hiss at him in frustration. "No one could know what transpired between the three of us in this room. Unless…"

"Now ye understand," Moore answered, pushing Vail tighter against the wall. "I crossed paths with Absalom Ravenskald not a week ago as I was preparing to return to ye. He had just procured a ship to take him to the Virgin Islands in pursuit of the pirate Levasseur. After a day's visit to Beaufort."

Moore smiled as the two men recoiled ever so slightly at the mention of the town that represented their greatest failure to date.

"Yes," the colonel said, pouring salt into the wound. "Still trying to resolve the issues created by your joint incompetency. We spent an evening in a tavern whose proprietor knows how to treat a man of Absalom's stature. A fine meal, the best claret, attractive serving girls, and I managed to ensure that—provided I take full responsibility for the operations of The Family moving forward—no permanent damage has been done. These allies ye speak of—Spotswood, Craven, Carteret—their fear of the Ravenskald family must be *used*. *That* is how we shall undo the past fourteen months' failures birthed from your stupidity."

Releasing Vail, sheathing his knife, and returning to the table, Moore drained his glass, taking two bottles of claret in his hands. "There is laughter in abundance upstairs. Can ye not hear it? Yet ye made me waste an hour in this cellar—site of your shame. I do not wish to see further either of your faces. We shall talk again tomorrow. Now," he added, gesturing to the spot where the basement's hatchway was hidden, "open that up and let me escape thee."

As Moseley quietly complied, Vail remained in the shadows of the wall where Moore had held him. As the foul drippings of the moss above slid down his face and filled his nose, he fingered the hilt of his own sizable knife, grinning the evil grin of the humiliated man whose mind is suddenly abuzz with visions of revenge.

Looking at the fledging town on whose sand and soil he now stood, named for Henry Somerset, the second duke of Beaufort, Absalom Ravenskald saw possibilities.

Endless, exciting possibilities.

With its access to the open ocean through Topsail Inlet, Beaufort, whose land was primarily owned by a local called Robert Turner, whose loyalty to The Family began during the Tuscarora War, had been the focus of many an explorer and entrepreneur who saw its potential for whaling, lumber, shipbuilding, and farming, in addition to its main industry—fishing.

When Walter Raleigh organized his second venture to the American colonies in 1585—funded largely by the Ravenskalds—he placed his seven ships under the command of Sir Richard Grenville, whose responsibility it was to form a military colony on the island of Roanoke, off the coast of what was then Carolina Province.

Grenville—known to be proud and ambitious, *like Alexander Spotswood*, Absalom thought—had overreacted over the disappearance of a silver drinking cup while he and some of his crew were the guests of the Algonquians in the village of Aquascogoc that June, which he ordered his men to sack and burn to the ground.

From there he had made a landing at Beaufort, then an unnamed fishing village that his crew of three hundred found to be notably rich in the offerings of the sea.

In both Beaufort and a few days later at the Wococon inlet and island near what was renamed Ocracoke one hundred and thirty years later, Grenville—his flagship *Tiger* purposefully grounded on a sandbar—had hidden two of the twelve sacred objects the Ravenskald family were intent on collecting. Raleigh placed them in his care before Grenville sailed from England.

He hid the Jeshua Cask—a vessel containing the dried blood of Jesus Christ— on Wococon. Absalom knew agents of the Star Quorum had removed it to somewhere in Italy sometime in the 1600s.

It was in the fishing village where Absalom now stood that Grenville had hidden the Tiber Vial. Hidden it so well that, despite his best efforts, the torture and death of two Portuguese fishermen, and the failed efforts of Moseley and Vail, Absalom had yet to locate it.

His gut told him it still had to be here.

Why else would Lord Carteret—for whom the subservient Carolinians had named the larger precinct—have arranged to have Henry Somerset poisoned in 1714? Becoming Palatine of the

Carolinas—the most powerful of the proprietors—would not have been reason enough. It would be years before Henry's children would be old enough to mount a challenge to Carteret, who would, in the meantime, have Beaufort all to himself.

Passing the rows of newly planted live oaks that would no doubt create a tapestry of comfort and respite in the twelve-block layout of Beaufort once they were fully grown, Absalom took note of the street names. Craven, named for Baron William Craven, Lord Carteret's weak-willed minion. Moore, for Colonel James Moore, the only member of The Family worth more than a handful of cow's dung, with whom he had recently met. Turner, for the town's founder. Queen and Anne, an homage to the now-dead daughter of James Stuart, who also had the honor in the Americas of giving her name to the War of Spanish Succession, from which the Ravenskalds had profited immensely.

Absalom was not surprised that there were no streets named for Moseley and Vail.

As he approached a whitewashed home near a creek, located close enough for a small boat to tie up at its front door, Absalom thought about the tobacco merchant, explorer, and spy that had collaborated with the Ravenskalds to fund the Grenville expedition.

Sir Walter Raleigh, founder of a secret group of Catholic loyalists and supporters of the Star Quorum—a group that included the playwrights Thomas Kyd and Christopher Marlowe—which a Jesuit ally cleverly named The School of Atheism, had ultimately outlived his usefulness. Marlowe's murder, Raleigh's death by beheading in London's Old Palace Yard on a fifteen-year-old charge of treason (treasonous to the Ravenskalds, if not to King James), and the imprisonment and ruination of the career and reputation of Kyd were all engineered by the Ravenskalds. They had funded Raleigh's 1617 to the Amazon, during which "Spaniards" reportedly killed his son, while they were traveling along the Orinoco River. The truth was that they were non-Spanish agents of the Ravenskalds, who had undertaken this series of actions in part to send a message to Sir Francis Bacon, Lord Chancellor of England, whose operations against the powerful family could not go unanswered.

Soon Marlowe's coded manuscripts would be in the hands of Absalom's family. As he waited here in Beaufort—at the back door of this solitary, whitewashed home—to meet a man who had professed to know the whereabouts of the Tiber Vial, his father Athelstan was preparing to procure the documents, needed to make full use of the twelve sacred objects.

The Ravenskalds intended to make the very most of them, separately and together.

Knocking upon the door of the house, Absalom drew his pistol and turned as a voice from behind him whispered, "Ye shall not enter my house. We shall talk out here in the open, for I have not much to tell ye."

Scanning the trees from behind which the voice had emanated, Absalom approached the largest of the cluster of live oaks, placing his pistol in his sash.

"Come forth now, good sir. I shall not harm ye. Or, if nature provides security so that ye shall tell me what it is I have traveled here yet again to try and know, feel free to remain where ye are. Though I thought ye were a braver man than that."

After a moment's hesitation, the owner of the house—and most of the town—Robert Turner, stepped out into the open, his hands stretched before him to show he held no weapon.

"Where is the object, Turner? The vial… Ye indicated to my agents that ye know."

"Aye, I know it well enough, Master Ravenskald… for it was my family that were guardians of it for many a generation."

Placing his hand upon the butt of his pistol, Absalom whispered, "*Were…*"

"What those two Portuguese fishermen no doubt told ye was true," Turner said, moving his legs and lower torso back behind the tree. "They had taken the vial to a ship anchored in Topsail Inlet at my request. They were returning to me when ye took them."

Shaking his head, Absalom replied, "They did not tell me for *whom* it was they worked. It took all of my considerable skill to extract the broad strokes of their errand. Which is why it took me so long to find ye. I thought Moseley and Vail would be the honey to lure their employer, though I was mistaken."

Spitting on the ground before his feet, Turner replied. "A pair of mangy dogs. If ye had sent Colonel Moore, ye would have succeeded."

"This I have come to understand. It cost a painful amount of time and considerable coin to uncover the trail to this house. To *ye*, Turner. Now… will ye tell me where the Tiber Vial hides, or shall I bring your promising future in this promising place to an end, despite your shield of oak?"

"Keep your pistol where it sits, sir," Turner said from behind the tree. "And your knife as well. I know ye hold it behind your back. There are half a dozen pairs of eyes—each with a musket just beneath them—on ye as we speak."

"Damn this town," Absalom hissed, bringing his arm around and holding it out in front of him to show the knife Turner had divined was in his hand. "Damn this precinct, this whole wretched colony... Will ye tell me what ye know?"

"Aye," Turner said. "That is what I told your agent, and I am a man of my word. Those poor Portuguese delivered the vial to a ship bound for the colony of Rhode Island. I know not who received it, or from where in the colony they come. I know only that the order to relinquish the object was one I could not ignore, for it came from the very highest of places."

Sheathing his knife behind his back, Absalom smiled, though it was a smile of continued defeat and frustration.

"Your guile and preparation saved your life today, Robert Turner. But know this—I will come back to Beaufort one day, and lay claim to the best of what ye build here in payment for the time and money of mine and my family's ye have wasted. Ye deserve worse than I gave those fishermen. And, on the day I collect my claim, I shall gladly give it to ye and then some."

As he walked away, Absalom heard Turner spit again.

It was all he could do not to turn around.

Damnable Carolinians—not one of them knew their place.

"**I** would well like ta be part a' the crew wit' the wine, Commodore, if ya please!"

Shaking his head while nearly laughing, Samuel Bellamy tried to seem the no-nonsense leader needed in such circumstances.

Bending down to look the youngest of his crew, eleven-year-old John King, in the eyes, Bellamy said. "I need ye on the *Whydah*, Mister King, to assist Quartermaster Fletcher, as ye have been."

Kicking the deck in frustration, King dropped his head, knowing better than to argue with the commodore's decision.

"A word, sir," Mister Fletcher whispered, quick at Bellamy's shoulder.

Moving to an empty space near the mizzenmast so they could talk in private, Bellamy said, "Time is of the essence, Mister Fletcher. We must assign a crew to our latest capture and point our bows for the Cape. There is a storm brewing and our mainmast cannot withstand another blow like that we suffered near Virginia."

"Unnerstood, sir," Mister Fletcher said. "An' I would not bother the commodore at such a time as this, but I was hopin' this prize might constitute my first command."

This is the last thing I need this morning, Bellamy thought. The capture of the ship now secured on their port side, an eight-gun sloop called the *Anne* out of Dublin—until an hour and half ago under the command of Captain Andrew Crumpstey—had been an unexpected opportunity seized upon more out of habit than strategy. Crumpstey, not willing to cross cannon with such a formidable opponent, had braced abox—maneuvering his ship so that the wind spilled from the *Anne*'s sails, signaling surrender—with little provocation from the *Whydah*. If it were not for her valuable cargo—seven thousand gallons of Madiera wine according to the manifest—Bellamy might have taken as many barrels as time would allow and gone on his way.

The damned barrels, however, were the problem. So well secured were they, with thick bands of cordage holding them in place, that all Bellamy's crew were able to bring above decks were a few dozen bottles, which the commodore had ordered Fletcher to transfer to the *Whydah*.

"I need ye aboard with me, to assure all goes well in the final hours before we make port on Cape Cod," Bellamy answered.

"Aye," Fletcher answered. "Like ye need young Mister King, I presume?"

A look of warning from his commodore set Fletcher to an apology. "No offense, sir. Jus' been lookin' forward. But I trust ye judgment now as always. Who may I ask will be takin' charge a' the *Anne*?"

"Mister Noland."

Former quartermaster for Paulsgrave's *Marianne*, Richard Noland had stayed behind, professing to have business in Boston that neither captain questioned after so many months of faithful, flawless service, when Bellamy's mentor had again sailed for Rhode Island three days earlier.

"Although," Bellamy continued, "when we have been refitted and resupplied, the *Anne* shall assuredly be yours. Now, Mister Fletcher. Look to the *Whydah* and see she is well prepared for this fast-approaching storm."

As Fletcher turned to go, Bellamy decided to stop him. "One more thing, Quartermaster. Captain Williams mentioned that ye entrusted one of his senior crew with more than half your take from the *Whydah*, for delivery to Glen Shira, in the Scottish Highlands, where ye learned this man was heading. These are dangerous times, sir—may I ask to whom the funds shall be delivered?"

"Ye may, sir," Fletcher answered, leaning in close. "Tho' 'tis a bit embarrassin' an' certainly private. I have a cousin, Findlay—a barber by trade—who has fallen upon the most tryin' a' times. His fiancé, a lovely lass called Rowan—caught the fancy of a rat bastard aristocrat name a' Murray. What he done ta the girl, sir, while keepin' her locked in a room in their palace—"

Bellamy raised his hand, feeling his cheeks go red. "Ye need say no more, Mister Fletcher. I trust the couple have been reunited?"

"They have, sir. I hear tell the righteous outlaw Rob Roy has made it his personal mission ta look after them."

Bellamy smiled. "Angus... Conall, that is... would be well and truly pleased to know what his uncle has done. Very well, then, Mister Fletcher. Ye know your work. See to it."

Watching Fletcher go, Bellamy turned his thoughts to whom he would select to crew the *Anne*. Scanning the men aboard her, he began to call out names. "Simon Van Vorst, John Brown, Thomas South, Thomas Baker, Hendrick Quintor, Peter Cornelius Hoof, and John Shuan—ye shall remain aboard with a few of the *Anne*'s crew, to see her home to port. There shall be no sampling of her cargo, nor tormenting of said crew, is that understood?"

Amid an enthusiastic cry of agreement, Bellamy looked to the sky.

Dark clouds were rolling in. They best make for the Cape without delay.

EL ESCORIAL, 28 MILES OUTSIDE OF MADRID, SPAIN, APRIL 26, 1717

The sun had just begun to rise over the Monasterio y Sitio de El Escorial en Madrid, sending a spray of jewel-like glimmers across the reflecting pool, as Isobel Farnese, the queen of Spain, crossed the Gardens of the Friars, a deep hood hiding her face from the few groundskeepers and clergymen milling about the expansive complex. Entering through the middle door of the main façade and crossing the Courtyard of the Kings, she took in the statues of the kings of Judah lining the exterior wall of the Basilica and made the sign of the cross.

Once inside the Basilica of San Lorenzo el Real, Isobel genuflected at the base of the Greek cross, its four arms, equal in length, marking the floor of this holiest of places and peered into the dome above her. Inspired by the dome of St. Peter's in Rome—although their support systems greatly differed—the one atop San Lorenzo el Real also served a different purpose for the people who visited and lived there, as did the basilica itself. In place of the romance of the Italians, who celebrated God and his divinity with soaring, breathtaking beauty, the Spanish embraced humility, utility, and the fundamental suffering of the Inquisition.

Suddenly missing her true home in Parma, Isobel made her way to the altar at the head of the cross, where she placed an offering of specially mixed herbs soaked in olive oil in a bronze bowl left for the purpose, as the trio of cardinals had instructed her.

Saying a prayer to Mary Mater for a mother's strength and resolve despite hardship, she ran her eyes over the granite and jasper altar screen and the paintings and statues that adorned it. Crossing herself before the tabernacle, she turned her head and looked through an archway into an adjoining chapel so she could bask in the beauty of Benvenuto Cellini's crucified Christ in white marble.

Slipping through a shadowed door and down a flight of red marble stairs, similar to those leading to the altar in the basilica above, Isobel stopped a moment to breathe—her heart was beating at a rapid pace, so overwhelming was all she had so far seen—and to appreciate the walls of Toledo marble with their gold-plated bronze ornamentations.

What a sight the Royal Pantheon was to Isobel's devout Catholic eyes. An octagonal mausoleum containing the bronze and marble sepulchers of twenty-six kings and queens—including Charles the First, Philip the Second, and Philip the Fourth—the crypt had a marble altar of its own.

None of these was of interest to her today.

Glancing over her shoulder to make sure she was alone, Isobel knelt before the sepulcher that read, in large raised letters on a bronze plaque decorated with intricate scrollwork, Elisabeth. Pressing the edge of the left-most veined marble section of the base, Isobel felt it give beneath her fingers.

Reaching into the hidden space behind it, she extracted a cask twelve inches in length and slightly more in diameter whose wood smelled of immeasurable age. She had paid a considerable price for the cask to an Italian merchant, using a portion of the treasures destined for the doomed Spanish plate fleet that sank off the coast of Florida in 1715.

She was still a week away from her marriage to Philip when Cardinal Alberoni brought her to El Escorial for several days of fasting and prayer. As soon as she was able, she took the opportunity to hide the cask as the mysterious traveler who had visited her as a child in Parma had told her she one day would. There could be no more perfect place for Isobel to do so than beneath the resting place of Elisabeth of France—also known as Isabella of Bourbon—first wife of Philip the Fourth, queen of Spain and Portugal, and regent of Spain in the years of the Catalan revolt.

Standing the cask on its end, Isobel contemplated what it contained—the dried blood of Jeshua ben Joseph, her Lord Jesus Christ and shining light of the Holy Catholic Church.

Resisting the urge to pull the bung from the top and peer inside, Isobel instead placed her hands in an attitude of prayer and began, "My Lord Jesus Christ, never let me be guilty of Thy Body and Blood by unworthy communion. For the sake of this same precious Blood, which Thou hast shed for me, deliver me, O Jesus, from so great an evil."

"*Amen.*"

So deep in prayer had Isobel been, so sincere her supplication, that she did not hear the footsteps approach from behind her.

Turning, standing, and trying to hide the cask beneath her cloak all in one motion, Isobel found herself face to face with Melchor Rafael de Macanaz, one of Philip's closest advisors, with ambition that rivaled her own.

He was a deceiver she thoroughly despised.

"Minister Macanaz," she began, adopting the posture, visage, and voice of the frail daughter of a Parmian prince for which so many in the Spanish court had fallen. "Is it your habit to interrupt the king's wife in the midst of her prayers?"

"Ah, ah, ah," Macanaz said, the smile in his eyes and the one formed by his mouth radiating an intent with which Isobel, being of fair face and shape, was well acquainted. "You cannot play the innocent with me, My Queen. I know what that cask you are trying to hide contains."

"Which is?" How she wished she had thought to bring a knife, although she knew she could not have brought herself to use it in this holy place even if she had.

"A portion of the jewels you demanded for your dowry. The jewels that, in the course of our securing them, delayed Capitan General Juan Esteban de Ubilla and the plate fleet. We need not speak of the outcome of that action, and the despicable fault of your greed."

Covering the relief that arose with his mistaken idea of what was in the cask with the genuine surprise she felt upon hearing that the minister was aware of her request—thought to be a private negotiation between Cardinal Alberoni on behalf of the Holy Catholic Church and Isobel's father—she managed to whisper, "But how do you know that?"

Opening his mouth like a leopard set to lunch on a gazelle he had just pinned beneath his paw, Macanaz let loose a laugh that echoed like the song of Satan off the bronze and marble walls and sepulchers. "I know many, many things, My Queen. For instance, I know that you and the ambitious cardinal who serves you—and you him—are conspiring to make the king's natural madness all the worse. You are no doubt removing a portion of your hidden wealth in order to bribe some official—or perhaps to purchase more of the herbs and ointments you are using to control your husband's moods."

Crossing her arms to still the trembling in her hands, Isobel said, "You say you know many, many things, Minister Macanaz. So far, I have heard only rumor and speculation—no better than that coming from the lowest of maids-in-waiting and minor countryside nobles. Tell me something you truly *know*, or leave me to my prayer."

Macanaz's dark brown eyes seemed to go black as he took several steps toward her, pushing her back against Isabella of Bourbon's tomb and the cask against its marble base, so it scraped and creaked beneath her.

"Very well, *Isobel*... or do you prefer Elisabeth or Isabella in such apt company as this?" He was now close enough for her to feel his breath upon her cheek. "For one thing, I *know* that your skills in the bedchamber are considerable. I *know* that your lust is like a man's, and I *know* that you give yourself willingly and often."

Feeling his hands upon her hips, Isobel hissed, "How dare you..."

Placing a long, ringed finger upon her lips, Macanaz whispered into her ear. "I dare because I also know that your secret is more important than your honor, or even your faith. I can feel your heart racing, beside this crucifix you wear, and it is not the pulse of fear. I shall keep your secret, Isobel Farnese, but you shall have to prove to me what I know about your skills—here and now, upon the tomb of one you so admire—beyond the shadow of a doubt."

Closing her eyes and sending a request to God for forgiveness for what she was doing in his name, Isobel lifted the skirts of the simple peasant's dress she wore beneath her cloak. She placed her hand on the crucifix that hung from her neck as Minister Macanaz undid his sword belt and began in earnest to confirm with thoroughness and exactitude all he professed to know.

OFF THE COAST OF MASSACHUSETTS, APRIL 26, 1717

"**I**t is nay any use, Commodore! The storm is far too strong, an' we are far too heavy!"

"I will not have it, Mister Fletcher!" Samuel Bellamy replied, grasping an axe in his nearly numb hand. "Club hauling still may work to keep her from turning her side to the waves. We must chop the fore and mizzen masts as well to keep her from layin' over. Will ye give me your assistance?"

Waving an axe of his own in response and heading for the foremast, Mister Fletcher looked like a man defeated. Samuel Bellamy knew well enough that there was not a man aboard the *Whydah* who did not feel the same.

Much was due to fatigue—the storm had steadily worsened as they approached the Cape—reaching its full height and fury—relentless rain, a piercing wind, and forty-foot seas—a few hours prior, shortly after they had taken the two-masted snow *Fisher* that was now near to capsizing off their port side.

Bellamy's decision to add another ship to their flotilla of two—the Madeira-laden *Anne* being the other—was not for her cargo of deer hides and tobacco, but the sure set of her sails, which indicated to Bellamy that at least one man on board knew the navigation of these waters well enough to assist them through the storm.

That man turned out to be Robert Ingels, captain of the *Fisher*, who complied with Bellamy's request, in return for assurance that the ship and half his cargo would remain with him upon arrival in port.

Turning his attention to the *Anne*, which was floundering to starboard, Bellamy was grateful that he had had the foresight to order each of the three ships' yardarms hung with lanterns so that the trio might better track each other. The last thing they needed was the roiling seas pushing them into one another, although, at the rate the storm-driven waves were pushing the lighter ships toward the shore, the chances of collision were fast diminishing.

Chopping at the mizzenmast with two others from his crew, Bellamy cursed the strength of the nor'easter. It was almost unnatural, this late-April fury.

Stepping aside as the mizzenmast came down, in almost perfect conjunction with the foremast that he had sent Mister Fletcher to dispatch, Bellamy held his breath as he waited to see how the galley would respond. His intention in dropping the anchors an hour earlier had been to keep her bow steady into the waves, to keep the ship from turning broadside to the waves and capsizing.

The shake and shudder of the hull sang back to him his folly—the anchors were not serving the purpose he intended. The *Whydah* was slowly starting to come about and the anchors were straining the hull to the point of bursting her seams.

"Chop away the anchors!" Bellamy ordered, taking a face full of seawater that made him stutter and gasp. The salt stung his eyes, nearly blinding him, and his first attempt at severing the anchor nearest to him was a clean, embarrassing miss.

"Allow me, sir!" It was John King, all of eleven years old, who was wielding a pair of boarding axes. "I have been practicing my stroke, Commodore. Thought it would be against some Royal Navy blighters—or maybe that sneaking pup Vane—but anchor cables shall do well enough."

"That's a good lad. Strike it with all your might, Mister King. And there just might be a promotion in it for ye."

As the boy went to work on freeing the anchor, joined by several others, whose arms and axes were far larger, Bellamy leaned into the gunnel as exhaustion began to take him.

"We are about out a' options, Commodore. What are yer orders?"

Wiping the salt but not the sting from his eyes, Bellamy tried to focus on the man before him. Luckily, he knew the voice well enough.

"We pray, Mister Fletcher. For our very lives depend upon it."

"Not much fer prayin', Commodore," the quartermaster replied. "Though I do 'ave some regrets I 'ave been chewin' on 'ard."

"Such as?" Bellamy asked, grateful for the diversion, for, other than prayer, he truly was out of options.

"Should 'ave sent all a' my share ta my cousin Findlay. Now it shall be at the bottom a' the sea, an' good ta no man there, I tell ya, and then the vultures—the land pirates, God curse 'em, shall descend upon the wreck, ta gather what ain't earned."

"Think not such dreary thoughts, Mister Fletcher," Bellamy said, just as a crash of thunder, followed hard fast by a bolt of lightning that split the sky, signaled a great gush of waves that set the bell to clanging and the hull hard to port.

"The cannons are comin' loose! Take cover!" he heard the sailing master, Mister Main, shout, as the collective cries of the men on both the *Anne* and *Fisher* increased to an ear-splitting shriek as they were driven toward the shore, capsizing within moments of each other.

Ducking involuntarily at the sound of what he thought was another clap of thunder, Bellamy sank to his knees as he realized that what he had heard was the main mast—her patch from weeks ago unable to stand the relentless strain—splitting with a groan as the *Whydah* was pushed with Hell's own fury toward the shore.

"Commodore Bellamy! Help me, sir... I do not want to die!"

John King stood before him, all the bravado of the insistent boy who had threatened to thrash his mother if she did not let him become a pirate gone.

"Come to me, lad, and I shall protect you," Bellamy said, opening his arms, then closing them with a father's love as John King clung to his torso. "Forgive me, Goody," the once commodore of the Pirate Republic—now a boy named Sam from Devonshire no different than the one wailing in his arms—whispered as he felt the deck beneath him begin to heave and break apart. "I came so very, very close to coming home to ye as the man I promised I would become."

Slipping his arm into a length of cordage that had entwined itself around the gunnel, Sam reviewed his life. Working the family farm, the beating he took from Colson—how odd they met as men not a week and a half ago... His failures in Portsmouth and victories on the sea. Meeting Paulsgrave and taking the Oath at the feet of a Catholic Cardinal... How it led to New Providence and Hornigold, Thache, and MacGregor. His partnership with Levasseur and the trouble it had caused... His election as commodore and almost immediate abandonment of the Fort and the ideals of the Republic, as he fought for something greater. Last, and nearly the most regrettable, was the tasks he had taken up through his meeting with the Star Quorum and how fully he was failing their mandates in his current situation.

As the straining of the ship produced a shriek that competed for primacy with the howl of the wind and the screams of dying, mutilated, and drowning men all around him, Black Sam Bellamy, the Robin Hood of the Seas, and Keeper of the Oath, at last closed his eyes against the inevitable arrival of Death.

As the relentless storm began to dash the *Whydah* to pieces against the shore, a cloaked figure on a ship a safe distance away carefully retrieved a box tied to a length of rope reaching seven feet down into the water on the starboard side of the ship. The box was steadily humming as it gave off a soft blue glow, which the man found almost mesmerizing. Placing a pair of gloved fingers on a small lever just below the spinning outer-most gear of a complex device known as the Ezekiel Wheel, he gave the lever a gentle push, smiling as the device began to power down.

The storm, which the Ezekiel Wheel had not conjured but suffused with an energy it would not have otherwise had—recalling to its user Ariel's assisting Prospero in conjuring the storm that opens *The Tempest*—immediately began to subside.

Satisfied it was now safe to do so, the man removed his gloves and ran his hands over the four bas-relief images of Biblical man, ox, lion, and eagle that adorned the device.

Aware of the prying eyes of the captain and his crew, who were emerging from below decks as the storm subsided, the man slipped the box into a velvet bag, which he tucked under his arm beneath his oversized cloak.

One cannot be too careful, he thought, watching the first of what would be over a hundred and sixty bodies begin to wash up on the rocky shore of Eastham.

There were a few living men as well, dragging themselves up the sandy beach. Just a handful—the chances that one was Commodore Samuel Bellamy were very slim indeed.

Everyone knew a loyal captain always went down with his ship. Even a filthy pirate like him.

One thing was clear—Marlowe's coded manuscripts of the *Jew of Malta* and *Doctor Faustus* were now at the bottom of the ocean, where time and tide would soon render them unreadable and then indistinguishable from the rest of the manifests and other meaningless papers on board.

The man, whose name was Athelstan Ravenskald, needed them not. He had another coded manuscript that served the same purpose—a quarto edition of Thomas Kyd's *Spanish Tragedy* with additional scenes by the Rosicrucian agent Shakespeare, although it was Sir Francis Bacon who had done the coding. He had done it for Marlowe's manuscripts and several of Shakespeare's as well.

Instructing the captain to make all haste in preparing the ship for departure—he was going to visit his son Adonijah on the Isle of Skye for an update on the other eleven ancient objects—Athelstan patted the device beneath its velvet protection.

Soon he would have the means to put the Ezekiel Wheel to its true intended purpose. It would again be Ariel to his Prospero. What mighty storms they would raise, on the sea and on the land.

Then he would at last emerge from the shadows, his sons at each of his shoulders, and all the world would kneel.

L ord John Carteret, governor of the Royal African Company and Lord Palatine—chief proprietor of the eight who collectively owned the Colony of North Carolina—was standing upon the ramparts of Dunvegan Castle, which stood upon a summit fifteen meters above sea level, staring out at the bay.

As he fingered the handle of the Abraham Blade beneath the hem of his coat, he felt the blood of Mammon and the venom of the *tanin*— the serpent that lived within the Aaron Staff—coursing through his veins. Sensing the competing energies of Adonijah Ravenskald, who possessed the staff and headed the Mammon Lodge in Dublin and those of a Scotsman called Malcolm, chief of the MacLeods who had claimed the castle and the lands around it on Skye for the past half century, Carteret had a sudden, smile-producing insight. The savagery of each—Adonijah's refined and hidden and Malcom's brutal and proudly displayed—mixed perfectly together within him, as did the mucus of the demon Mammon and the venom of the *tanin*.

Thinking back to his visit to the Grand Lodge of the Masons in London several months earlier, in the guise of Anubis, Carteret smiled wider as he saw the Ravenskalds' plan—of which he was such a prominent part—swirling and coming together over the rough waters of the bay.

If they had to negotiate with yet another brutal savage to ensure its success, it truly was no matter.

In addition to spending more time with his mentor, Adonijah, it was good to be away from the stench and stagnation of London for the better part of a week. Malcolm's household staff had placed Carteret in richly appointed quarters on the fourth level of the castle's tallest tower, just down the hall from the second-most powerful member of the most powerful family in the world.

"Laet oos coonclude oor parlays, Laird Raevenskald, an' saet aboot oor indaevidual paths, eh?" Malcolm said, in his thick and damned near indecipherable brogue, same as all the savage Scottish bastards. "I am eel-suited tae play'n' the host. I mooch praefer tae bae straengthenin' oor holdin's, ken? They haev coom wit' nae small shaedin' a' blood."

"I understand what you are saying," Adonijah answered, although Carteret did not know how—literally or figuratively. "You are a most impressive man, Chief Malcolm. Has there ever been a time that the Sìol Tormoid and Sìol Torcaill have worked so well together?"

Carteret was impressed. Not only was Adonijah able to understand the savage's accent—he even spoke a bit of Gaelic. Carteret, who spoke several languages, including German—much to George of Hanover's delight—preferred the modern to the dead, or nearly so. Adonijah's reference to the two sides—or seeds—of the MacCleod line, which had feuded aplenty in the past, working in such close harmony was his way of complementing Malcolm's leadership in a way that even a simple-minded Scot of the Western Isles would understand.

Adonijah continued. "Your loyalty to the Stuart pretender is admirable, as is your distrust of the MacDonalds, MacGregors, and MacKinnons. And I assure you—as soon as we are able to manage it—their de facto bullyboy Rob Roy will be finally, brutally undone."

"Ock," Malcolm said, spitting over the ramparts toward the bay. "I wish ye loock wit' that. Rob Roy's goot the de'il's faevor, I taell ye. If it wair hae that haid coom wit' the MacDonalds an' McKinnons against oos, nae even the faery flag that flies tae this day oopon the highest tower a' this castle—given tae the fourth chief, Iain Ciar by the faery princess he was granted a year an' a day wit'—would haev saved oos. Rob Roy has the faery blood. Hae has tae. Noon caen catch haim. Noot even that numpty roaster Montrose. Nae forget, Laird Raevenskald—twas after the Battle a' Carbisdale in 1650 that James Graham, the fairst Marquess of Montrose, fael oopon haes knees at Ardvreck Castle baefore oor own Neil MacCleod."

"How could I?" Adonijah asked with a laugh. "It was a Ravenskald that paid the gold to Neil's wife Christine that convinced her to lure Montrose to the dungeon and ultimately to his death at the hands of the Covenanters. If you are insinuating that this admittedly difficult history between the Montroses and MacCleods means that the Fourth Marquess of Montrose will fail to give us his full loyalty and aid, I guarantee you, Chief Malcolm—you are mistaken."

"That may wael bae," Malcolm replied, adjusting his kilt and sporran, "an' I maen ye nae offaence. I joost cannae guess what sooch a piece a shite as Rob MacGraegor—faery blood er nae—would haev tae offer the de'il, the way hae flies froom ally tae ally. Cannae ken a bit."

It took all of John Carteret's will not to correct Malcolm's woefully incorrect assessment. The devil *did* bestow his favor on men—he was living proof of that—but never upon the likes of a Highlander thug and cattle-thief such as Rob Roy.

Further, to suggest that a Highlander was any less than another because he flew from ally to ally was less dangerous and therefore more laughable. Though it was true that the MacLeods had been fighting with the MacDonalds and their allies throughout the sixteenth century, culminating with their defeat of the MacDonalds of Sleat in 1601—and some daft idea of a silken faery flag had naught to do with it—the secret negotiations and back-stabbing in the face of censures and imprisonment by English kings of clan chiefs from *both* sides proved that none was more noble than another.

The same situation was beginning to unfold with the Caribbean pirates. Kings could not afford to look the other way when their profits were being affected—and George was no exception.

Carteret—with the help of Baron William Craven and the Family—was making sure of it.

"You need not give Rob Roy MacGregor a single thought more, Chief Malcolm," Adonijah said, his tone signaling to Carteret that he was losing patience with this history lesson in clan rivalries. "I simply need your assurance that Clan MacCleod will continue to come to the call of the Ravenskalds in the Western Isles without question and with full fealty. I will sail tomorrow to the Isle of Mann, to await the arrival of a key ally and an important object he is bringing to me at Castle Rushen, before returning to Skye to meet with my father. You shall provide protection for them both as they near the isles, as agreed. Yes?"

"Aye," Chief Malcolm MacCleod replied, spitting again toward the bay, which was beginning to churn a deep, dark grey with agitation and expectation. "By the by, 'twas Godred Crovan, comrade a' Harald Hardrada, the last a' the Norwegian Viking kings, who returned the faery flag froom Harald's hands tae those a' Godred Sigtryggsson, who was not long aefter, an' by its power, named king a' the Isle a' Mann."

Lord Carteret pulled his coat tighter around him as a biting wind rose up from the churning bay to invade the castle's ramparts. If only MacCleod's ridiculous stories could protect him from its chill. The supposed faery flag flapping from a tower high above him was nothing but a brown silk memento taken from Syria in the fourth century AD by a Ravenskald knight. The family later presented it to King Harald Hardrada in Norway under the pretense of it being a powerful talisman to gird his shriveled loins as he and Tostig Godwinson, the brother of King Harold the Second, made war on England in the summer of 1066. The fact that Harald Hardrada, along with Tostig, was slain at Stamford Bridge that September should have been proof enough of the worthlessness of the flag, but the Scottish clung to their myths as beetles clung to dung.

The sooner he was back inside his tower rooms the better. He had secured the services of a mildly defective daughter of a local sheep farmer for the week, and it was time to turn her to greater uses. Fingering again the handle of the Abraham Blade—it had been no small relief when Adonijah had returned it to him at the end of his time in Dublin—he ran the tip of his tongue along the length of his lower lip. How grateful Mammon would be for a pale-skinned, generously breasted nonsavage the likes of the farmer's daughter.

And if her defective mind would not fully comprehend what an honor her death was under such illustrious circumstances, Carteret would happily explain it to her as he slit her frail white throat and pulled her still-beating heart tenderly from her chest.

After the ritual, he would be fully energized and ready to assist Adonijah—and his father Athelstan, with whom he was anxious to speak—in the coming fight with the Star Quorum and their army, the Scarlet Knights of St. Grotth.

Nodding to the immense power of nature evidenced by the roiling of the waters of the bay, Carteret turned for the tower, thinking of the ancient object soon to be on its way to Castle Rushen.

It was the leather-lined skull of the long-dead leader of the Essenes.

Carteret would find a way to possess the fabled Baptist Bowl, curse of the Templars and one of the most powerful of the twelve ancient objects. If all went well this evening, he would have an invitation to enter Castle Rushen upon the Jacobite traitor's arrival there. Stealing the skull meant betraying Adonijah, although his foolish plan to install George Seton as a spy in the Masonic Lodges through the false gesture of bringing them the skull was a betrayal in and of itself—of the Mammon Lodge, of their master Mammon, and of Lord John Carteret.

Adonijah would forgive him in time, or he would have to die.

"**I** cannae do it, Rob!"

"If ye do not, how caen ye say ye are a man, Finlay? Take this knife. We haev only a few hours a' darknaess left. Ye shall bae a sair sample of manhood tae yer beloved Rowan if ye turn back froom this task."

Upon returning to Glen Shira after his escape from bullyboys in the employ of John Murray, the first duke of Atholl, Rob had lived with a single thought in his mind.

To kill the nephew of another of the heads of the Murray plague, David Murray, Fifth Viscount of Stormont. And, what was more, to give Findlay Fletcher a hand in that well-deserved revenge.

Findlay, whose mind had become sharper and resolve stronger— or so Rob had thought—had trained hard with Rob and his men for several weeks before the decision was made for the two of them to enter Scone Palace under cover of darkness and dispatch the ravenous bastard who had nearly destroyed Findlay and Rowan's lives.

"Yer beautiful lass is noot healed," Rob said, cursing the time they were wasting. "Keep yer heid. Ye know wael enuff how the sheddin' a' the blood a' those who harmed haer has helped mae Mary. Shae could noot haev survived John Graham's terrible actions against haer had she noot done what shae has. Rowan is in nae condition tae undertake this haerself. So ye moost. Heid doon, arse up!"

Pushing the proffered knife away, Findlay shook his head. "Ock, Rob. We are nae the same as ye an' Mary. I am a barber, nae a leader a' men. An' Rowan, even baefore what shae endured, was nae a fighter. We are grateful tae ye booth, boot this is nae oor path. I know this haever is far froom what ye expaected, an' I am sair sorry fer it, boot mae Rowan, mae bonny, bonny lass, wael naever heal if she wair tae know that I killed Murray's naephew. Shae would smael it on mae hands nae matter how often, how haird I washed thaem. I moost gaet back tae Glen Shira… tae look tae Rowan's health an' rebuild mae life as a barber. That bae mae path. Killin' is noot. Else I am nae baetter than hae is. Tis gaein bae awricht once the pain has gane away. Mony a mickle maks a muckle. That is troo a' our actions as it is wit' oor coin."

Running his eyes from the pair of knives he held to the tower room where he knew the nephew slept—a room that shared a wall with the one in which he held poor Rowan—Rob tried his best to understand all that this odd and rather remarkable barber had told him. So long had he been a warrior, a fighter, a seeker of revenge, dispensing as a result his own brand of brutal, bloody justice that the sense Findlay was speaking took time to penetrate the tall, burly walls he had built around his heart.

"An' yer sure aboot this, Findlay? Completely, securely sure?"

"Aye, Rob. I am."

Sheathing the knives and exhaling his last remaining doubt, Rob turned toward home.

"Thaen wae baest bae on oor way. Mary and Rowan are fixin' a meal a' haggis an' greens fer after the workin' day, an' they should noot see oos late in oor arrival at the table."

I should have sailed with the morning tide as advised.
Robert Daniell, outgoing deputy governor of the Province of South Carolina, thought of the salt air and reviving breeze being enjoyed by those on the fishing boat on which he had refused passage hours earlier, finding himself envying them and cursing his own stupidity in equal measure.

He had had his chance to escape the tirade now washing over him, and he had chosen to remain and endure it.

What a load of stuff and nonsense.

"Are ye listening to me, Daniell? Or are ye already lounging on your island off the coast?"

The roiling weather system that stood in the form of a man on the far side of the desk in the governor's office was Robert Johnson, newly arrived colonial governor of the province.

Now seventy years of age, Daniell thought it his right to speak up for himself and his legacy in the face of Johnson's dire assessment of the state of things, although it was far wiser to weather the storm in silence and take up his retirement on his comfortable island homestead.

"Ye were no better than that damnable malcontent, Craven, sir. Who is a damned sight better than his Lord Proprietor brother and *his* master Carteret for having spoken out against them and their greed. I tell ye, Daniell. Their time is winding down. I watched my father in this very office a decade ago stand up to those elements that seek to weaken this province."

"Sir Nathaniel was a man to be admired, Robert," Daniell answered, trying his best to sound sincere. "As are ye. I do not think ye appreciate the challenges ye face. This is not the unified—at least on paper—Carolina of the first decade of the century. There are rifts... Competitions... Jealousies... I would be happy to help ye navigate them."

Robert Johnson's laugh was like poison funneled into Daniell's ears.

"*Navi*gate them? Damn it all, man—ye have, if not *caused* them, then certainly made them *worse*! Your dealings with this so-called Family... and the accursed family behind them... Colonel James Moore most of all. Instead of suing for peace with the Indians to the west, which would have far better assured the prosperity of Charles Town and the whole of the east of this province, ye allowed Moore and his brother to wage an unjust war for personal profit and power. I assure ye, sir, as I said—the time of those who have personally profited at the expense of this province is winding down."

"Ye mentioned it, Robert. Yes. Ever so clearly. But how will ye change it?"

Expecting silence, Daniell instead found a thick packet of papers thrust into his hands.

Did Johnson expect him to read them, or were they merely a prop to accompany the next monologue in the new governor's exquisite piece of theatre?

If Daniell had bet the latter, he would have lost the pot.

"South Carolina will no longer be held in thrall, Daniell. Ye hold in your hands a plan to encourage settlement in the frontier to the west to make Charles Town's shipping more profitable. It will also create a zone of defense should a *legitimate* Indian threat arise. My contacts on the continent are putting forth a fund to bring the best Protestant families to our shores."

Genuinely interested in this ambitious—although assuredly foolhardy—plan, Daniell glanced at the cover page staring up at him from his lap. "I see here... um, yes, yes... free land, determined by the number in the party, including slaves and indentured servants. Brilliant." He flipped the page with growing enthusiasm. "For every hundred families who settle acreage together, a parish shall be formed, from which two representatives will take seats in the Commons House of Assembly." Handing the bundle back, Daniell looked Johnson in the eye. "Ye truly believe ye can do this."

"I do," Johnson answered, placing the papers in the center of the desk. "It is already set in motion. Once we form the parishes, the growing population of prosperous South Carolinians shall be sending money and goods back to Britain at sufficient levels to force the proprietors out. It will make much more sense for George to secure the province for himself. For the Crown. For the good of Britain, instead of a select, malevolent few... There is, though, a single practical matter to which I must first put my attention."

As if on cue—this was, after all, just more theatre—there was a knock upon the door and Colonel William Rhett was entering the room.

"If I am disturbing something, Governor..."

Daniell barely restrained himself from answering. That would have been embarrassing, and he had been embarrassed enough for the day.

Waving the fierce naval fighter and former privateer, slaver, and ivory trader into the room, Governor Johnson turned his gaze upon Daniell.

"If ye will excuse us, sir—Colonel Rhett and I have much to discuss that would be woefully inappropriate to make a newly retired governor privy. Enjoy your island paradise, sir. Do think of us toiling servants of the Crown and province now and again, would ye? But not too, too often, I pray…"

Nodding at the smugly smiling colonel as he passed him, Daniell paused on the other side of the door, leaning his ear in to listen.

"It is a joy to see ye again, Colonel. Please sit. My father spoke often of your assistance in the defense of Charles Town in 1706, and I have been most pleased to receive reports of your exploits in recent months."

"Thank ye, Governor. Only doing my duty."

Oh hell… another consummate actor, Daniell thought from the shadows on the far side of the door.

Johnson's tone turned serious. "I further understand that ye have a secret ye wish to share—an unburdening of your heavy conscience, as it were—regarding a certain unfortunate incident involving the torture and murder of two Portuguese fishermen in Beaufort."

"Aye, Governor. I do."

Daniell leaned in further.

It seemed he had been wise, after all, to remain in both the building and the doorway that day.

PART THREE

IMPERCEPTIBLE CRACKS IN THE CUP

EASTHAM TAVERN, MASSACHUSETTS COLONY
APRIL 27, 1717

"Well, well, well... if it ain't old Thomas Davis... We thought that ye had drowned!"

Looking up from his cup at a back table in the Eastham Tavern, Thomas Davis, survivor of the hurricane that had taken the lives, as far as he could reckon, of every member of the crew of the *Whydah* save for he and one other, cursed his luck at the sight of the seven haggard-looking men arrayed before him.

Are ye all that is left of the *Anne*?" he asked, dropping his hand to the butt of the pistol he had hidden beneath his coat.

"Aye... that we are, mate."

"And Richard Noland?"

"Careful what ye tell him, Simon. Davis ain't one a' us, ye know."

Looking the man who spoke the words, John Brown, squarely in the eyes, Thomas Davis smiled. "I think Mister Van Vorst knows whom he can trust. Is that not right, Simon?"

Calling to the barkeep to bring three pitchers of ale and seven mugs with all possible haste, Simon Van Vorst indicated that the rest of their bedraggled party, including John Brown, have a seat. Pulling up chairs and falling wearily into them, the other five—Thomas South, Thomas Baker, Hendrick Quintor, Peter Cornelius Hoof, and John Shuan (a Frenchman who spoke no English)—ravenously poured and guzzled the ale, while the barkeep went for more.

"Listen carefully, Davis," John Brown said, leaning in close so the smell of the sand and sea embedded in his clothes burned in Davis's nose, "Cap'n Noland did not prevail. Turns out he was not loyal to our cause."

"That's right," chirped Hendrick Quintor, letting out a belch. "Soon as that storm started, Noland took the side a' one a' the bastards the commodore left upon the *Anne*—name a' Alexander somethin'... Irishman, I think. Startin' beratin' us fer indulgin' in the Madeira."

"John Brown, 'especially,'" added Thomas South.

"Stow yer flappin' gums, would ye?" Brown spat out with a growl. "We was all equally in our cups an' swarthy."

Slipping his thumb over the hammer of his pistol, Davis asked, "So what became of Richard Noland? I sense it was not the storm that saw him deceased."

All eyes were on John Brown, and Davis had his answer.

83   To Be a Proper Pyrate

"How did ye all manage to survive it?" Davis asked, placing his hand over the top of his cup as Thomas South raised the pitcher to refill it.

He wanted to be sober for what was to come, though he could not say what it was.

"I chopped the mainmast to keep us from breakin' apart," Thomas Baker proudly offered.

"I read from the Book a' Common Prayer by candlelight below decks wit' a crewman from the *Anne* name a' Thomas Fitzgerald," Peter Cornelius Hoof added, making the sign of the cross upon himself.

"An' what about you, Davis?" John Brown asked. "Seems ta me ta be a bit of an irony that ye alone of all the hundred and sixty upon the Whydah would survive, seein' as ye never did want ta be amongst us."

John Brown, for all his drunken bullying, had a point. It was in December of the previous year that the *St. Michael*, a cargo ship out of County Cork, Ireland, had had the ill fortune to cross paths with and find herself stopped by the *Sultana* and *Marianne*, under the command of Samuel Bellamy.

Finding himself sore in need of a carpenter, Bellamy insisted that Davis join them, despite his protests, promising to let him go once the commodore had enlisted another with his skills.

True to his word the commodore had been, although the crew, appreciative as they were of what Davis could do, overrode him. It was this bastard sitting before him, John Brown, who had whispered in his ear, "We would whip or shoot ye at the mast before lettin' the likes a' ye go."

Rather than presume to know why fate had chosen to spare him, Davis said, "I was not the only one. John Julian, the sixteen-year-old pilot from the Mosquito Coast, survived the storm as well."

"An' where might that damned-lucky Julian be at the moment?" Brown asked.

Flicking his free thumb upward, Davis answered, "In an upstairs room celebrating his survival with an escaped slave girl recently arrived from Barbados. As ye must no doubt have seen, the beach is crawling with Codders scooping up our riches, so we chose to keep a low profile."

Brown belched and nodded. "A most unfortunate situation. Word is the gov'nor of this colony, a blighter an' blowhard name a' Samuel Shite, is sendin' some wormy colonel an' his mapmaker sidekick ta oversee recovery."

"The word ye received is correct," Davis said, eyeing a trio of shadows in the doorway of the tavern. "Although the governor is named *Shute*. The colonel is called Bassett and the cartographer is Captain Southach. They are due to arrive within days, supported by the fifth-rate frigate HMS *Rose* and a sloop named the *Mary Free Love*."

After half the table made remarks about needing a bout of free love—from Mary or some other whore, never mind the name—Peter Cornelius Hoof, making once again the sign of the cross upon himself, slammed his hand upon the table, setting the cups—empty and full—to rattling. "With that much muscle descending upon us, we best fetch Julian, acquire some shovels an' barrows, an' get down ta the beach. A few flashes a' the blade an' pistol will set the Codders ta scatterin'."

As the survivors cheered their assent, Davis quietly removed his hand from his pistol and placed it on the table, beside his other, as the three shadows approached.

He was not sure if it had been John Cole, in whose barn he and John Julian had spent the previous night, or perhaps Samuel Harding, whom the pair had passed on their way to the tavern as the smiling local dragged a sack of treasure from the shipwrecks toward his own barn early that afternoon.

It did not matter which. One or both had ratted them out.

As the oblivious men around him laughed and drank, Thomas Davis eyed the fast-approaching shadow in the center of the trio, which had pulled a sword and pistol as his companions did the same.

"In the name of the governor of this colony, the right honorable Samuel Shute, and with my vested authority as sheriff of Eastham," the shadow barked, "ye all are under arrest."

Looking up from her desk amid the seventh-floor complex of glassed-in offices and workstations in a severely utilitarian federal building—even for the U.S. government—Magdalena "Maggie" Sorrus forced a smile as her three-in-the-afternoon appointment approached her door.

"Come in, Doctor MacGregor," she said, pointing to a chair that was, again, incredibly and at the moment embarrassingly, utilitarian. Other than her fellow office workers, of which there were only three full time and a consultant, no one ever came to see her, and the rest of the staff—all men—usually just stood in her doorway.

"Please... Kirstine is fine," her visitor said, accepting the chair with a forced smile of her own. "You are SA Sorrus?"

God, she looks like she's been through Hell, Maggie thought, closing the door behind them, although she had arranged for the office to be empty during Doctor MacGregor—Kirstine's—visit. *That's because she has.*

"I'm sure that Maggie will suffice," she replied, perching herself on the corner of her desk, a few feet from where Kirstine sat. "I am not going to waste your time. Not a moment of it. You've been through far too much for any of the usual government formalities. First things first... can I get you anything? Coffee, water, a semi-stale but edible donut or bagel?"

"I had some lunch in my new apartment. Thanks."

"Your new apartment. How's that working out?"

After Haxx, Jake, and their mysterious, well-trained insider—he had to have been, and Quarry Peak Psychiatric Hospital's security team had to know it as well as DTEAU—had extracted Kirstine from the site, it was deemed impossible for her to return to her former residence.

The knowledge she possessed was now a matter of national security, and it was clear that the bad guys would keep coming until they got whatever it was they wanted.

"It's much nicer than my old one," Kirstine answered. "Although all of the gadgetry—the security, the security detail... It's a little overwhelming for a simple postdoc in pirate studies."

Maggie nodded. "I can imagine. But all of it is necessary. Have you looked over the paperwork for your independent grant? As far as anyone who checks, it will be clear that the National Endowment for the Humanities is fully funding your work for the next year and that you are listed as on sabbatical from the Smithsonian."

"And is all of that true?"

Been through so much she is no longer capable of bullshit. Duly noted.

Maggie shifted position slightly. She was about to go even further off script than she had planned.

"Essentially, yes. Where the money for your studies and apartment is coming from is complicated. Best to put it out of your mind. And, should we get these guys within the next year, it is not outside the realm of possibility for you to get your position back at the Archives— although I think you will have other, better options to consider before that occurs."

Starting with an accepting nod, Kirstine suddenly began shaking her head. "I don't know what I know, Agent. This seems like a lot of effort and expense. These... *people*... tried to extract my memories and they couldn't. Though they came close. But I can't imagine what was in that rusty old box at my grandmother's on the Outer Banks that could be so important..."

Now. Before the boss or anyone else comes back. Tell her, Maggie. She called you Agent. Better build trust. Immediately.

"I am going to level with you, Kirstine. Complete and utter honesty. It's just us girls, so to speak. And I know what you went through. *Intimately*. But we'll get to that. To answer your question, we believe that the ciphers to Angus MacGregor's journals are somehow locked within your memories. Officially, that's just a theory for now and, trust me, I will tell you more as we go, but we are all but positive that that's the case. Occam's razor... the simplest explanation is the truest. They have digital copies of the coded journals... nearly killed Jake Givens for them... and the only possible reason for hooking you up to that infernal machine was to get the cipher keys."

Kirstine's eyes lit up—ever so slightly—at the mention of her savior. "How is Jake? I haven't been allowed to see him. When can I? Is he is a new apartment somewhere too?"

The questions came out in a gush.

They had clearly become close. And she was harboring some guilt.

"We hope to get you both together soon. He is back in New Jersey, under the care of his father who, as I think you know, is a retired chief petty officer with a long career in Naval Intelligence. He is extremely well connected. He's the reason Jake knew about the content of the journals... I know he feels terrible for putting you in danger... Anyway,

Jake is no longer any use to these people, and to go after him merely for revenge would be a chance that they are not going to be willing to take."

"Okay," Kirstine said, a hint of relief in her voice. "But I honestly don't understand any of this. Is the information in these journals really that volatile?"

Maggie. Enough now. No more stalling, my friend. Give it to her straight.

"Yes." Just that simple, one-syllable affirmative was enough to open the floodgates. Having admitted it, the rest would now be easy.

"There is a very powerful family. Going back to the Western Isles of Britain, at least to the first century AD. A family that has interdicted itself into every major war, every royal dynasty, every sector of our lives with increasing manipulation and effect as the centuries wear on. They play both sides. They script and direct world events like master filmmakers—whom they've long employed for predictive programming in film and TV and for conducting social conditioning experiments. They are the architects of the darkest aspects of social media and data mining. Their wealth is beyond anything either one of us could understand. They have now *transcended* money—their power is beyond any financial ledger's bottom line. No world leader gets elected without their approval. No major merger happens without their overseeing the process and getting a share of the profits. They are the heartbeat behind the military–industrial–intelligence complex. The European and American banking giants, the so-called secret societies, the Illuminati, Rosicrucians, the elite clubs like CRL, TLC, Bilderberg, Rome, even Bohemian Grove events in California... all of these are under the control, or at least the influence, of this family. And they grew exponentially in power in the 1700s, starting with the Golden Age of Piracy—your specialty—and the French and American revolutions."

Kirstine, listening attentively with a look of quiet knowing—due to the information buried deep within her memory, Maggie knew— whispered, "The Ravenskalds."

"Yes." Another single-syllable affirmative. *Keep going, Maggie. It will only get easier from here.*

"No one outside of the Domestic Threat Early Assessment Unit knows this—you're the first Kirstine, with everything that comes with—but our core mission is to monitor and do our damnedest to thwart the grander designs of The Ravenskald Group. Or, as most people know them, TRG."

Kirstine nodded. Their commercials about their work in biomedicine, space technology, food production, and just about every other sector of life were ubiquitous.

And utterly phony. A front.

As if reading her mind—and her body and eyes; Kirstine knew she was one of the best profilers the FBI had ever developed—Maggie answered, "It is all propaganda, what the world sees—the high-tech planned community of Storm Haven, in New Jersey, being the biggest lie of all. It's a security surveillance state, Kirstine. And they are planning more than two dozen others—each to have its own state of the art nuclear power plant running on a very advanced, very controversial power source."

"My God..."

"God is absent in all of this," Maggie said, shifting her legs, which had begun to cramp, she was crossing them so tightly. "Replaced by King Solomon Ravenskald. Solomon the wise, lording it over the tentacles of a Lovecraftian leviathan-kraken from his offices atop Ravenskald Tower—otherwise known as Solomon's Temple."

"They think it's all a game."

"To them, it is. Therefore, for the rest of us, we have to be top-level players. This usurpation of God is not just metaphorical. Those journals this guy from New Jersey found off the coast of Beaufort, North Carolina—we haven't been able to identify *him* yet, which means TRG most likely hasn't—they contain spells, incantations, and the details about twelve ancient objects from Biblical times that can be used for all kinds of nightmarish occult activities. Do you believe in angels and demons, Kirstine?"

Clenching her fists until her knuckles went white, Kirstine thought of the strange entity she had met in the mind machine, who called himself PF.

Nodding, she decided to keep the reason, for now, to herself.

"Good," Maggie said, genuine relief in her tone and on her face. "It will make all of this easier. I have been chasing TRG for years. What they are doing—just in terms of policy, governance, and finance is unconstitutional at the very least and in reality insurrectionist. People look for the coming of the one-world government, the New World Order. It has existed from the start. No need to combine countries into zones. No need to make more of the UN than its humanitarian good-intentions—more propaganda from the point of view of TRG—or to do anything that would actually make the bread-fed, circused masses sit up and take notice.

"They deal in subtleties. In shadow. Fomenting mini-insurrections through protests of elections at the local and state levels is a favorite trick of theirs, as is using front groups and indoctrinating lone wolves through social media and the dark web by the creation and spread of fake news—a practice that the Nazis and then the Russians excelled at. Our guys learned from the best of both of them. Pre-9/11 it was all about environmental and animal rights groups. Ivy League do-gooders, ease to manipulate. Only one of them really survives and matters, because they are protesting the nuclear energy facilities planned by TRG, and that's the No Tech Alliance, headed by Andy Milligan, a former MIT professor and global warming guru. The Right-Wingers destroyed his career, nearly gave him a mental breakdown, so he went militant.

"I'm kind of rooting for him.

"TRG, through their infiltration of core sectors of the MIIC—through what are called the DEDs... Haxx can educate you on each of the six of them—has brought the worst aspects of science fiction mind control and manipulation into reality. You experienced it, Kirstine. That fucking machine they hooked you up to..."

Based on her look of sincerity, the way her eyes moved, and the tension suddenly rolling off Maggie's body in persistent waves, Kirsten knew it was time to ask something that had been on her mind almost from the start of the meeting.

"You said you knew what I went through. *Intimately*, you said. Have you been in that machine, Maggie?"

The answer was almost silent. "I have." Then, in a moment, the FBI Special Agent and elite profiler was back. "A case a year ago. Tracking down a company called Dream Coin that used a version of the machine you were in to get data on anything high finance. Made hundreds of millions and set in motion a domino effect of stock market and cryptocurrency manipulations we are still feeling the effects of before we were able to stop them. It ended ugly and I was nearly one of the casualties... Anyway, back to the dangers of the .TRG juggernaut.

"When their psychiatric staff and personality profilers—you met Doctor Friedrich Reinhardt, who is one of their most gifted—identify a particularly strong candidate for moving the pieces on the board in measurable ways, they recruit them. A few examples, to keep this concrete and nonspeculative—Jim Jones and the Peoples Temple, David Koresh and the Branch Dividians, Marshall Applewhite and Heaven's Gate, Bhagwan Shree Rajneesh and his Oregon Commune, Shoko Asahara and Aum Shinrikyo. Once recruited, the head shrinkers put them through intense psychological conditioning at Quarry Peak Psychiatric Hospital and in their shadow labs elsewhere in the world. The events surrounding the final weeks of Trump—culminating in the January 6, 2021 storming of the Capitol— are a direct result of these highly refined and field-tested operations."

"Jesus Christ," Kirstine said, her nails now digging into her palms. "I wish I could say I thought it was bullshit. So tell me something I *can't* believe… Rumors of mind control… Manchurian candidates… the Kennedys, MLK, John Lennon, Ronald Reagan…"

"It's all true, Kirstine. A small percentage of serial killers as well. We have an in-house specialist for that special breed of psychopath, named Kevin Connor. He has seen some really shitty things and still manages to be decent."

"Okay… *okay.* How about Eisenhower's treaty with ETs in the 1950s? Valiant Thor? Underground bases? Phil Schneider, Bob Lazar… Alien abduction and hybridization…."

Maggie gently put her hand up. "Those are not subjects we have time to tackle today. First of all, they are a subset and, second of all, there are different levels of dosage when you want to take this trip. But, like I said, as we continue with our collaboration, depending on how far down the Rabbit Hole you want to go, I can send you files on any and all of it. Haxx has set up a secure connection between our terminals here and yours at the apartment."

"Noted."

"Good. Our public profile is to prevent terrorist events by identifying their seeds very early on. DoD and DARPA are the front-runners as far as the algorithms and AI but we are the boots on the ground. In that regard, our team has had some wins. We have really done some good. But TRG is our Golden Goose. Lucifer to our Michael. The dragon to our George.

"So… what do you think of all of this?"

Leaning forward, Kirstine asked, "How the fuck can I help?"

Standing on the shore in the dreadful heat of the African jungle, Andrew Colson looked out at the Royal African Company slaver, called the *Hannibal*, anchored in the bay and thought long and hard about signaling to her captain, Collin Hume, to send a longboat for him.

Since arriving two days earlier, Colson had tried and failed on four separate occasions to gain an audience with Chief Daagakutsu of the Ashanti. For more than a decade, Colson had been the main voice of authority from afar—*owura oburoni* in the Akan Twi language, meaning *master foreigner*. His name, like his father's before him—he had made the journey here with Lord Colson just before his twentieth birthday—had always been enough to allow Hume and his bullymen, such as Devon Ross, to obtain a steady supply of bodies for the transatlantic trade in exchange for weapons, the finest of European items, and other desirable goods.

So desirable in fact, Daagakutsu had not only sold enemies captured in war and those offered to him in tribute, but many members of his family.

Now, after having traveled so far at a time when Colson could ill afford to be absent from the increasingly brutal war being waged between the Masonic and Mammon lodges, he was told twice each day that Daagakutsu was in isolation in his village. No matter the fineries and further means to consolidation of power Colson had offered to the Ashanti officials who barred his way, Daagakutsu refused to see the man whose company had made him the most powerful Ashanti on the Gold Coast—the paramount chief of his people's formal alliance. Not even the great Osei Tutu and his holy man, Komfo Anokye, could mount a challenge, contenting themselves with sitting upon their golden stools in the capital village of Kumasi.

Yet he refuses to see me, Colson thought, silently fuming as he stood like an idiot upon the shore. *Has John Carteret already had his ear?*

Resigning himself to failure, Colson stooped to light the lantern that would signal to Hume that he was ready to depart.

Then he heard a rustle in the bushes behind him.

"*Owura oburoni*," spoke a quiet, melodic female voice. "It is not safe for you to be here. Though speak we must. Quickly. Join us in the bushes and we shall help you as we can."

Us. Join *us*.

Was this a trap? Not probable, although Daagakutsu would think nothing of sacrificing a child to further his outsized ambitions.

How weary Andrew Colson was becoming of ambitious, evil men.

Finding his courage hiding deep in the pit of his intestines, and summoning it to his heart, Colson entered the bush-line, where he saw the young girl who had called to him, standing beside an aged holy man, painted and feathered, covered with gold dust, and grasping a six-foot staff adorned with shells, beads, and rattles.

"I am Andrew Colson, of the Royal African Company. And you are?"

Nodding her head to honor and ease the mind of their guest, the girl said, "I am Abenaa. I am the daughter of the supreme chief Daagakutsu. This man is Kwasi, an Obeah master whom my father has banished from our village, although, two years ago, he was our chief advisor."

Two years ago, Colson processed. *The time of Devon Ross and the calling of the Jumbee.*

"Do you know why I have come?"

"We do, *owura oburoni*, and it fills us in equal measure with pleasure and with dread." Kwasi spoke this, as he approached Colson, who could feel a power emanating from the Obeah priest—a quality of intense energy that was pure, perfect light instead of the dark in which he had for so long immersed himself. "Your dealers in devilry wrought a terrible illness upon this land by forcing Daagakutsu into conjuring the Jumbee. Do you understand that you are responsible? Do you understand that only you can put this right?"

It was one thing to have known it, to have known it strongly enough to have traveled to this place he had avoided for so many years, preferring to reap the rewards without seeing their inestimable price. But to hear it from this holy man—to see it in the eyes of the girl who stood beside him... Colson felt as though he was standing at the edge of the abyss, and they were pushing him into the pit.

"I do," he said. "It is why I have come—although you know that. I feel in my heart that you have known it for some time. Will you help me put this right?"

"We shall," Kwasi said. "I must remain here, to keep the delicate balance that is my sole reason for being, but Abenaa... you must take her with you. Make her your ward. I see inside your heart, and you are no longer *owura oburoni*—though *oburoni* you shall ever be. Abenaa shall share with you all she knows. What she has learned from me and what the gods have shown to her directly. Will you do this?"

"I shall."

"This is good. And you must do something else. My grandson, Caesar—he is living among the agents of the Star Quorum, the red-robed with whom I arranged his passage from St. Croix with a pirate of good heart."

Colson's eyes widened. "How was it that your grandson was on St. Croix?"

Abenaa answered. "After Kwasi and my father quarreled, my father sold Caesar into slavery through your slave trade. He proved to be more than the governor of Port Royal, Jamaica had bargained for."

This last bit brought a smile to their faces that Colson could not share.

"I shall tell you this in confidence. I am no longer with the Royal African Company. Lord Carteret, its governor, is as much my enemy as Daagakutsu is for you, Kwasi."

The Obeah priest nodded. "The spirits reveal all things needed to be known, *oburoni*. We would not be talking to you now if you had not done what you have. You would be lying dead in the sand with a poisoned dart embedded in your throat. My grandson is safe for now. He shall serve a purpose amongst the pirates. A purpose he understands. As, in the present, through your penance, your heart is being cleansed, you shall serve as another of his guardians, though remaining at a distance until the appointed time. As I said, he is where he belongs, but there is aid that you must give."

Colson found himself dropping to one knee, only partially knowing why. "Tell me how to do it, and I pledge it will be so."

"I see the winged and evil Mammon lived within you," Kwasi said, touching his staff to Colson's shoulder. "In time, the poison will leave you. Abenaa will assist you. There is another—a demon-thing like Mammon, though once he was an angel, and he struggles toward the light. As your penance and new practices progress, you shall meet him. Together with Abenaa and Caesar, you shall be an instrument in undoing what Daagakutsu set in motion. Do you understand this, and accept it as spoken?"

Feeling an energy coursing through his body, starting from the spot where the staff still rested, Colson answered, "I do. With all that I am and shall become."

"The ancestor spirits have heard you," Kwasi replied, removing the staff and shaking it so the rattles, beads, and shells produced a powerful, gut-churning sound. "It is to them that you now answer." Shaking the staff more forcefully, Kwasi began to tremble, his eyes rolling upward in his head so all that Colson could see was a glowing pale blue light. As he spoke, his voice became ethereal. "There is a ship that soon shall come to dock here, which is called *La Concorde*. She travels from Nantes in France with a crew of seventy-five."

"I know this ship of which you speak. She is a slaver, owned by René Montaudoin. His numbers rival those of the Royal African Company."

Still under trance, Kwasi intoned, "Her Captain, Pierre Dosset, has many sickly crew. Their illness is not only in their bodies—they shall take the gold dust so important to our peoples. More than their share. Daagakutsu shall allow it, for the power that it brings him."

"The *Hannibal* is a fierce fighting ship. Shall we engage them?"

Shaking the staff so it became a blur before Colson's eyes, Kwasi said, "You must not alter what must be. *La Concorde* has a destiny, of which our Caesar is a part."

With those final, prophetic words, Kwasi vanished into the jungle, leaving Abenna and Colson, who lit the lantern without speaking, signaling to Captain Hume it was time to launch the longboat, which he did with all due haste.

FORT OF NASSAU, NEW PROVIDENCE, THE BAHAMAS
MAY 10, 1717

At the very moment Colson and Abenaa were stepping into the longboat five thousand miles away to take them to the *Hannibal*, and on to England, Edward Thache was standing, hands clasped tensely behind his back, on a rickety rampart overlooking a pair of crumbling earthworks at the Fort of Nassau.

"This relentless heat begins to rot the fort anew the moment we make repairs!" he lamented, motioning for Conall MacBlaquart to step closer so he could dictate more items in need of immediate attention for their never finished list.

"The western wall needs to be mortared—this time correctly! I want those earthworks below us refortified, with twice the number of sharpened poles to delay an enemy's approach. These cannon… they will be cleaned and test fired before the end of the day. Are ye getting all of this down correctly, Conall?"

"Aye, Maister Thache. That I am," Conall answered, dipping his quill in his inkpot and scribbling away as fast as his hand could work.

Thache had been increasingly agitated in recent days, with lack of word about the whereabouts of Bellamy and Levasseur and the inability of Captain Jennings to command the necessary respect of the crews that came and went from the harbor. To make matters worse, with the arrival of spring, Hornigold—restless and feeling every bit the decrepit grandfather everyone took him to be—had taken twenty men and put out to sea, leaving Thache to help Jennings as best he could.

"What about me, Ad-meer-al?" Caesar, who had fast become Conall's shadow, now asked, raising his hands and twirling twice around so that Thache would be sure to notice him.

"I told ye, Little Man," Thache answered, crouching down to look Caesar in the eyes. "I am but a meager sailing master. I have no ship, much less enough of them to be an admiral. One day, perhaps—and when that day arrives, ye shall be with myself upon the flagship."

Caesar laughed with glee at the prospect. "And Capee-tano Conall MacBlaquart as well, Ad-meer-al?"

"Indeed," Thache said, enjoying this welcome diversion from his mounting frustrations. "Capee-tano MacBlaquart will command the second-best ship on the seas! Is that not true, Capee-tano?"

"Aye, mates. Tis true as true caen bae," Conall answered, relieved to see Thache, for the moment, smiling.

It was not to last.

From the shadows of a doorway just behind them, Captain Jennings had emerged, his white-knuckled hand clutching a missive.

"I am sorry for breaking your merriment," he said, looking embarrassed. "God knows we could use a little more of it in the fort. But I have just received word. I..."

"Out with it, Captain, I pray ye," Thache urged, all joy erased from his heavily bearded face.

"It is Samuel Bellamy. According to this report, taken from a Royal Navy supply ship by one of our sloops, the commodore has been lost in a storm in the north Atlantic. He, at least two ships, and more than one hundred and sixty souls were taken by the sea."

Holding out the paper as if his word were not enough, Jennings wished he were elsewhere as Thache began to weep as his eyes pulled the words from the page.

"There is more," Jennings added. "A bit of hope in all this tragedy. It also says that nine of the crew survived, washing up on the beach at Eastham, in Massachusetts Colony."

Not making eye contact, Thache said, "Do what ye can to bring them home to Nassau... will ye? Take up a collection amongst the crews. Whatever it costs... We must bring them back, to tell us in detail what befell our mates. I have been in the north Atlantic in late April... the storms can be harsh, yes, but it would take a behemoth to best a sailor such as Bellamy..."

Again wishing he could blink his eyes and find himself elsewhere, Jennings answered, "It is not so simple. They are gaoled in Boston, awaiting trial for piracy. If they are convicted, they will without a doubt be very publicly hanged."

As a white-bearded grandfather looking back on this difficult year, Conall/Angus would clearly recall the dark grey shadow that passed in that moment over Edward Thache's face. A shadow that would not lift for even an instant in the remaining eighteen months of the soon to be infamous pirate's life.

"This injustice shall not stand," Thache whispered. "If I have to burn every ship in Boston, I shall see them safely home."

Fearing the look in Thache's eyes even more than the menace and meaning of his words, Conall said, "Maister Thache... Edward..."

Turning to face his well-meaning student—the able quill to his loaded, primed, and ready to fire cannon—the heartbroken pirate replied, "Edward Thache? That man is no more. From today I shall be Blackbeard, and those that hear that name shall tremble at the sound."

"**M**arius. Marius… please. Your wailing is no better than Louis's. And, should you wake him from his nap, you shall truly know what misery can be."

Philippe the Second, Duke of Orleans, and Regent of France, had been engaged in the complex game of assessing the national numbers with his chief financial counselor, the loud but brilliant Scotsman John Law, who had set up the Banque Générale Privée, when Marius Adenot—tutor and best friend to the seven-year-old Louis the Fifteenth—burst into the chamber.

"Eleonore has been sent to Italy! To a *nunnery*!" the young man, whose face was a reddened blob of tears and yellow snot, had yelled, not bothering to knock or ask forgiveness for interrupting these two important men.

"I think I should take mae leave," Law said, gathering up his ledgers.

"You shall stay," Philippe said, taking the ledgers from his financial counselor's hands and dropping them on the desk. "This shall only take a moment." Turning to Marius, he asked, "How can this be? Were you suddenly lax in your caution? For eighteen months, you have met and lain with the beautiful Eleonore without the least whisper of suspicion coming to my ears. Something must have changed."

Shaking his head, Marius answered, "Nothing. I swear it. I would never put you and your reputation in any danger. Nor that of little Louis…"

"*Oui.* Little Louis. He must never see you, his tutor, like this. Gather yourself together. We find ourselves with a dilemma. Give me a moment to think."

Wiping his eyes and nose with a section of sleeve already damp and discolored—much to Philippe's chagrin—Marius took a seat in the corner and tried to keep his sobs from spilling out too loudly.

After a moment or two spent tapping his signet ring on the desk to help his mental processes, Philippe slapped his hand upon the desk. "Of course! It is clear my dear Marius that Eleonore's uncle, Nicolas, who as you know is not only Viscount of Melun and Vaix, but the former financial superintendent to our former king, Louis the Fourteenth, and therefore well-connected and capable of doing you harm, will not rest until you pay for what you have done."

Nodding weakly, Marius said, his eyes pleading in conjunction with his outstretched hands, "I know this all too well, what nobles such as the viscount can do. Which is why I have come to see you. What am I to do? My work here with Louis…"

"Is much appreciated, Marius. It is. Although it must now come to an end. You see only danger, while I see opportunity. This is why I am regent of France and you are a tutor. You can be of service to me yet, young Marius. I wish you to shadow Cardinal André-Hercule de Fleury. Where he goes, you must follow."

Intrigued enough by the proposal to cease, for the moment, his sobbing, Marius asked, "Is the Cardinal under suspicion?"

Philippe shrugged his shoulders. "This I do not know, which is why I enlist your help. Rumors in the courts of France are nothing new. Gossip here is as much a national pastime as the theatre. I want to know with whom he meets, where he travels, anything he does that does not seem in harmony with the duties of a servant of God and the Church. Can you do this for me, Marius? If you can, I shall see if I can reason with Nicolas. And, if not, perhaps, if you work well in this new duty, I shall send you to Italy with the means to make a rescue of your lovely flower before she becomes a nun!"

Approaching the desk, Marius fell to his knees at the regent's feet. "You make my heart sing with hope, my Duke. I shall not fail you."

When Marius had gone, John Law asked, "Who could haev ratted the loovers oot, I woonder?"

"It was me, of course," Philippe answered, opening one of the ledgers. "Did you hear what he said about knowing what nobles can do? His brother Henri was killed at sea during the War of Spanish Succession. He has never forgiven the upper classes for it."

Law nodded. "A Scotsman kens the value of raevenge baeter than moost. Do ye ken hae weel turn on you?"

"Quite the opposite," Philippe answered. "He is a coward. Not the smallest strength of conviction. He was offered a chance to spend his life in service to God when he was eight, and he refused. No. He is becoming far too close to Louis. Louis calls for him, not me, when he has a nightmare or falls and skins his knee. I will begin to cycle the whiny runt's tutors with greater frequency, having learned the lesson."

Hearing a knock upon the door, Philippe smiled. "Our appointment has arrived. I take it this subject stays between us?"

"Aye," Law replied.

Standing, Philippe pointed to the chair that Marius had recently occupied, indicating that the newly arrived Abbé Guillaume Dubois should bring it to the desk and join them.

"What news, Dubois?" Philippe asked, pouring his guest some wine. "Has the transaction been completed to my instructions?"

"Indeed, it has, my Duke," the abbé replied. "Since the signing of the alliance with Britain, which I personally oversaw, doing your will has become exceedingly easy. The people trust and love you. The matter of acquiring the largest known diamond in the world for you—which you no doubt richly deserve—is just the latest of tasks accomplished."

It had been at the suggestion of Law and the Duc de Saint-Simon that Philippe, through the person of Abbé Guillaume Dubois, had persuaded the Regency Council to purchase a one hundred and forty-one carat diamond for £135,000 from the merchant and trader with India, Thomas Pitt. This princely sum had allowed Pitt, the former president of the East India Company province of Madras, to turn down the position of governor of Jamaica, a place he did not ever intend to see.

"When it arrives next month, it will make an excellent addition to the crown jewels, my Duke," the abbé added.

"It weel indeed," Law then said. "An' tae honor ye further, the Council has agraed that the diamond shall bae knoon as Le Régent."

"Gentlemen," Philippe whispered, raising a glass of Burgundy's best, "I am humbled by what I hear from you today. I shall endeavor to never disappoint."

Touching glasses with his agents, Philippe swallowed with satisfaction the delicious wine and thought of Eleonore Fouquet—how the viscount's spoiled, pampered niece would soon find herself in a simple habit, with rough-cut hair, sans jewelry and perfumes, living in a simple cell for all the rest of her days.

And he found he did not care.

Ailish MacDonald, newly arrived in Boston via Glasgow and London, was already weary of the larger world and longing for the quiet of Glen Shira in the Scottish Highlands, although she knew she had weeks of travel to the Caribbean still to face.

"What haev ye doon, lass?" she asked herself, stepping off the gangway of a ship called *Comfort*—which had been anything but. Grasping her small bag of belongings, Ailish waded into the crowd of scurrying merchants and sailors as though they were the waters of Loch Voil near the village of Balquidder and Loch Fyne near Glen Shira, where she had spent so much time lamenting Angus's departure more than two years earlier and the later news of his death.

News that, she had recently learned from her cousin Duncan, had been false.

Angus was alive and well, living among the pirates in the Caribbean.

After nearly being raped by James MacGregor, eldest son of Rob Roy and Angus's deceitful and jealous cousin, Ailish had insisted that Duncan help her get to the Caribbean, where he had gone in March 1716 to carry out Rob's order to murder Angus. He would have done it too, were it not for the intervention of one of Angus's guardians—a leader in the Jacobite cause called Samuel Bellamy.

Ailish looked forward to shaking Sam's hand and thanking him for saving the life of the man she now knew without question owned her heart.

Her journey thus far had been both eye opening and exhausting. It had begun weeks before in Glasgow, where she had traveled with Duncan with the permission of both Rob Roy and her parents. Because he was traveling there only to meet with a handful of merchants about summer supplies, it was deemed wholly safe and probably a good way for Ailish to get out from beneath the dark clouds that had been over her head since Duncan had returned with his fabricated narrative of Angus's death.

Arriving in London, she found herself fascinated by the arches of London Bridge and the tall, sword-like spires of London's many churches, mostly named for saints—most of all Christopher Wren's imposing St. Paul's Cathedral, which dominated the view from the Thames and offered her some small comfort in this very foreign place.

Two days after arriving, Ailish said goodbye to the spires of London for the trans-Atlantic passage to Boston on the very same ship that Angus had sailed on, the *Bonny Anne*—although she would not know this until Angus shared it with her one evening many months in the future. For the duration of the voyage, Ailish had kept almost wholly to herself, the fingers of her right hand grasping almost continually the three-inch piece of mountain ash, *caorrunn*, tied around her neck with red thread that Duncan had given her for protection when they parted ways in Glasgow.

Taking in the sights and sounds of Boston, Ailish knew she was far from home indeed. And the smells… how different they were from the pungent yet grass-sweet odors of the livestock, the woodsy smell of heather, and the peat fires in the chimneys of the Highlands.

As she took it all in the best she could—this would be her temporary home for nearly a week until the ship on which Duncan had arranged her passage, the *Mockingbird*, would depart—Ailish heard a commotion up ahead. Ducking between the stands of a fish seller and a net maker, she felt her body tense at the sound of the harsh, barking voices of what she guessed were soldiers commanding one and all to make way for a parade of prisoners.

Within moments, the incarcerated men in question appeared, chained together in a ragged line. There were seven all together, their hair and beards long, tangled, and filthy and their bodies lean and pale from lack of food.

"What's this all about?" the net maker called across to the fish seller, paying Ailish no mind.

"Pris'nah transfah," the fish seller answered, spreading a thick layer of salt over the day's offerings. "Them's the men from the shipwreck ah them pirates. Big ole converted slavah an' anotha, commandeered an' commanded by the Robin Hood ah the Seas, Commodore Samuel Bellamy his-self. Whom the sea sadly claimed as heh own. Come down heah from Eastham 'cause our prison's more secu-ah."

"Aye," said the net maker, returning to his weaving. "I can attest ta that. Shame 'bout Bellamy—a good an' righteous man from what I've heard. An all those othas… Was a wicked, wicked storm, it was. Ain't ever known the likes, not that time a' ye-ah…"

As the seven prisoners were led past the spot where she stood, Ailish heard one say to another, as she processed the news about the death of Samuel Bellamy, "I hear John Julian, that Mosquito Coast breeder, has been sold inta slav'ry."

"True 'nough, Hendrick," the man behind him replied. "He an' that escaped Barbadian sugar-reaper he was gettin' pers'nal with upstairs in the tavern. An' old Tom Davis has been taken ta sep'rate quarters in the gaol for a trial of his own. That one might get off. Slippery fish if evah thehr was one."

As the soldiers called a halt for a moment's rest not five feet from where Ailish was tucked away, the one that looked to be in charge pulled a paper from his belt and read the list of names. "Answer 'aye' when called. John Brown, Simon Van Vorst, Thomas South, Thomas Baker, Hendrick Quintor, Peter Cornelius Hoof, John Shuan."

After each name came the cry of "aye" as instructed. All but the last, who answered *"oui."*

The one who had called "aye" after the name John Brown motioned for the lot of them to form a semi-circle as their guards took advantage of an offered drink of water from a bucket and ladle courtesy of a pair of buxom barmaids outside one of the taverns.

Shaking his head, John Brown said, "Davis better not rat us out. Ya said too much about the difficulties wit' the captain, Hendrick. An' ye Thomas South... ye was no better."

Before anyone could answer, the soldiers barked at them to get back in line and silence themselves.

As the ragged procession reformed, Ailish found herself only a few feet from the last man in line, whom she knew spoke no English. Stepping forward as far as she dared, she asked the man just ahead of him— Peter Cornelius Hoof, a name easy to remember for its pleasant sound—if he happened to know Angus MacKinnon.

"Aye, girl. I do. Or did. Sailed together now an' again. Though he don't answer ta Angus no longer. Now he be Conall MacBlaquart. 'Sposed ta be a secret he be alive, though nothin' gets by ole Peter Cornelius Hoof—that'd be me. No idea where he be. Took sides wit' Edward Thache an' Gran'pa Hornigold in the split 'tween our commodore, Samuel Bellamy, rest his soul, an' a Frenchie called Levasseur. If ye seeks the lad, best ta go ta Nassau."

As she thanked him for the information, the commander of the soldiers yelled "Forward!" and they were gone.

As Ailish stepped farther into the crowd in search of a place to lodge, a kindly looking man in a black coat with two long, wide ribbons of white hanging from his collar approached her. "Bless you, my child. You look lost and a little afraid. Can I offer you assistance?"

Ailish, grasping the length of mountain ash around her neck, nodded. "Perhaps. I am in naed a' lodgin' fer saeveral nights."

"I am happy to assist you. Blessed is he who doth righteousness at all times. Your brogue speaks to places far away. What brings you to Massachusetts?"

Instantly trusting this stranger, Ailish said, "I am sailin' soon tae Nassau—as soon as I earn the money—tae bae reunited wit' mae one true love."

Tapping the bible in the crook of his arm, the stranger said, "Nassau... 'Tis an evil place. A reeking island of vipers breeding demons of the seas. *Pirates*. Like the troubled, devil-devoted men that have just passed. I know my way around witches and their offspring well enough. It is my mission to see to their salvation before the Lord's justice is done and they are hanged." Offering his arm, he added, "Be careful, young lady. I hope your love is not an aider of these pirates. May I ask your name?"

"'Tis Ailish, a' clan Donald a' Balquidder an' Glen Shira. An' ye?"

"I am Minister Cotton Mathers. I welcome thee to Boston. Now, let us find ye food, and a proper place to bed. Tomorrow we shall find ye work, so your innocent hands be not idle."

A week had passed since Captain Jenning's had received and shared the news of Samuel Bellamy's death and the arrest of nine survivors from his crew in Massachusetts.

Edward Thache, who, since his declaration upon the parapet to answer to no other name than Blackbeard, had been nearly unapproachable. He would sit upon the beach awaiting the arrival of the longboats launched from newly arrived ships anchored in the inlet, demanding to speak to the captain, whom he accosted and tried his best to coerce into sailing to Boston with him.

Not a single captain would dare to risk his ship or his men on such a foolhardy endeavor. The Royal Navy presence was thick off the shores of Massachusetts, Bostonians were fiercely loyal to the Crown, and, as they were all too quick to confess, they wholly detested pirates.

Sitting behind the desk in Edward Thache's quarters, Conall MacBlaquart was readying his quill to take a letter. Blackbeard had been unusually vocal in recent days about the soon to be written contents, which Conall was afraid would upset the delicate balance of pursuit and tolerance the Royal Navy displayed when it came to the pirate republic and the independent crews that prowled the waters along the length of the Atlantic coast.

Giving a stir to a newly opened bottle of ink, Conall cursed his courage and, lighting a candle in the corner of the desk, said, "I oonderstand that ye are oopset. Sam was the baest a' us. Boot the Crown weel react with sooch violence against oos if wae start tae burn—"

Slamming his hand on the desk, causing a bit of the ink to spill, Blackbeard replied, "If God or Nature herself spared these 9 mens' lives, what right do the puppets of a false king have to take them? I will have satisfaction or I will have vengeance, Angus. There is no other path. We shall speak of it no more, am I clear?"

"Boot Maister Thache!"

"Dammit, Angus! Ye call me Blackbeard, or ye shall suffer the consequences, same as any other! Now... cease from speaking and *write the damned letter.*"

Mopping up the spill and dipping his quill in the ink, Conall answered, "Aye. Whainever ye are raeady."

Placing his foot upon a chair, Blackbeard worked his long beard and its braids and bows with his calloused fingers. After a few seconds' contemplation, he began:

To Governor Shute, Massachusetts Colony:

Greetings and salutations. I pray that these words find ye well. I cannot but trust that they do, as any so called nobleman sitting fat in his mansion, fed by his greed, while innocent men rot in his cells has no reason to be anything other than well. I have a question for ye, Governor Shute: How dare ye claim to honor the law, trying the nine survivors of a recent shipwreck off your shores, by trial with no doubt corrupt judges in your employ, when God himself saw fit to spare their lives from what must have been a most Hellish storm?

Surely, Governor Shute, ye can see the injustice done, and shall, upon concluding your reading of this letter, set things right with a turn of the gaoler's key! For—and I say this with all sincerity—should ye keep to your plan to continue to spin this treacherous web, ye will be wise to ready yourself, and those under your protection, for the very demons that gave rise to that storm to unleash themselves upon ye!

Swift shall be my vengeance. I tell ye, Governor Shute—the blood that ye bleed shall never cease its flow. I shall not be satisfied 'til all of Boston is on its knees. When ye hear the sound of my guns as they fire upon ye, it shall already be too late to ask for compassion or mercy, as I do here for these nine worthy men.

Now that ye fully understand the terms and the stakes, I trust that these nine men shall soon be set free. Should ye choose to *ignore me, make no mistake, Governor Shute. It will take a wagonload of hogsheads to collect the torrents of blood I shall spill.*

Even now, we are prepared to attack ye. Our swords, pistols, pikes, and axes are sharp dragon's fangs, craving the flesh of those who would ignore us.

I am not an unreasonable man. I shall forestall our attack, awaiting word from ye on what ye have decided. But know this, Governor Shute—ye had best ready yourself for Hell should a single one of those innocent crewmen hang! Not your mansions, nor your riches, shall be enough to protect your life when I bring my chaos down upon ye! Again ye shall be warned: There will be no opportunity to bargain, no chance to save your life. God shall not hear ye, his angels shall abandon ye, and none but demons shall remain to laugh at your destruction at my hands!

Do what is prudent and just, Governor Shute, or the final sound ye shall hear upon this earth is my cold, vengeful laugh as I watch your colony burn.

Ye have been warned—
Blackbeard, 16 May 1717

Shaking out his cramping hand—Blackbeard's words, slow to start, had soon morphed from a silent stream to a rushing river of anger and invective—Conall lifted and gently waved the paper on which he had written, word for word, Blackbeard's threats. Once he was satisfied the ink was dry, he asked, "Shall I see tae its daelivaery, Mai—Blackbeard? There is a ship bound fer Massachusetts saet tae sail upon the morning tide."

Taking the letter from Conall's hands but not reading it, Blackbeard replied, "Ye have not changed a word of what I said, have ye, Angus? I must know the truth."

Moving around the desk and taking the letter back, Conall shook his head. "Not a word. I swear it."

Nodding his head in satisfaction, Blackbeard motioned him away. "See to it then. And be sure those to whom ye hand it are capable of delivering it directly to Governor Shute. I shall not wait forever before I make good on my threat."

Exiting the room, Conall heard Captain Hornigold approaching from the opposite end of the hallway, entering Blackbeard's quarters with a buoyant greeting and offer to share a bottle of newly acquired claret.

Perhaps hae caen talk soom sense inta him, Conall thought, not managing much in the way of hope.

It would be several hours later before he would learn the substance of the subsequent conversation between the captain and his closest confidante.

Benjamin Hornigold, at the request of Henry Jennings, was once again in command of what was left of the Republic of Pirates. He had returned from the East Indies to find the crews in disarray and no longer griping about his shortcomings as they had prior to voting him out in favor of Samuel Bellamy.

Although Blackbeard was too loyal to the former commodore to come right out and say it directly to Conall as they shared a meal that evening, it was clear that Captain Hornigold was tired, soul sick over the past year's events, and not at all up to the task before him, any more than had been Jennings and Blackbeard himself.

"The fort is an outward expression of the crumbling notion of a possible pirate republic," Blackbeard said, stabbing a piece of blood-red meat with his fork and shoving it into his mouth. "I do not see our once committed commodore lasting very long here at all. He is less than pleased with me for threatening Governor Shute. Ye sent the letter… *yes*?"

Suddenly feeling his appetite wither away as a thin line of blood leaked out of Blackbeard's mouth and onto his beard, blending with the color of the ribbons he wore at Samuel Bellamy's urging and now in his memory, Conall answered that he had.

Although he silently regretted having done so with all his heavy heart.

For Ramón Perellós y Rocafull, noble from Aragon and grand master of the Knights of Malta, the periods when his fellow members of the Star Quorum were out in the world, about their sacred business, and not in council in the chambers within the fort were a time for drilling the ever-expanding units of the Scarlet-Shrouded Knights of St. Grotth. Grand masters such as Rocafull had handpicked these elite warriors of unquestionable faith and loyalty from the ranks of the order since its founding, when their name was the Order of Knights of the Hospital of Saint John of Jerusalem, or Knights Hospitaller. They had not only protected the hospital—they were key participants in the sieges of Ascalon and Jerusalem in the 1100s.

Leaving Jerusalem after the kingdom had finally fallen in 1291, the Knights Hospitaller spent years of brutal campaigning in Smyrna and elsewhere, eventually taking the Greek island of Rhodes, which they used as their base of operations—fighting off two sultans and endless hordes of Barbary pirates—until 1522. In that year, Suleiman the Magnificent sent four hundred ships and nearly a hundred thousand men to expel the Knights, who found themselves outnumbered at better than ten to one.

It was not until 1530—after Pope Clement VII had struck a deal with Spain's Charles the Fifth involving the annual tribute of a Maltese falcon—that they had moved to their current headquarters on Malta.

Through their centuries of fierce fighting and migrations, grand masters had chosen the best—far less than a tenth—of their knights to don the scarlet shrouds of the protectors of the Star Quorum in the name of their patron, St. Grotth, about whom the members of the order—even their grand masters—knew little.

As to the Star Quorum, the Scarlet-Shrouded Knights were protecting The Seven, as they called them, since the secret council was first organized in 1209, following the sack of Constantinople. The looting of the city, seat of the Byzantine Empire, had made it clear that Ravenskald-backed rulers and Crusader armies were jeopardizing rather than defending the Holy Church in their quest to collect the twelve sacred objects that were still the cause of endless bloodshed around the globe half a millennium later.

That first meeting of the council, ringed by the original unit of six hundred Scarlet-Shrouded Knights under the command of Grand Master Guérin de Montaigu, occurred in a chamber beneath the tombs in the Old Basilica of St. Peter, not far from where the remains of the apostle and first pope lay enshrined.

Legend had it that St. Grotth himself had attended this initial meeting, having selected, with the blessing of Pope Innocent the Third, a trio of Cardinals to sit upon the council—Giovanni di San Paolo, Gregorio Carelli, and Guido de Papa [a practice that continues to the present]. Filling out the seven seats were the Albigensian crusaders Simon de Montfort, 5th Earl of Leicester and Geoffrey I of Villehardouin, as well as the chronicler Roger of Wendover and the priest and natural philosopher Simon Langton, brother of the Archbishop of Canterbury, who was said to be named for the magician Simon Magus.

Watching the nearly thousand men as they drilled upon the grounds that overlooked Christiansted Harbor, Rocafull contemplated the events of the past two years. Of all the political machinations and secret operations the council had set in motion, their forced alliance with the pirates of France and the Caribbean had been for Rocafull the most concerning. Despite the declared allegiance of many of them to the Catholic Church—either through their assistance of the current trio of popes or their declaration as Jacobites in support of the Stuart claim to the British throne—they were not to be trusted. In the end, at the very moment it mattered most to the cause, they would serve only themselves.

The revelation of the location of a portion of the Star Quorum's war chest on the far side of St. Croix by the traitor Archibald Hamilton to the rogue pirate Vane the previous summer had caused endless ripples and aggravations for Rocafull and the other members of the council. The grand master had used his influence with the British Royal Navy to have Hamilton removed as governor of Jamaica and sent to London to stand trial for acts of piracy. Security around and on the island had been enhanced, costing much in time and resources best used elsewhere.

Worst of all, Olivier Levasseur and his allies had failed to prevent Vane from obtaining the level of power and influence that orphan son of a whore currently enjoyed.

Rocafull had heard that, despite their close cooperation in unseating Benjamin Hornigold from command of the fort in New Providence—the grand master knew well enough their terming it a *republic* was nothing but a fleeting, hopeless dream—Levasseur and his main ally Bellamy had ultimately parted company. Although the command to do so had come from the council, Rocafull knew in his heart that neither had been disappointed.

Looking out to sea, he thought of each of the Start Quorum members with whom it was his honor to serve. Assuring that their choice for king or queen of France, Spain, and Britain held or would soon secure their respective thrones kept the trio of Cardinals more than occupied. Anthony Sayer, Grand Master of the newly united Free Mason lodge in London, was tasked with holding at bay the Mammon Lodges of London and Dublin—a task the four archangels themselves could barely hope to manage.

Then there was Archibald Sinclair. Since his ancestor Henry, a powerful earl of Orkney, member of the Order of the Thistle, and a Templar Knight, had accepted a seat on the council in 1399, just before his voyage to North America on its behalf, a Sinclair had always been a member of the Star Quorum. The last earl of Orkney, William Sinclair—Henry's grandson—was also the builder of Rosslyn Chapel, and a staunch defender of the cause against the Ravenskalds. Archibald oversaw the scattered remnants of the Knights Templar, who, over the centuries, had absorbed themselves into a number of secret organizations, including the Rosicrucians and the top levels of Free Masonry.

Michaelangelo Tamborini, Superior General of the Society of Jesus, held the remaining seat. His work with the Chinese, while causing the Society a great deal of scandal and calls for its dissolution, were vital to battling the forces of evil that the Mammon Lodges and other dark sects were unleashing upon the lands and seas in their quest for the twelve sacred objects.

Allowing himself a small smile of satisfaction at the precision with which the Scarlet-Shrouded Knights of St. Grotth went through their drills, Rocafull knew that the call would soon come for him to divide them into small, unidentifiable units and disperse them into the world. Their destinations would be where the forces of Light and Dark were keeping several of the sacred objects or where the historical records—which were no more than well-worn legends in a few cases—purported them to be.

The most elite of the units would be assigned to protect James Frances Edward Stuart in Rome as well as a small island off the colony of Rhode Island—*how fittingly named*, Rocafull thought—to protect a mysterious, sightless monk named Trogon Ophidian and the secrets—and no doubt objects—he possessed.

Traveling with them would be a man Ramón Perellós y Rocafull trusted even less than the pirates with whom he insisted on keeping company.

Yet, because he possessed both the obsidian mirror and the Fatima Hand, Abraxas Abriendo was indispensable to the cause, so Rocafull had sent a summons for the well-pedigreed but all too egotistical magician to return to St. Croix in preparation for whatever was to come.

No matter what it was, the Scarlet-Shrouded Knights of St. Grotth—as well as the Knights of Malta—would be at the forefront of the fight.

"Lift your right hand just a little higher. Higher… Good. Bring the pointer and middle fingers closer together. Just like that. Now. The other hand. The one with the secret object. Keep it cupped by your dagger… seems natural enough to do so. Especially for you. Firm. But relaxed. Hold that thing steady in the palm of your hand. Pinch it beneath the muscle of your thumb and flesh just below your fingers. Good. Not going anywhere now. *Up here*! Keep looking me in the eye… That will keep *my* eyes up high on yours, where they belong. Now, open the empty hand while releasing the object into the pocket by the dagger."

Blackbeard growled in frustration as the coin he was palming clattered to the decking on the rampart of the fort.

For the twelfth consecutive time.

"This is nonsense, Abraxas! It is *not* what I asked you to teach me!"

In the few days since the letter regarding the nine shipwreck survivors addressed to Governor Shute of Massachusetts had left the island, Blackbeard had been like a caged beast, pacing the ramparts, yelling at the workers and keeping watch for a ship bearing an answer that—if all went exceedingly well and expeditiously—was still several weeks away.

He was becoming insufferable, even to those who understood and shared his sense of loss over the death of Samuel Bellamy.

So it was that with no gentle manners Benjamin Hornigold had prodded Abraxas to engage Blackbeard in some lessons that would prove useful should Shute refuse to release the shipwrecked sailors—which they all knew was the probable outcome—and the man formerly called Edward Thache would secure a ship and head for Boston.

Abraxas was grateful for the diversion. The task of looking after Caesar was rather easy, especially with Angus/Conall's help—and as far as teaching the former slave about magic, Caesar's grandfather Kwasi was so adept at Obeah, and had taught so much to the boy, Abraxas felt on most days more like the student than the teacher.

"I can teach you the kinds of simple conjuring tricks that will reinforce the effect of your height and width, that long beard with its braids and bows, the three brace of pistols, and the slow fuses beneath your tricorne," Abraxas had explained.

To his surprise, Blackbeard had accepted.

"Listen to me, Abraxas Abriendo," the pirate hissed, not bothering to pick up the coin from where it had come to a halt after rolling several feet. "I do not desire to make objects *seem* to disappear... What I desire... what I demand from ye... is to teach me all ye know about powder and fire and wind so that I may make my enemies *actually* disappear—into the depths of the sea!"

In a matter of seconds, Abraxas contemplated his choices. He could give in and teach Blackbeard things he was not yet ready to learn. He could move more quickly through the lessons, although his pupil had proven over the last several days that he was far from adept at even the simplest sleight of hand. He could give up. Walk away. He was wasting his time in waiting on New Providence as it was. Finally, he could persist in doing what absolutely was not working.

Snapping his fingers to make all but one of the choices dissolve, Abraxas said, "You cannot hope to control the elements of fire and wind if you do not have a mastery of simple hand control. Of concentration and intention. Would you allow a powder monkey to bring a fuse to the touchhole of the cannon without him first learning all the parts and pieces and how the damn thing has the power to do the destructive, deadly things it does?"

"Of course not," Blackbeard answered, as Abraxas knew he would. "And, as much as I dislike them, I understand your methods. *Intention* I have. In abundance. It is *concentration* that I lack, because I am so *intent* on saving those nine men's lives or making all of Boston pay the price!"

"You tell me what you want to do. We can proceed as I deem best, or we can go our separate ways, as we did in Jamaica all those years ago."

Staring at the coin where it lay on the decking, Blackbeard grunted and retrieved it. "We shall continue with your methods. Your sleight of hand was always impressive when we were boys—until ye slipped up with my father..."

"Only because of your sister!"

"*Step*sister. Do not remind me, or mention her again, or I shall quickly succeed in making *ye* disappear!"

Abraxas laughed. "After you succeed with the coin, you are welcome to try larger items, although I will *never* fit in the palm of your hand, no matter how abnormally large it is! Now... concentrate. Your intention is to succeed at this task. Nothing else matters beyond it. Good. Begin by showing the coin. Lift your right hand just a little higher. Higher... Excellent, my friend. Now make it seem as though you are passing the coin from the one hand to the other... Keep looking me in the eyes..."

It took two more increasingly tense efforts, but finally, as they were both about to give up hope for good, Blackbeard succeeded in making the coin fall into his pocket as he opened his other hand to show the coin was no longer in it.

"Bravo, my friend! You have done it. Tomorrow we shall take up something slightly more to your liking... it involves a special sort of paper, lightweight, coated secretly with a flammable substance."

Before Blackbeard could answer, a voice rang out from the beach below where they stood on a rampart of the fort.

"Abraxas Abriendo! I am Captain Oliver Hart, of the ship *Good Providence*, and I bear a message from Saint Croix. Ye are to accompany me with all haste back to the island by order of—"

Waving his hand at the captain, Abraxas said, "I know well enough who issued the order and you should know well enough not to say it aloud! I shall be down within minutes." Turning to Blackbeard, he said, "Your next lesson will have to wait. In the meantime, keep up your practice of the principles of sleight of hand. If this summons means what I know it does, we must all be at our best, using every trick we can manage."

Entering the fort, Abraxas left Blackbeard in a state of contemplation about what the magician meant.

BLOCK ISLAND, OFF THE COAST OF RHODE ISLAND COLONY, MID-MAY 1717

At times, the best way to remember the dead is to remember the most important moments spent during your time together.

For the past three hours, Captain Paulsgrave Williams was trying to do just that after receiving the news of Samuel Bellamy's death from the leader of the Jacobite cause, who had been kind enough to leave his pupil in peace in order to grieve, as he must.

Sitting in a well-appointed guest cottage on the estate of his dead stepfather—yet another casualty of The Cause—Paulsgrave thought back to the moment of his meeting with Sam in Boston and his willingness to join the Jacobites. Inextricably linked to Sam's commitment was the bond they shared over the harms the British government had visited upon their families. In Sam's case, his humiliating beating at the hands of Andrew Colson before the spoiled boy's father forced the Bellamys to leave the family homestead in Devonshire for which they had been the custodians for generations. For Paulsgrave, witnessing the death of his stepfather for the "crimes" of being Scottish and Catholic turned his heart and mind forever to The Cause. He had left his wife and two children, his mother—twice now a widow—and three sisters, and a thriving trade as a silversmith without pause or regret, and had rarely looked back.

Indeed, although they lived in Newport, a mere forty miles to the northeast, Paulsgrave had not contacted them, telling himself it was far too dangerous. Although that was true, there were other reasons as well. Did he bear any resemblance to the man they called a husband and father? He was too afraid to look into their eyes to find the truth.

Placing his hand upon the Marlowe manuscripts he had saved from destruction while inadvertently saving his life, and those of his crew on the *Marianne*, Paulsgrave thought back to the rescue of the Manchurian warrior Xiang Yu from the gallows in Boston for the crime of protecting a fellow slave in 1713. Then, two years later, in that same city, they had rescued Angus MacGregor and Joseph Stanton.

Angus had been proving himself ever since. Paulsgrave saw in his eyes and his actions the same kind of loyalty and determination that he had seen in Sam's, which had led to his now dead friend's taking the Oath on their ship *Expedition*, administered by no less a man of God than Cardinal André-Hercule de Fleury, France's highest-ranking Catholic.

As for Joseph, his was a soul needing saving, and Paulsgrave would find a way to do so.

Running his hand over the cover of Marlowe's *Jew of Malta*, and cursing the coded information it contained for causing, in some way he could not yet accept, the death of his closest friend, Paulsgrave turned his mind to Sam's private, exquisitely personal, meeting with his childhood nemesis just before his death. Although Sam had not said so, it had felt to Paulsgrave as though they had somehow managed to resolve the differences between them.

A meeting at sea, so close to Sam's demise.

Could it have been the hand of God?

"You know this to be true," came a soft, aged, melodic voice behind him.

"Master Trogon," Paulsgrave said, acknowledging his visitor by wiping the tears from the corner of his eyes and standing. "How long have you been standing there?"

"Only a couple of moments," the man replied. His thick silver-grey beard falling to the middle of his chest and coarse hooded robe, which hid the deeply etched age lines upon his hands and face, belied the powerful position he held. "It is odd, is it not, my pupil, how losing one's sight makes you more sensitive to the presence of another than those who can see?"

Pulling a chair along the floor so his teacher could track its movement, Paulsgrave said, "Sit please. I will pour you a cool cup of water."

"That would be most welcome," Trogon Ophidian replied, sitting squarely in the chair without touching it beforehand to be sure of its location. "I wish you to read to me from the *Dr. Faustus*. We have much work to do to ensure your friend was not killed without purpose."

Finding himself suddenly distracted to the point that the water he was pouring from a pitcher into a wooden cup overflowed the vessel's sides, Paulsgrave whispered, "I *knew* it. Though I could not—"

"Not *could* not.... *Choose* not," Ophidian replied. "For the thought was more than you could bear. Rightfully so. You must not allow a single thought of revenge to cloud the purity of your actions." Pausing a moment, he added, "I apologize for my timing. You have made a mess."

Wiping up the spilled water with a cloth, Paulsgrave once again found himself astounded by his teacher's acute sense of hearing. The overflowing water had hardly made a sound and at least fifteen feet separated them.

"Who did it?" he whispered, walking the cup of water across the room.

"You know that as well," Ophidian replied, grasping the cup with precision as though he could see it. "And further, that the storm was most unnatural. Which means—"

"One of the Ravenskalds possesses either the obsidian mirror or the Ezekiel Wheel. Last I knew, Abraxas Abriendo possessed the mirror. And the Fatima Hand…"

Handing back the empty cup, Ophidian said, "Blessedly, that is still the case.Therefore, it was the Ezekiel Wheel the Ravenskalds employed. An ancient and terrible weapon fallen into evil hands."

Slamming his hand into the table where he had placed the cup, causing it to topple to the floor, Paulsgrave asked, "Do you believe they attempted to steal the manuscripts?"

Leaving his chair, Ophidian walked directly to the spot where the cup had rolled and picked it up. "I do not. I have long known that Athelstan possesses Kyd's *Spanish Tragedy*, in which Sir Francis Bacon encoded the same vital information. He simply did not want *us* to have the Marlowes and their hidden knowledge." Approaching the table, he asked, "What is it now, my pupil?"

Paulsgrave shook his head in shame. "Samuel, several times, asked your name. I would not speak it. I told him it was too dangerous. But I… I think it was that I enjoyed knowing something about all this madness that he did not. After all, he was the one called before the Quorum. What a fool I was. I could have given him that. It is only just a name. And not a given one at that."

Placing his hand on Paulsgrave's, Ophidian whispered, "Your decision was correct. Some names do not matter. They change over time. Mine is best unsaid. Now… I have allowed you time for your grief. It is time to return to action. My student in Spain is facing greater obstacles in her quest to control the throne, and the Scarlet-Shrouded Knights shall soon be ready to deploy to assist her and the other of our allies. I shall take the books into my possession once we have spent the week gleaning from them their secrets."

Taking the cup from Ophidian, Paulsgrave answered, "And then what shall I do?"

"Do not use that cup again, my pupil."

Stopping the pitcher he now held over the cup just before the water spilled from the lip, Paulsgrave said, "Why not? It is perfectly fine." Commencing with the pouring, he soon felt a slow trickle of water on his hand.

It would later take him a dozen minutes to find the hairline crack, although Trogon Ophidian had known it was there from the moment that it fell.

Placing the cup upon the table, where it continued to trickle out its contents, Paulsgrave nodded in silence as his teacher said, "As to what you must do, it soon shall be revealed."

"Praise to God you have arrived, Olivier. Come and join us at table. We are about to discuss the most urgent of matters."

A few hours earlier, as Olivier Levasseur's flagship, the *Postillion*, and her escort, the *Oiseau de Proie*, captained by the Manchurian warrior Xiang Yu, sailed into the bay from their months-long mission off the Spanish Main, the French captain and Jacobite agent was surprised to see two other ships at anchor, neither of which he recognized.

Placing the crews of their ships on full alert, Levasseur and Yu took a longboat to the fort, where Grand Master Rocafull gratefully received them. After arranging for food and drink for the two captains and others, Rocafull took them into the chamber where the members of the Star Quorum met when the council was in session.

The voice that Levasseur heard upon entering the room was that of Cardinal Giulio Alberoni, advisor to the throne of Spain. To his left sat Filippo Antonio Gualterio, advisor to the Old Pretender, and, to his right a Franciscan friar who was still years away from twenty by the look of his innocent face.

"This is Guillermo Vincolaré," Alberoni said. "Guillermo, this is Capitaine Olivier Levasseur. You may have passed one another in the halls when the council was last in session..."

Introductions made, including Levasseur's of Xiang Yu, Grand Master Rocafull indicated that the two captains should take a seat. He then directed the line of servants entering the room to place their covered trays and pitchers on a table ten feet away and be as quiet as possible as they prepared the evening meal.

"So," Levasseur said, "what ees thees urgent matter of wheech you speak, for wheech you praise Dieu for my arrival at thees moment?"

"Cardinal de Fleury has gone missing," Cardinal Alberoni answered. "And we are, as you can imagine, greatly concerned for his safety."

"*Mon Dieu*! Where was he last seen?" Levasseur asked, resisting the urge to rest his tired legs by placing his heels upon the table.

"In Paris. That we know for certain. Although he was scheduled to travel on a ship to Spain on a most important mission several weeks ago. The ship arrived, but he did not."

Leaning into the table to show his frustration, Levasseur answered, "Then why are you all seeting here, een zee one place we know the Cardeenal ees not, readying yourselves for thees evening's meal?"

Seeing his fellow Cardinal's cheeks flush red with anger and embarrassment at the insult, Cardinal Gualterio placed his hand upon Alberoni's, cuing him to refrain from speaking lest he should say something they all would regret.

"The members of the Star Quorum," Gualterio began, his voice even in tone and barely above a whisper, "have various mechanisms for keeping in contact. I believe he boarded that ship, and our enemies took him from it. As to why we are all sitting here, it pertains to the urgent matter of which my fellow Cardinal spoke."

Before Levasseur could respond, Cardinal Alberoni shouted into a darkened corner, "Abraxas Abriendo, if you would please come forth!"

"Abraxas! *Mon Dieu!*" Levasseur responded as the grizzled magician emerged from the shadows, holding the obsidian mirror in one hand and the object known as the Fatima Hand in the other.

"Enough, Olivier!" Cardinal Alberoni said, glaring at the Frenchman with an intensity that almost made the proud captain avert his eyes. "I will send you away and find someone else to assist us!"

"Apologies, Your Emeenence. I meant *non* offense. I am honored to asseest een any way that I am required by your command."

"Very well then," Alberoni answered, his tone softer. "Sit quiet and learn what you can." To Abraxas, he said, "You may begin when you are ready, Master Abriendo."

"Thank you, Your Eminence," Abraxas answered, placing the mirror on the table. Placing the Fatima Hand in his cloak, which he then removed and draped over a chair, he removed two white candles from a pocket, which he lit and waved over the mirror three times while mumbling a dozen indistinguishable words.

Placing the candles to the right and left of the mirror, the magician said, "As I open the door of the mirror so that we may see our answer, I ask you all to close your eyes and think of the face of Cardinal de Fleury, as though it were a portrait in oils lit by a single close-by candle."

Non, non, non, Levasseur thought, half wishing he had not chosen to come here. *I shall peek just a leetle, old weezard, so that I can see what conjuring you are doing!*

Placing his hands on the top and bottom of the mirror, Abraxas began to intone, "*Sanco tupanché, tecco du mané, té-liggo, té-liggo nupanché. Sanco du mené, heelo du ché ché. Sanco tupanché, tecco du mané, du mané, du mané. Vibra sume ché ché. Sanco tupanché, tecco du mane...*"

Three times he whispered the incantation, each time with increasing conviction. Peeking through his half-closed eyes, Levasseur saw the mirror begin to emit a soft blue glow, just as Abraxas said, "Yes, yes... continue to picture the face of our missing friend. He indeed has boarded the ship. It is night, and they are sailing out at sea. The Cardinal is gazing at the horizon, deep in contemplation. What is this? From behind him, keeping to the shadows, is a young man. He looks frightened... at war with his himself and his soul. I see a flicker in the moonlight. A knife! He holds it loosely... nearly drops it... but he steels his resolve... It is at the neck of de Fleury! The young man whispers something in French... I cannot make it out... but the Cardinal nods. Keeping the knife at de Fleury's neck, the scoundrel produces an unlit lantern and whispers more French. De Fleury lights the lantern, which he holds over the side of the ship, passing his hand in front of the light three times."

Slapping his hand on the table, which drew several angry looks, Rocafull hissed, "Signaling a ship. The rogue!"

"Indeed," Abraxas said, taking his hands from the mirror and waving them over the center of its polished obsidian service with a series of complex gestures, as though he were inscribing invisible symbols. "I see a wisp of the skull and crossbones in the fog..."

"Pirates!" Cardinal Alberoni whispered, crossing himself.

Nodding sadly, Abraxas said, "The image has faded away, but I believe we have our answer as to what has happened to the Cardinal."

"But eet tells us nothing about where he ees!" Levasseur shouted, consequences be damned. "Zee waters are *très, très* wide indeed, *mes amies*, even for *moi*!"

"Forgive the Capitaine's outburst, Master Abriendo," Alberoni said, not bothering to look at Levasseur. "This information, while not fully what we had hoped, nevertheless answers several questions. Are you prepared to undertake the second part of what we have asked?"

Lifting the mirror and heading for the door, Abraxas said, "I am. Please come outside with me."

Several moments later, the group stood upon the beach near the harbor. Pointing above them to a bright group of stars, Abraxas said, "There shines the constellation Cassiopeia. If I gaze upon it in the surface of the mirror like this, I should be able to see... Yes! Yes. There it is, just as the wise ones said!"

"Do you see them both?" Cardinal Gualterio asked, his voice atremble. "The balm and the comb?"

"I see only the Magdalene Balm," Abraxas answered. "It is on an island. Well hidden. Both the island and the Balm. It is far to the north. Follow the light of Cygnus and you shall find it."

"We are grateful, Master Abriendo," Cardinal Alberoni said. "Although disappointed once again. You see nothing of the comb? You are certain?"

"The mirror has gone dark," Abraxas answered. "Someone is shielding the comb from our sight."

"And we know who that someone is," Grand Master Rocafull muttered. "And that damnable demon Ravenskald no doubt has the Cardinal as well."

"Conjecture, Ramón, which is the devil's maze," Cardinal Alberoni softly said. "Careful you do not find yourself lost in its twists and turns."

"How do we proceed?" Cardinal Gualterio asked.

"If I may?" Grand Master Rocafull asked. Given the go-ahead with a nod from both the Cardinals, he said, kneeling and placing his fist over his heart, "The Scarlet-Shrouded Knights of Saint Grotth are at their peak of discipline and fitness and are ready to be dispersed. We shall find Cardinal de Fleury no matter the obstacles and sacrifices we all have to make. I promise you this as a Knight of Malta and a servant of Saint Grotth."

"God shall bless you in this venture, Ramón, as he does in all our righteous deeds," Cardinal Gualterio said. "And as for the Magdalene Balm…"

"Now I know why *Dieu* was praised upon my fortueetous arrival here," Levasseur said, all trace of bravado gone from his voice. "I shall sail weeth all haste to zee north, followeeng Cygnus zee Swan."

"God goes with you, Olivier," Cardinal Alberoni said. "As shall the Franciscan friar Guillermo Vincolaré."

"*Très bien!*"

"And Master Abriendo."

"Abraxas? *Mon Dieu!*"

PART FOUR

A SONG OF SWANS AND SECRETS

Captain Charles Vane did not care for complications.

Although his life since he and Henry Jennings—whom he now considered an enemy—had stormed the Spanish fort off Florida and taken a load of recovered treasure from the sunken plate fleet in 1715 had been nothing *but* complications.

Hornigold's ambition to forge a pirate republic in the Bahamas. Former governor Archibald Hamilton's arrest in Jamaica and transportation in chains to London. Vane's split with Henry Jennings. The recovery of the treasure in St. Croix, the proceeds of which had not taken them nearly as far as he had thought. The failure of Ross and Stanton to learn the location of a map that would lead Vane to some or all of twelve ancient objects over which the two sides of this grand and gruesome game of international chess were warring. Twelve objects, the possession of even a few of which would provide the bargaining power he needed to secure his place on the board.

With each failure, each broken alliance, each instance of insubordination by Ross and Stanton—he was ready to keel haul them both—the more complicated Vane's daily life had become.

Take this latest embarrassment. Not long after the oil-and-water pair had returned from their failed mission in Boston—sending them together was a gross miscalculation for which Vane had yet to forgive himself—and Stanton's subsequent flogging for being the architect of the fuck-up, Vane had been the recipient of a vague and threatening message. Signed "R," the two-page missive informed him that its writer was well aware of the theft of the treasure from St. Croix and the attempt by Ross and Stanton to learn the location of the map.

The letter had concluded with, "Now ye owe us. My associates and I shall have our satisfaction. Ye shall hear from me again."

A second letter had arrived two weeks later, also signed by "R," directing Vane to proceed to the coast of North Carolina colony, near the Albemarle, to receive a delivery in the form of two human beings.

"R" would explain what he was to do with them once Vane had taken possession of whomever it was he was referencing.

So here he sat, three days idle, in a precarious position just outside the shipping lanes of the mid-Atlantic, awaiting the arrival of Christ knew whom. Whomever it was, it would no doubt be another, rather severe, complication in Charles Vane's life.

"Cap'n, do ye 'ave a moment?"

Devon Ross was standing just behind him.

About to create, Vane knew in his gut, another complication.

"What is it ya need, Mistah Ross?" Vane answered, not turning around but instead making a motion over his shoulder that Ross should move to where his captain could see him.

"This collection we are makin'. Based on the location, an' who I think this 'R' is, I believe that Lord Carteret is involved. As ya know, 'e is the reason I came ta the Caribbean. An', I 'ave ta tells ya, Cap'n, 'e ain't 'appy wit' me as a' late. I ain't learned nothin' a' the location a' the Jacobite Seton, escaped from the Tower a' London eight months ago an' who has managed ta elude capture by constantly changin' his route a' travel."

Looking Ross in the one eye not covered by his frightful leather mask, Vane replied, "Ya 'ave a way a' upsettin' ya employahs. Findin' Seton ain't my concern 'til I am asked. Ya serve one too many mastahs, Ross. I do not 'ave ta remind ya why we are in this shitful position..."

"'Course not. An' I want ta makes it right, fer both a' ya."

Vane was suddenly interested. "'Ow do ya prahpose ta do that?"

"If we could offer ta Carteret a bit a' the Saint Croix treasure..."

"All spent fer the cause, Ross. Anythin' else?"

"Ship sighted! Headin' fer us hard, Cap'n!"

This came from the crow's nest, way up high on the mainmast.

They had some time before their delivery arrived—if indeed that is what the ship heading toward them was doing on this course—but not much.

"Talk fast, Ross. Our cargo might be arrivin'."

Two hours later, as Vane mulled the various scenarios Devon Ross put forth—none of which he liked—a ship came alongside, flying a flag comprising a white cross on a red field.

The flag of the Swiss Confederacy.

Across the deck of the ship now strode a tall man in merchant's clothes, though the rings he wore and the shine of his buttons and boots betrayed a man significantly more wealthy than any mere merchant.

"I seek the man Charles Vane," the stranger said, his accent neutral and sonorous.

"I am he," Vane replied, trying to match the new arrival's proper pronunciations. "I await delivery, as per the letters sent by the respected gentleman who signs his name 'R.'"

"The man to which ye refer is me. Absalom Ravenskald. As to the planned delivery, I have decided to make other arrangements for our reluctant pair of guests. They shall no longer be your concern. Although, when I first obtained them, I flew a flag like yours."

Vane felt his heart sink. He had heard the Ravenskald name all his life, and from Devon Ross more than he would have liked. Now the plan had changed.

Never a promising sign.

To make matters worse, Ravenskald would blame him for something he had not done and therefore from which he could not hope to profit.

"If not ta deliver ya *cargo*, why then 'ave ya still made a point ta meet me?"

"Ah… I have angered ye! Now the true rough and tumble Captain Vane emerges. Believe me, sir… It is much more preferable for me to speak to ye as ye are, and not as ye believe I wish ye to be."

"I much prahfer it as well."

Absalom laughed. "Excellent. Now, if ye shall invite me aboard the famous sloop *Ranger*, we shall have, as ye pirates call it, a parlay."

Several hours later, as the ship that brought Absalom Ravenskald to him was sailing away, Charles Vane, feeling the effects of several drams of hastily swallow rum, looked at the map clutched in his hand.

The very map of the north Atlantic islands he had sent Ross and Stanton to learn about in Boston.

Now here it was in his hands.

One damnable complication ended, with another taking its place.

Looking back on recent events, Vane once again saw where misplaced compassion had gotten him. The merchant captain who had told him about the map must have gotten word to the Ravenskalds that he had shared what he should not.

That is why it is wiser ta kills 'em outright an' be done wit' it.

In addition, Vane now knew that Lord John Carteret was indeed displeased… and not just with Devon Ross.

Ye shall be judged by the comp'ny ya keep.

Taking the treasure—meagre though it was—from St. Croix was proving to be the whore-mother of endless complications, each one of her offspring a sharp-toothed, breast-bitin' bitch latching onto Vane.

It was not treasure the map would bring him, Ravenskald had said—although wealth beyond imagining was Charles Vane's for the taking should he not fuck this revised assignment up.

With purpose and haste, Vane was to sail for Rhode Island colony, where he was to lie in wait for La Buse himself, the vulture Levasseur, who was due to meet with a person of interest to the Ravenskalds on a small length of sand called Block Island south of the colony.

"It is of the utmost importance," Ravenskald had warned, "that ye engage with Levasseur—mark well that he sails with a second vessel, under the command of a fetid *Chinaman*—before he reaches port. He will have on board at least two items of interest to us—an obsidian mirror and a carved wooden hand, although there might be more. The man who bears them—Abraxas Abriendo— fancies himself a wizard. Ye will kill him, though not kindly or quickly. He has caused us innumerable griefs."

"An' the rest? Levasseur and the Chinaman?"

"Kill them however ye like. Take their ships… whatever is on board is yours, following our inspection. Our only interest is in the mirror, hand, and like items that we will know when we see them. Fail us, and I shall show ye what the fury of the Ravenskalds can do to a person's soul."

Then the parlay was over, Ravenskald having the pressing need to sail with his two guests—hidden aboard his vessel—to the western isles of Britain for what he termed a "family reunion."

Glancing at the map in the flickering candlelight, Vane saw writing in the corner that he recognized. It was from William Shakespeare's *The Tempest*, which he had been reading, along with the bard's other plays, in the collection he had taken from a Captain Benning of the merchant ship *Voyager* in February of the previous year.

Benning, whose throat had been slit by Joseph Stanton without orders from his captain.

Yet another complication.

Holding the paper close to the fire, Vane read aloud the words spoken by Caliban in the second scene of the third act:

> *This isle is full of noises,*
> *Sounds and sweet airs that give delight and hurt not.*
> *Sometimes a thousand twangling instruments*
> *Will hum about mine ears, and sometime voices*
> *That, if I then had waked after long sleep,*
> *Will make me sleep again; and then, in dreaming,*
> *The clouds methought would open and show riches*
> *Ready to drop upon me, that when I waked*
> *I cried to dream again.*

A description of an island Vane could fast call home.

If the bees would just keep buzzing, I could read the hive…
If the bees would just keep buzzing, I could read the hive…
If the bees would just keep buzzing…
The bees…

"Ohmygod, ohmygod, I need to FIND the BEES! Jesus… ohmy god!"

Doctor Kirstine MacGregor awoke with a start, to find herself back in the barn behind her great-grandmother's house on the southern Outer Banks of North Carolina. Beside her was her cousin, Callum, who had just used a rusty old screwdriver to pry open a wood box containing pieces of history.

Her family history, which had led her to her life as an expert on the pirates.

Reaching into the box, she grasped an acorn and oak leaf brooch. She had not known it then, but she knew it now—it had belonged to Angus MacGregor's father—killed for delaying his oath of fealty to William of Orange. Angus had worn it—first to Boston, then to the Caribbean, then upon his travels on the seas and in the American colonies. Angus then gave it to his son. His son, whose name was…

Callum! *Like my cousin!* Although, unlike the often poison ivy–covered pig-nosed bully that stood beside her, Angus's Callum was a hero… a Jacobite who fought on Drumossie Moor in the Highlands of Scotland in 1746. A hero thirty years later, in an Indian dispute known as Lord Dunmore's War on the banks of the Ohio River…

Holding it to her lips, she placed the brooch back in the box. What she most wanted was to secret it away in her pocket, although she knew Callum would never allow it. Wiping the sweat from her hands so the oils in her skin would not damage them (how does a nine-year-old *know that?*) she pulled out the papers. So many, and so old. Ships' logs and officers' journals. Hand-drawn maps with latitudes and longitudes marking secret places… Fortresses and castles. Temples and cathedrals. Islands, forests, and deep, forgotten caves…

Amidst them, as interesting as they were, she caught a glimpse of a first page of a log. Written upon it, in an elaborate hand, was "1716. The Coast of St. Croix. Christiansted Harbor. Logs of Capitaine Olivier—"

How did she know all this? All this detail. *How?*

Mygod, mygod, mygod... I am back in the mirror machine! Back in Quarry Peak! Back as a captive of Doctor Friedrich Reinhardt and Nurse Rachet... Stiles... Nurse Anita Stiles. Help me! Help me!

"Help me!" Kirstine cried, snapping up in bed.

There was someone sitting beside her. She somehow knew his face.

Hiya, Kirstine. No need to be afraid. I'm a friend.

His voice was in her head.

"You helped me—"

Ah, ah, ah. Speaking is for regular girls. You have a gift, Kirstine. That's why the cruel old Nazi doctor... and the serpents who pay his wage... want you. Use your mind, *like PF showed you.*

PF. You helped me escape from the hospital.

The humanoid form in the chair—for she knew it wasn't human— nodded, causing its long, curly black hair to shimmer and shake like he was Paul Stanley, KISS's glam rocker frontman.

I did. Listen... we don't have a lot of time. When you screamed for help, it triggered an alarm and, although I am just a few anomalous pixels on the DTEAU security cameras, a few of them possess the... let's call it bloodline... to see me when they get here.

Why am I seeing these things?

Because I need you to really look *at those dusty old pirate papers, Kirstine. Look at them closely, and tell me what you see. That's it. Close your eyes. The bees will lead you back...*

She was back inside the barn, with the papers in her hands.

They were just a lot of symbols. No longer numbers and words.

Almost speaking aloud, she said with her thoughts, *I don't understand...*

Oh, but you do, Kirstine. That's precisely the point. Olivier's codes... That's Olivier Levasseur, by the way... be sure to take a look at all your notes on him... Taught to him by the magician Abriendo, who was taught by the descendents of Bacon and Newton. Occultists and alchemists. Codes not breakable by the NSA or the Navy's most gifted cryptologists. Beyond the logics of quantum computers... Every one of those papers you found there in the barn was written using that code. Angus's journals as well. Olivier taught him. Then the magicians schooled Angus and they made him an adept.

So if they're in code, and I can read them...

Then... PF let loose a laugh that tickled the curves of her skull.

The *inside* of her skull.

I somehow know the code.

It was then that the sounds of sirens filled the air and there was pounding on the door.

Standing as he dissolved, PF psychically whispered, *Close. But even better. Kirstine, you are the code. That is, the code's inside you. A part of you. 'K... I gotta fly. Oh... and tell Jake... I am not his competition. Nor do I think 'he's got this.'"*

She was suddenly in her bed, with Haxx Alvarado and SA Maggie Sorrus standing near PF's empty chair, guns drawn and FBI flak vests reflecting the morning light, looking incredibly, almost laughably, concerned.

"Non, non, non! I weel not accept thees. I do not be*lieve* thees!"

Abraxas Abriendo, upon realizing that Olivier Levasseur and Xiang Yu were unaware of what had befallen Samuel Bellamy two months earlier, had resolved to spare them for as long as possible.

It had not gone as planned.

Insisting that they engage with a merchant ship off the coast of Virginia for needed sheets and cordage, Levasseur had learned from the captain, who had, in his anger and frustration, yelled at the Frenchman as he was preparing to return to the *Postillion*, "I hope ye are swallowed by these righteous Atlantic waters the same as that bastard Bellamy!"

"You knew, you *worthless weezard*, and you deed not theenk to tell me?" he had asked Abraxas, once back on board.

That had been a week ago, and Abraxas had found it prudent to transfer his things to the *Oiseau de Proie*, under the command of the more understanding Xiang Yu.

Then, a day earlier, as they sailed off the coast of Cape Cod, Xiang Yu ordered the lowering of a longboat, which he entered alone, along with light provisions and his pair of Chinese swords.

Back aboard the *Postillion*, Abraxas found Levasseur silent as to what Xiang Yu was intending to do.

"We have beeseezness of our own, old weezard," Levasseur had said in answer to Abraxas's tenth query. "Focus on thees, and not on Xiang Yu."

The business of which Levasseur was speaking was his desire to know the origins of the obsidian mirror, having seen the blue light emanating from it during the activities on St. Croix.

Thinking it wise not to scold Levasseur for his indiscretion, Abraxas removed the mirror from its custom-shaped box and lay it on a table between them in the captain's quarters.

"In the time before time," Abraxas began, his voice transforming into the melodic, soft-toned lilt of the master storyteller, "the Aztec god of illusion and sorcery, Tezcatlipoca, created a 'smoking' mirror, made from obsidian—*this* mirror—to trick and then banish his rival Quetzalcoatl, the feathered-serpent, mediator of earth and sky. These two prideful, powerful deities had engaged in a war of creation and destruction of the suns of the ages of earth, water, and wind since their birth at the time of the Universe's great awakening. In order to reach the feathered-serpent god's home deep within the jungle, where he had incarnated—in the time of the rise of the Ravenskalds in Orkney—in the humanoid form of the ruler of the fabled city of Tollan, Tezcatlipoca transformed himself into a jaguar. As he crept through the jungle toward the city, the watchful ones could identify him by the yellow and black stripe across his face.

"Although they warned their ruler Quetzalcoatl about the coming of his rival, the feathered-serpent god, who had defeated his jealous enemy thrice prior, did not bother to defend himself. Then, when confronted with the obsidian mirror Tezcatlipoca had created, which hung now from the dripping jaws of the jaguar, Quetzalcoatl found himself in a trance, unable to resist his rival's order that he conjure a horrific hurricane—as you know, another of the mirror's awesome powers—which did great damage to Tollan and many other surrounding cities.

"For this reason, Quetzalcoatl was pulled from his humanoid form and banished back to the ether for untold centuries. As for Tezcatlipoca, he used the mirror again and again at the behest of the Ravenskalds, who had found a way to control him as they soon would Mammon and Moloch."

Sitting in silence as Levasseur took in all that Abraxas had told him, the wizard placed his hands protectively over the mirror as he heard a light knock upon the closed and bolted door. Half in a trance of his own, Levasseur stood and opened it, not asking whom it was.

By the time Abraxas saw that it was the Franciscan friar Guillermo Vincolaré, the mirror was already back in its box and under the table.

"Ah, Guillermo," the wizard said, motioning to a chair at the table. "You just missed the story of the origins of the mirror."

"I know it in detail from my dreams," Guillermo answered, his voice tinged with embarrassment. "The fearsome jaguar turned many a dream into a nightmare for me. I am sorry, though, that I missed your rendition. Perhaps another time… I have come for another reason…"

"Tell us, then," Levasseur said, retaking his seat. Although still not quite himself, Abraxas noticed that Levasseur's trance was wearing off. "And we weel asseest as we can."

"I was instructed by Cardinal Alberoni to wait until we had reached the coast of the Massachusetts colony to instruct you, Master Wizard, to open the Fatima Hand."

Attempting to suppress the look of shock he knew was in his eyes, Abraxas said, "I do not know how, Guillermo." Then, pausing for a moment in realization he added, "Though I am guessing that, thanks to your dreams, you know *exactly* how to do it. And, further… what it contains."

Nodding his head with all humility, Guillermo gently held out his hand. "If you please, Master Wizard."

Taking the Fatima Hand from a deep pocket of his cloak, Abraxas refrained from handing it over. "What of Capitaine Levasseur? Did the Cardinal offer any guidance regarding if *he* should be included?"

"He did, and he is, or I would not have spoken to you of it in his presence."

Levasseur smiled. First, because of the friar's sharp tongue—so at odds with his dulcet Italian tones—and second because La Buse was no longer on the outs with the council.

"Very well," Abraxas answered, placing the carved wood lower arm and hand into Guillermo's own.

[*Note*. It would be indiscrete and a breach of trust to disclose how the Fatima Hand can be opened. Given its crucial role in the current state of the world and the future of humanity, it is best to skip to what the trio found after Guillermo had done so. *JM*]

"Empty. As I had feared." Guillermo placed the pieces of the Hand upon the table.

"We have been betrayed!" Abraxas said, running his finger inside the exposed opening in the length of wooden arm after peering into it with a candle. "Capitaine Levasseur—you must take us to Block Island south of Rhode Island with all due haste."

Levasseur, trying to process what had just occurred, and what it meant, shook his head. "*Non*, weezard. Xiang Yu—"

"Can join us there. Send him word to do so," Abraxas said, his eyes now ablaze with a yellow-orange fire.

"I shall send someone to fetch heem, *oui*. Although our orders—from zee sacreed counceel eetself—are to proceed to zee isle of zee swan weeth all haste."

"And we shall," Abraxas said, standing, his voice taking on the crackle and power of the fire in his eyes. "Once we have spoken with my master, Trogon Ophidian."

Rob Roy MacGregor sat upon a low stone wall on his land, his hands not far from the claymore and pistol also atop the wall, placed to either side of him.

Why he thought he might need them, he could not say, but his life had been lived based on his instincts, a situation that had admittedly caused him as many losses as wins.

Looking out over his land—the barn and cattle pens, the cottages where he and half a dozen of his kin now lived, Rob—as had become his almost constant daily practice—considered all that had happened to them in the past few years. His feud with the Duke of Montrose over missing money the duke had loaned him to purchase cattle had put Rob in a precarious position, seeking allies where he could. His alliance with John Erskine, Earl of Mar and loyal Jacobite, had led to humiliating losses at Sheriffmuir and Preston in 1715, and the earl's undoing. When the Old Pretender had returned to France two months later, Rob found himself almost wholly unprotected, leading to his alliance with the Duke of Argyll—who had abandoned George to fight in support of James Stuart—whose arrival he now awaited.

Having had his allegiance to the Jacobite cause called into question by the Old Pretender because of certain letters his nephew Angus had sent Ailish from the Caribbean, Rob had ordered her cousin Duncan—Rob's most trusted man—to sail to the Bahamas and murder him for his indiscretions.

No one knew the truth but Duncan and Rob.

Aligning with Argyll had renewed the feud with James Graham, the Duke of Montrose, and his factor—also a Graham, though his name was John. How much Rob had learned about the ruthlessness of his enemy when, having moved his family and closest allies from Balquhidder to a more strategic, easy to defend plot of land here in Glen Shira, he kidnapped John, only to find that the duke refused to pay a ransom.

Again, Argyll was there to help. Although the help came, as always, with a price—look after Findlay Fletcher, the half-mad barber whose fiancé was an unwilling guest in Scone Palace of the nephew of another of Rob's enemies: David Murray, Fifth Viscount of Stormont. What a pleasure it had been to steal guns from Scone, meant for the Loyalist cause, as well as Findlay's fiancé Rowan, who was, after months of imprisonment, rape, and God knew what other depredations, more out of her head than Findlay.

Rob's lass Mary had taken Rowan into her care, and her journey to healing had begun.

Following the unsuccessful attempt of another of David Murray's nephews to retrieve Rowan from Rob Roy's cottage—the treacherous bastard meeting a ball from Mary's pistol rather than his cousin's desired target—Clan Macgregor, still forced to use the alternate name of Campbell, had found itself sitting in a pot of slowly boiling water, ever the valuable bargaining chip.

That, Rob reminded himself, was on him and him alone, for constantly changing sides. The latest result—his being kidnapped three months ago by *another* of the Murrays, John, first duke of Atholl, so that the bastard might earn favor with King George, who rightfully doubted his allegiance due to the fact that his family had at times *fought for the Jacobites*—could have easily been his doom.

Yet Rob Roy MacGregor, Highlander and slave to no man, fought and plotted on.

Pushing himself off the wall at the sound of a horse about to crest the nearest hill, Rob decided to leave his weapons where they lay.

Staying loyal to John Campbell, Second Duke of Argyll, was his only way out of the mess his actions and intuitions had created, and he did not want to send any message other than that to the fast-approaching rider.

"Mornin' Rob," the duke yelled, bringing his impressive bay charger to a halt near the wall.

"What news, John?" Rob asked, wishing to delay not a moment with small talk.

"'Tis nae what wae hooped an' all that wae expaected. The MacGraegors weel nae bae included in the king's Indemnity Act. Tho' Carnwath, Nairne, and Widdrington and almost twaenty oothers haev baen let go froom the Tower a' Loondon an' Newgate Gaol an' moost a' the Highland clans haev received a pardon fer the uprisin's in fifteen, ye are held accountable fer moost a' the lingerin' troobles hair in the Highlands, Rob."

Resisting the urge to yell, Rob whispered, "Oonly the MacGregors are exaempt?"

Argyll shook his head. "Nae, Rob. Matthew Prior and the Harleys haev also baen excluded. Boot that is nae matter, eh? We need tae bae careful aboot ye, Rob. Montrose an' the Murrays weel seize this opportunity tae coom after ye again."

Retrieving his claymore and pistol, Rob thanked the duke for personally delivering the message before sending Argyll on his way with an assurance that he would proceed with all due caution in all matters, while stopping short of guaranteeing he would consult with Argyll before he proceeded with a plan.

About to enter his cottage minutes later, Rob stopped at the sound of a horse, whose gait and whinny were markedly different from Argyll's bay charger. It was a workhorse, no doubt carrying a simple messenger of some kind with a missive or verbal speech that would add an even greater degree of complexity to Rob's increasingly troubled life.

"Hallo, Rob!" the young rider said, untying a heavy-looking bag from the horn of his saddle and handing it down as Rob returned the greeting.

"What bae this?" Rob said, his grasping hands revealing that the bag was full of coins.

"It cooms from a coosin' a' Findlay Fletcher's, a pirate oot on the account wit' the famed Robin Hoods a' the sea, Bellamy an' Williams. Shairin' the wealth like all good clansmen should, eh?"

"Aye, Ewan. Spoken troo. Carry on, lad, an' long may yer lum reek!"

"Yers as weel, Rob."

As the rider rode away, Rob undid the cord that held the heavy bag closed, his eyes wanting to see what his hands had felt.

Indeed, as Ewan had said, coins and other treasure filled the bag.

Cinching the bag, Rob leaned against the doorway, his mind suddenly full of images of his nephew Angus, whom he had sent to his death to protect himself and his other kin and allies.

What if he had made a mistake?

No one knew the truth but Duncan and Rob.

Calling for Findlay, who was working out in the barn, before he changed his mind and kept the bag of treasure for himself, Rob turned his attention to the recent disappearance of Ailish MacDonald, as well as the cloak that Rob had given Angus, which Duncan had returned as proof of Angus's death. A cloak that had belonged to Rob's brother—Angus's father. The cloak carried now the bloodstains of father and son, wherever it was.

Pressing Duncan for answers after he had returned from Glasgow without the girl, Rob had found his once closest friend even more distant and tight-lipped than usual. As to Ailish, he said that she had chosen to remain, having secured work in a tavern. Rob found that hard to believe, though her parents did not share his doubts, so Rob had not pushed. Duncan had not been the same since his return from the Caribbean, favoring a shoulder whose wounding he would tersely explain away with some excuse about cramped quarters and the cold sea air.

Had Ailish somehow secreted away the cloak, as a remembrance? That had to have been it.

Leaving the comfort of the doorway to meet Findlay halfway across the yard, Rob began to ponder the possibilities of how to keep his family and the others in his charge safe from what was sure to be a vicious coming storm.

"**H**ave at it again, Captain Masters! All guns on the starboard side! And the rail guns full of shot... hard to the sails and do not cease until she is splintered and aflame!"

Colonel William Rhett, commander of the eight-gun sloops *Henry*—his flagship upon whose deck he now stood—and the *Sea Nymph*, under the capable hand of Captain Hall, was enjoying the spectacle of destroying a wormy, barely seaworthy pirate ship they had been scouting for several days.

In truth, if Deputy Governor Robert Johnson was not aboard, Rhett would have let the pirate ship pass, certain as he was that she would sink on her own before reaching whatever Caribbean hideout to which she was heading.

Of course, he had invited Johnson aboard *precisely because* he knew the pirates would be exactly where they were and he did not intend to let them—or this opportunity to further prove his prowess to the newly installed politician—pass.

Since they had initially met on the last day of April, Rhett had found much to admire in their new deputy governor. His predecessor, Robert Daniell, loyal as he was to Colonel Moore and the Family, would have proven an obstacle to Rhett's ambitions, which, despite him being a few months shy of his fifty-first year and his fiscal future being of no concern after decades of success on the seas, were more grand than ever.

"I say, Colonel Rhett," Johnson said, his eye stuck to a spyglass, "she is on the verge of sinking. Why waste further powder, ball, and shot?"

"To provide a lesson in abject brutality, Governor. The same lesson in brutality the Royal Navy would be wise to readopt. It is their present softness, their mercy to these *hostis humani generis*, which has placed South Carolina in the position it is in."

"Yes, I quite agree," Johnson answered, lowering the spyglass as the nameless pirate ship burst into flames and the screams of her crew began to reach the *Henry* in earnest. "Although it does not end with the navy. I intend to finish—and extend—what my father started here in my position a decade ago, before the Lords Proprietors thwarted his plans. I intend to end the reign of the Cravens and Carterets of this world. To expand to the west, to make our promising colony so strong as to challenge—and perhaps absorb—our sister colony to the north, raped and plundered as she is by this so-called Family."

"Ah, yes," Rhett answered, torn between his delight in watching the pirate ship begin to sink as a ball of blue and orange flame and lending his full attention to the deputy governor. Realizing he was skilled enough to concentrate on both, Rhett said, "Colonel Moore and I see eye to eye on little. I find him arrogant. His games with the natives, in both colonies—along with his cohorts Moseley and Vale—I also find distasteful. Furthermore, the man that truly rules them… Absalom Ravenskald. I told ye of the horrific actions he undertook in Beaufort to try and procure some secret or other from those fishermen. The bloody, ghoulish aftermath of which it was left to *me* to scrub from the decking below us…"

As the captains of the sloops barked orders to prepare to depart to their one-hundred and thirty combined crewmen, Governor Johnson took the instrument of his own ambition by the shoulders. "Worry not, Colonel Rhett. Absalom Ravenskald's rule over the Carolinas will also end. For now, ye must concentrate on patrolling the shores for pirates. Continue to dispatch them with the level of brutality ye have demonstrated for me today—and yes, I know why ye invited me along—and I shall provide the resources ye require. When South Carolina assumes her place of greatness, along with Virginia and Massachusetts, as our port here entitles us, ye shall be remembered and rewarded, sir, for your service."

Watching the last few feet of the mainmast of the now unrecognizable pirate ship slip below the boiling, churning waves, Colonel Rhett began to feel as though he had come back home at last.

Xiang Yu had no sooner returned to the *Oiseau de Proie*, anchored off Cape Cod, when the message arrived from Levasseur ordering him to rendezvous on Block Island.

Reaching Rhode Island half a day after Levasseur, Xiang Yu had been anxious to get the Frenchman alone so that he might unburden his heart as to what had occurred in Massachusetts.

Levasseur, who had dined with Paulsgrave Williams the previous evening, insisted that Bellamy's mentor and friend be included in the talk.

"My reason for returning to Cape Cod was a simple one," Xiang Yu began. "To rescue Goody Hallett and bring her back with me, in order to protect her from her father."

"Protect her?" Paulsgrave asked. "What has the brigand done?"

"I know we have little time and pressing issues before us, so I shall be as straightforward as I am able. Not long after Samuel left in anger and shame on the heels of Hallett's rebuttal to the idea of an engagement, Goody made a realization. She was pregnant with his child. When Hallett found out, he was furious. He disowned Goody in the public square, proclaiming her a penniless sailor's whore, before having her arrested and whipped for pregnancy outside of marriage. He and several of his equally angry, abusive mates then turned their attention to me. This was the result."

Xiang Yu removed his shirt, revealing dozens of pale pink scars interdicting the elaborate tattoos on his back.

"Ye never told us!" Paulsgrave protested. "Although Samuel saw them. He mentioned them to me, in New Providence. I think he knew who had done it..."

Xiang Yu nodded. "He was in many ways the wisest of us. As I say, my intention was to remove Goody and the child from wherever they were and bring them back to the *Oiseau de Proie*. It was not to be..."

"*Mon Dieu, mon amie*," Levasseur whispered. "Tell us."

"Goody had the child in the local gaol. It was a girl. I do not know the name. The jailer was a kind man, a family man, who took pity on them both, and hid them in his barn, though even this slight reprieve was not to last. Goody awoke one morning to find that the baby had choked on a few strands of hay. In her grief, she hung herself near to where the dead child lay."

To the quiet melody of the weeping of his friends, Xiang Yu continued.

"When I learned this news, I confronted the monster Hallett, beating him near to death. Again, his mates intervened—though not one dared to lay a hand upon me. I know he will survive, although he will find his life—the simplest of things, like lifting a fork or walking to the piss pot—to be nothing but pain and anguish."

"It is best Samuel did not know this," Paulsgrave said, wiping his eyes with the heels of his hands. "I am grateful to ye, Xiang Yu, for all ye have carried, endured, and done."

"*Oui*," Levasseur said. "Now you are zee best of us, *mon amie.*"

Gathering up their grief and stowing it deep inside the holds of their hearts, the three men entered the chambers of Trogon Ophidian, who had granted them time to discuss what they reported was an urgent, private matter.

Turning toward them from his place by the fire, the blind man said, "There is a great heaviness between you. I am sorry for your losses."

As the three man sat around a table full of food, Trophon stood, although he did not join them. "We have much to discuss, my friends. Tomorrow, you will sail to an island off Nova Scotia to make sure that the Magdalene Balm is safe and where it should be, as the mirror indicated. I have detailed maps and instructions for navigating the traps and finding where the Templars hid it more than a hundred years ago, although, if an ally is guarding the island as he should, you shall not need them.

"Our enemies, the Ravenskalds, have several of the ancient objects—the Aaron Staff, the Abraham Blade, and, as I have reason to believe, the Ezekiel Wheel. The Jeshua Cask is safe with one of my students. The Baptist Bowl is in the hands of a Jacobite who shall deliver it, God willing, to the united Masonic Lodges in London within weeks. I have the Tiber Vial, which I have hidden. And, as you are well aware, Abraxas Abriendo is the custodian of both the obsidian mirror and the Fatima Hand."

"Although not the Joseph Scroll!" Abraxas shouted, entering the meeting room, an embarrassed and weary-looking Guillermo Vincolaré just behind him. "Dirty liar! Rotten deceiver! You profess to trust me, Master, yet you have removed the scroll..."

"I told you to wait on zee *Postillion* until summoned, fooleesh weezard!" Levasseur said, standing. "Why do you not leeson?"

"It is *alright*, Olivier," Trophon said in such a manner that it suddenly was. "Abraxas is correct. I did lie. I did deceive him. Although not from lack of trust. Absalom Ravenskald may know by now that the Tiber Vial is here. Which is why I am sending it with you to the island, called Seaswan, to hide it beside the Magdalene Balm. You shall take the Marlowe manuscripts we paid such a precious price to obtain for safekeeping there as well. We have learned all we can from them for now. I know you are strong, Abraxas. And capable. Although I also know the power of the Ravenskalds and the demons to which they pray. If they came for the mirror and hand, I could not risk them getting the scroll. Which, I need not remind you, is of no use until we have gathered in one place the eleven other objects. We are far from accomplishing that. No one knows the location of the Judas Coin or the Sheba Comb."

"You know the location of the Joseph Scroll?" Paulsgrave Williams asked.

"I do," Trophon answered. "And it is safe. Safer even than if the Scarlet-Shrouded Knights of Saint Grotth were guarding it, because the person who possesses it is unaware he does." Turning his head so his empty eye sockets were directly in line with Abraxas's eyes, he said, "Please do not be angry, my student. We have not time for that."

"Understood, Master Trophon. What do you command of us?"

Stepping toward the table, Trophon said, "The matter of the balm and vial is of utmost importance, of course, and that plan is now in place. The disappearance of Cardinal de Fleury is also of great concern. I am sure that it was the doing of the Duc d'Orleans. His recent alliance with Britain and the other steps he has taken in a variety of fiscal matters lead me to believe that he may be working with the Mammon Lodge and the Ravenskalds. Regardless of who aided the duc in the kidnapping, Cardinal de Fleury must be found."

"I shall find him," Xiang Yu said. "I owe the Cardinal my life. Three years ago, in France, he gave me a mission—a reason to be. He gave me answers to questions that I had been asking since a secret sect of warriors with a purpose I did not understand took me from my parents in Manchuria when I was four, raising and training me in their ways in the brutal peaks and passes of the Himalayas. My tattoos are their story, which the Cardinal decoded, inch by inch over many nights. I owe him much."

"So it shall be," Trophon said. "And when the business on Seaswan Island is complete, Olivier and Paulsgrave, if required, will join you in the search. I know that Cardinal de Fleury means just as much to you both. As for our young Friar Vincolaré, he is safest here with me. In truth, we have much to discuss and for which to prepare ourselves. Now, my friends, I suggest you avail yourselves of this meal I have had prepared, reveling in your comradeship, for many hardships await."

As the men dug in, Trophon Ophidian sat back beside the fire, the flames of which, as bright and strong as they were, could not vanquish the chill in his blood.

"**T**hus is brought to an end the first official meeting of the United Grand Lodge of Masons, on the Feast Day of John the Baptist. Let the record state it as such."

Grand Master Anthony Sayer stepped down from the dais, removing his robes as the attendees dispersed.

"It is hard to believe that an ale house called the Goose and Gridiron has been chosen as the site for the Grand Master to hold these monthly proceedings."

Looking Lord Bolingbroke, who had made the comment, in the eyes, the Grand Master replied, his tone tinged with impatience, "This is not why the site was chosen, Henry. The Knights Templar met here in the eleven hundreds. As to the name, Goose and Gridiron is a corruption of Swan and Lyre, a band of musicians who met here on occasion. If you would feel more at home at one of our sister houses—Drury Lane, Westminster, or Apple-Tree Tavern in Covent Garden—choose one. But this is where the most important work is being done, Henry, if you still wish to be a part of it."

"Of course I do, Antho—oh, yes, um… Grand Master Sayer. This building is impressive. Five floors and a basement. Plenty of room to do the good, important business of the lodge. My apologies. In my ignorance I have offended ye. I wish to make—"

Sayer turned away as a well-dressed man entered the room.

"Ah… our brother Andrew Colson! Welcome home! Ye have missed the meeting, but we have much to discuss."

He looks different, Bolingbroke thought. *Lighter somehow…*

"I am sorry I am late, Grand Master," Colson answered. "Provisions had to be made for Daagakutsu's daughter, Abenaa. It is not safe at present for anyone to know she is here with me in London. Hello Henry. Good to see ye have not worn out your welcome. I saw as well, as I approached the ale house and entered, that ye have posted plenty of guards."

"Indeed," Sayer answered. "I will not again allow the soiled soul of Lord John Carteret or his agents of Mammon to enter our domain. His performance as Anubis frightened many of our members, a dozen of which have transferred to other lodges, where they feel they shall be safer. We cannot continue to use a prop in place of the Baptist Bowl— the bastard was right about that."

Colson shook his head, concerned with all he heard. "What news of George Seton?"

"It is not encouraging. He should have left the Orkneys by now, where a Templar agent has given him the bowl to bring to London. But we have not received confirmation that he is on his way."

"He can be trusted," Colson answered. "If he were not, Henry and I would not have incurred Lord Carteret's wrath by arranging for his release from the Tower. Have his bank ledgers and estate documents been secured?"

Sayer nodded. "Thanks to your retrieval of the Masonic codes from the Tower. I do not doubt his trustworthiness, Andrew. Our enemies are powerful. Carteret and the Ravenskalds have much to gain by securing his holdings and obtaining the Baptist Bowl. We shall pray that all goes as planned—that mine is but a needless worry. Now... I have made a decision. I have selected ye, Andrew, as warden of the Free Mason Grand Lodge, and Henry, ye shall serve beneath him. Starting with our next meeting, ye shall hold the level, symbol of the office, taking position to the west, representing the column of strength, Jachin, the right-hand pillar which stood at the door to Solomon's Temple."

As Bollingbroke feigned good cheer at the news, Colson dropped to his knee in front of Sayer. "Your faith in me will not go unrewarded, Grand Master. I am working with Abenaa to learn the ways of the Obeah and to have the last of Mammon's rancid essence removed from my soul. I will serve faithfully as warden, keeping the sacred oaths and seeking to undo all the darkness I conjured with my pride."

The Grand Master indicated Colson should stand. "I know that ye made peace with Samuel Bellamy before he died, which will hold ye in good stead with our Jacobite allies, up to and including the Old Pretender. A new era is dawning for the world, Andrew, and I am pleased to have ye working as a servant of the Light."

James Francis Edward Stuart—James the Third in England, James the Eighth in Scotland—known as the Old Pretender, a moniker he despised, was tired. Tired of sustaining losses on the battlefield. Tired of betrayals and lies. Tired of moving from place to place every handful of months for well over a year. After returning to France after a pair of demoralizing defeats in Scotland in 1715 (where he had grown up), it was deemed by his advisors, including Cardinal Filippo Antonio Gualterio, that he would be safer and have more resources available in a Papal territory. First, it was Avignon and then Pesaro, until a recent invitation from the pope to come to Urbino had given him the briefest flash of hope that he could settle in and focus on obtaining the throne without being a wanted man on the run.

Flanked by his two primary advisors—Richard Hamilton and Dominic Sheldon, both of whom held the rank of general—James was sitting in a comfortable chair in a room full of Renaissance art in the Palazzo del Re, part of a complex of several palaces and other buildings in the Piazza dei Santi Apostoli. Owned by the renowned Muti family, Pope Clement the Eleventh had arranged for the rental of the palazzo—paid for in full by the papacy—for use by the rightful king and his court.

As grateful as he was, James found the muscles of his back and arms tensing as he smelled the smoke from a censer full of incense and heard the chanting prayers of the pope's attendants as he entered the room.

Perhaps it was Clement's long, aquiline Roman nose or his ever-present sneer that made James feel this way. More likely, it was knowing that his debt to the pope—and to the Holy Roman Church—would be steep, taking the rest of his life to repay.

What kind of king would he be when his throne was rightfully restored if he was beholden to the Church and sneering popes such as Clement?

Seeing the pope hold out the hand containing the Ring of the Fisherman—which popes starting with Clement the fourth had worn since the middle of the thirteenth century—James stood and immediately knelt. Having kissed the rings worn by Cardinal Gualterio and other want-to-be popes since he was young, James knew exactly what was expected. Reading the inscription, "CLEMENT. XI. PONT. MAX.," etched above the image of St. Peter casting a net from a boat, James gently kissed the ring and bowed his head.

"Rise and sit, my son," Clement said in his heavily accented Italian. "We have much to discuss."

As James retook his seat, Clement made a motion with his hand. Two attendants appeared from a corner behind James, carrying a gold-filigreed divan with red velvet cushions to just behind where Clement stood. Making himself comfortable, the pope made eye contact with Sheldon and Hamilton, indicating they should also rise, kneel, and kiss the Fisherman's Ring.

"I understand your struggles, my son," Clement said when the formalities were complete. "Remember, I was not always the pope. I was born a simple man, christened Giovanni Francesco Albani, here in Urbino, and in far simpler surroundings than these. I became a priest, working hard to improve my position in the hierarchy, and here I sit, host to the rightful king of all of Britain and Ireland. I have chosen this palazzo, this city, with care, knowing that you are weary of the constant need to move your court and yourself. The basilica of Santi Apostoli is conveniently located just down the street for your daily worship. Concentrate on rebuilding your court, my son. You have the full backing and authority of the papacy, but you must continue to pressure the usurping English king."

"Your Holiness," James said, suppressing any sign of the rancor he felt at Clement's juvenile attempt to build camaraderie by spouting on about common ground and history, "I am most grateful for all you have done. I already feel at home in this palace. I do have concerns, however. To truly establish my court, to see it prosper and strengthen into what it must be in order for us to find success both upon the battlefield and in other courts with whom we must make allies, will take considerable funds."

"You need not worry, my son," Clement replied, half a smile seeking to change his visage from a sneer to something pleasanter for a second, before retreating. "Your champion, His Eminence Cardinal Gualterio, has succeeded in securing for you an annuity of eight thousand Roman scudi. We will, of course, contribute resources beyond this sum as well, as needed."

This was welcome news indeed, and James felt his tension begin to ease, to the point that he could look upon this man with something less than derision. After all, Clement was a learned man who supported the arts and sciences, who had directed efforts to preserve antiquities from Rome's dark and storied past. He had done a great deal to expand the holdings of the Vatican Library.

Most importantly to Cardinal Gualterio, and therefore to James, Clement had funded both expeditions and excavation of the expansive catacombs of Rome, which had yielded numerous writings from the earliest days of Christianity that were crucial to understanding and benefiting fully from the twelve sacred objects the Star Quorum was committed to gathering.

Once its trio of Cardinals had examined and assembled them, the Holy Roman Church would be invincible. Gualterio and the others often remarked that the very might of the archangels was contained in the collective power of the objects.

Then, James the Third and Eighth, Old Pretender no longer, would benefit directly, almost unimaginably, from a wholly Catholic world and his central place within it.

As though summoning Gualterio with his thoughts of him, James smiled—fully, sustainingly—as the Cardinal entered the room, crossing directly to Clement and kissing the Fisherman's Ring.

"You bring news, Filippo?" Clement asked, genuine interest in his dark brown eyes.

"I do, Your Holiness. The Duc d'Orleans, seeking to distance further the boy king from his mentor, had André-Hercule de Fleury kidnapped while he was en route to Saint Croix from France. We have dispatched trusted allies to find him. Arrangements have been made to protect the objects currently in our possession, for efforts are underway to steal them from us."

"This is distressing news, my friend. What do you know of those who hold de Fleury?"

Stooping and leaning in so he could lower his voice, Gualterio whispered, "According to what our wizard saw in the mirror, it was pirates—perhaps the very agents of the Ravenskalds and their Mammon Lodge."

"They grow in strength every day." Clement's sneer was now causing the lines in his face to sink even deeper than James thought possible. "Filippo... What do you advise?"

"I have taken the liberty of requesting that Grand Master of the Knights of Malta and member of the Star Quorum, Ramón Perellós y Rocafull, send a detachment of fifty Scarlet-Shrouded Knights of St. Grotth to Urbino to guard the piazza. They should arrive within the month. They shall be discrete, of course."

Standing to signal that the meeting had come to an end, Clement said, "Excellent. The Papal Guards shall suffice until then, along with the men no doubt well trained by these two generals here. My son, are you comfortable with this plan?"

"I am," James answered, suddenly feeling as though the endless waiting, relocating, and suffering of humiliating defeats was morphing into something that almost looked like the far off outlines of victory.

In that moment he realized he was exactly, finally, where God meant him to be.

Olivier Levasseur had been standing anxious watch upon the bow of the *Postillion* for the better part of an evening, having entered Mahone Bay in the north Atlantic just as the sun was beginning to set. Endlessly pouring over the maps and instructions Trogon Ophidian had entrusted to him as he waited, Levasseur marveled at the elaborate tunneling and trap systems the Templars and their allies had employed over the centuries. They had learned their craft working in the ingeniously designed shafts and passages Solomon had created beneath the Temple Mount in Jerusalem—some said with the help of enslaved *djinn* under the command of a malevolent being called Iblis.

Olivier knew better than to laugh at such an idea. The Sheba Comb, one of the missing ancient objects, honored another *djinn*, Bilqīs, who had beguiled Solomon and bore him a son. Menelik, who went on to become emperor of Ethiopia, was responsible for guarding the Ark of the Covenant, recovered by the Templars along with the skull of John the Baptist (soon stolen from them by the Ravenskalds and eventually used to frame them) and other important religious artifacts.

The Templars and their descendent and ally organizations, applied the techniques learned and skills acquired in two decades of work beneath the Temple Mount to locations all around the world, from forts, to chapels, to the sites where they hid their vast riches and most sacred treasures, such as Seaswan Island.

The tunneling systems and traps had saved the lives of hundreds of the fabled warriors-monks when, in 1313, they fled France and went into hiding ahead of the arrests, sham trials, and murders of hundreds of their comrades, including the Templar Grand Master, Jacques de Molay.

Levasseur had learned these skills building secret fortifications on Tortuga, St. Croix, and other islands, where those wishing to protect what was theirs could create flood traps with ease.

During those years of apprenticeship, he also learned the ciphers he was teaching to Angus MacGregor/Conall MacBlaquart.

As he contemplated the path that had led him here, Levasseur's attention shifted to three equally spaced flashes of light from a lantern in the tree line.

The signal that it was safe to approach the island.

An hour later, he and Abraxas, along with their pieces of precious cargo, stepped foot upon the island, where twenty well-armed men met them, weapons drawn and faces set in grim determination to fulfill their task of protection of the island and all it contained.

"Ah... Levasseur! Abraxas! Welcome to Seaswan!" From the shadows behind the soldiers stepped a man they both knew well— Archibald Sinclair, descendent of Henry and William, and holder of one of the seven seats of the Star Quorum.

"Archeebald!" Levasseur answered. "Zese islands are happy to have zee Templars return to them at last, *oui*?"

"It feels as if that is true, my friend," Archibald answered, indicating to his men that they could drop their weapons and disperse. "The ghosts who haunt this island, and the others, are many, just as our secret brothers the Rosicrucians wrote of in their plays, and they are restless. You may hear the wails of the slaves killed to protect the treasure from deep within the ground or see the blue and orange lights of the souls of those who perished undertaking the elaborate works here and on Seaswan's sister island."

"I sense them," Abraxas whispered, absent any hint of the bravado he used in his stage act.

"They approve of your arrival," Sinclair replied, indicating that they should follow him into the tree line. "Our encampment is well away from prying eyes, in the center of the island. I have a dinner prepared. After we have eaten, I shall examine the items you have brought. I have longed all my life to touch the Tiber Vial. And the manuscripts... they are of great interest to me as well, beyond the coded secrets they hold, for why do we fight wars if we cannot appreciate art in our rare moments of peace! Come my friends!"

After a memorable meal and a good night's sleep, the three men awoke just before the dawn and made their way to a formation of rocks that one would not find if he did not know to look for them, so well were they hidden amongst the brush.

Exposing a trap door leading to a long tunnel, which was platformed at even intervals, after a series of complicated procedures it would not be prudent to detail in these pages, Archibald Sinclair lit a lantern and invited Levasseur and Abriendo to follow him.

When they reached the bottom, Sinclair extended his hand. "Give me the manuscripts and the Tiber Vial, Olivier. And you, Abraxas—I am to take the Fatima Hand as well. You shall keep the mirror. At least for the present."

As Levasseur handed over the bag that contained the items of which he had been the brief custodian, he heard Abriendo let out a squeal immediately eaten by the earth, so deep down into it had they descended.

"I will *not!*" he cried, turning his body away as if to better protect what he deemed as his possession. "It may not contain the scroll, but it has a power of its own. A power only I know how to—"

"Nonsense," Sinclair answered, his voice both calm and strong. "You are talking to a member of the Star Quorum, Abraxas—not some former privateer turned pirate with visions of hard-fought naval victories and out-of-his-grasp grandeur burning his rum-soaked brain. My blood is the same that flowed in those that took up the Templar flag and holy mission after the Ravenskalds' betrayal and ensuing slaughters in the early thirteen hundreds. It was my ancestor, Henry, who brought the ancient object I am about to show you here—and others not under the protection of the Quorum, hidden upon a sister island—eighty years later, under great peril. So do not presume that you *know how to* do *anything* with these items beyond the little knowledge with which you have been entrusted."

Seeing Abraxas tense, and knowing what he would soon endure if Sinclair chose to abandon his calm, Levasseur whispered, "Look, you seely weezard... Do as zee Templar has commanded. He has managed to eensult us both, but you do not see me acteeng like a child! Zee Star Quorum has allowed you to keep zee meeror. Do not make zhem change zehr minds!"

"Very well," Abriendo answered, handing over the Fatima Hand. "I meant no offense. One gets used to having one of the objects and it becomes frightfully hard to part with."

Taking the offered object while placing his free hand upon the wizard's shoulder, Sinclair nodded in sympathy. "That is why it is best that they remain here, deep underground, untouched. They each have an energy, an intelligence, which the Ravenskalds are employing their unholy monsters to find." Twisting a nail in a beam just above his head, the Templar took a step back as a door opened from somewhere in the ceiling. Reaching inside, Sinclair withdrew an alabaster box the size of his fist. "Now, look upon this, for no man has had the privilege of doing so since Sir Henry brought it here in thirteen ninety, having received it from agents in Galilee."

Looking upon the pure white box, Levasseur took in its scalloped edges. "May we see zee balm eenside?" he asked, his normally forceful voice a reverent whisper.

"None of us can," Sinclair replied, placing the box back inside the hiding space, along with the manuscripts, Tiber Vial, and Fatima Hand. "It is fused shut. Only the Abraham Blade can open it."

"Then we shall get eet from zee Ravenskalds!" Levasseur said, his full, insistent voice returning. "I swear eet!"

"I look forward to that day," Sinclair answered, securing the trap door through a series of secret steps. "Ah, Abraxas—do not look so forlorn. If you have patience, my friend, once we are out of the tunnels and the entrance is secure, I shall tell you what I know of the Joseph Scroll, for you will have a central part to play when we at last are ready to use it."

Levasseur would swear to Xiang Yu and a few trusted others in the coming weeks that Abraxas's smile was so bright as they exited the tunnel that they did not need the lantern.

Once they had returned to camp, Sinclair called for food and invited his guests to sit in a pair of comfortable chairs beneath his tent. Pouring wine, he said, "You, Abraxas, must go to London when opportunity allows, where you will find on Fleet Street a seller of rare manuscripts and items from antiquity by the named of Adolphus Vellum-Verlag. He knows more than anyone alive about the contents of the scroll." As Abraxas nodded his acceptance of the assignment, Sinclair raised his glass. "I propose a toast to the work of this day, and to all those—including Samuel Bellamy—who have sacrificed their lives so we can keep these items out of the hands of our enemies. Let us also drink to the success of our Templar brothers on Orkney, who by now should have delivered the Baptist Bowl to a trusted agent who shall bring it to Anthony Sayer, Grand Master of the now United Freemason Lodges of London. You shall meet with Sayer, Abraxas, when you are there, and you shall then be able to boast of having been one of the only persons on this planet to have seen five of the twelve objects."

As they drank their toast and began their meal, a break in the clouds revealed the constellation Cygnus, shining forth in a cold grey sky.

They took it as an omen of the victories to come.

"I cannot do it anymore. The stress of it shall break me!"

Elisabeth Farnese, the queen of Spain and recently anointed keeper of the Catholic faith in Europe, sat on the floor outside her bedroom, weeping into her hands. Beyond the locked doors, her husband, Philip the Fifth, was screaming out the window about conspiracies and betrayal, attaining new heights—and lows—in his growing madness.

Taking his charge by the hands, Cardinal Giulio Alberoni, recently returned from St. Croix, looked into her blood-shot eyes. "The court physicians will soon have him under control and asleep, Isobel. The sudden onset and ferocity of the attack caught them by surprise. I should have been here, to see it coming..."

"Nonsense," Elisabeth replied, squeezing her protector's hands. "I am his wife. I should have seen it. I fear the laced wine and the *leche para dormer* will not work this time, Your Eminence. I have never seen my husband so wild and unreasonable as this."

"Walk with me, Isobel. Hearing his accusations shouted to all of Madrid through the door of your own bedchambers does you no good."

Accepting the Cardinal's invitation, Elisabeth waited until they had passed through several hallways before speaking. "Your Eminence. There is a reason why I did not see the coming madness in my husband. I was preoccupied... God forgive me, I am failing Him, and you, and His most Holy Church!"

As another fit of weeping overtook her, Alberoni led Elisabeth to a cushioned seat beside a fountain, the center of which featured two rotund dancing angels carved from marble.

"How I wish you could be as these angels, Isobel. You deserve such peace. Not this wretched life of secrets and ill use of your body that you have committed to for the sake of God and his church. No one could tell how far our Philip's madness would progress. But it is you who now run Spain, and you must believe that you were chosen to do so."

"I cannot touch my child, Your Eminence," Elisabeth whispered, a fresh gush of tears spilling from her eyes. "Charles Infante has turned eighteen months old. He needs his mother to be with him, not midwives and nursemaids, as in the past. He calls for me, and I cannot go to him. And Philip's other children... they deserve for me to be their mother and I cannot."

"And why not, Isobel? What is the darkness that has taken over your heart? I do not believe it is the madness of your husband, for, if that were the case, you would love them all the harder for his absence in their life."

Making the sign of the cross and kissing the crucifix that always hung around her neck, Elisabeth slipped to the floor, grasping the Cardinal's knees as she pleaded, "Cardinal Alberoni! I have done something... something terrible... a necessary action in order to cover a mistake, but it was I alone who made this mistake, in my hubris and love of self!"

Taking her hands and guiding her back to the seat, Alberoni asked, "What is it you must confess, my child? Whatever you have done, God shall forgive you. The stress that you have borne is more than anyone should have asked of you. Our Lord and Savior knows this, for who has endured greater trials than He?"

Placing her head upon his shoulder so she could whisper in the Cardinal's hear, Elisabeth related all that had happened in the crypts of El Escorial six weeks earlier.

"I am so, so sorry, Your Eminence," she said, lifting her head and looking in his eyes, where she would judge the truth of what he would say.

"I have known about the Jeshua Cask for months now, Isobel," he began, his voice soft and forgiving. "Guillermo told me where it was. Do not be angry with our gentle friar... he was doing his duty, same as you. I asked him not to tell the others, for I knew in my heart that where you had hidden it was where we were wisest to keep it. I did not, however, give any thought to the immense burden you carried by guarding it as you have. Although I do not know the circumstances that led you to know of its existence and whereabouts, I know that it was God's divine grace that made it possible. As I have said, you are the chosen, Isobel. And God never fails in His choice. As to Minister Macanaz... his actions are unforgivable. Reprehensible. I must think on how to proceed in this matter, for it is delicate, but rest assured that justice shall be done."

Isobel kissed him on the cheek. "Thank you, Your Eminence. Your understanding and forgiveness are more than I deserve. As is your faith in my actions and in me. Yet I feel compelled to make a request of you, although I have no right."

"What is it you need, my child, now that you have forgiveness?"

Sitting up straight and wiping her eyes, revealing the queen that all of Spain recognized she was, Elisabeth said, "I request that I be allowed to keep the Jeshua Cask in my possession. It is my insurance that Philip and his advisors—led by Melchor Rafael de Macanaz—do not dispose of me once I have served my purpose, as I fear they already believe I have."

"You may indeed," Cardinal Alberoni replied. "Although the question of if it is to remain in El Escorial is one I must ponder. Whatever is decided, you shall have a say. Now... If you wish to remain useful in the eyes of Philip and his ministers, attend to your children. And then attend to your king."

Giving her guardian and advisor a hug, Elisabeth stood, brushed her crumpled skirts, placed her hair back in its place, and walked toward the children's wing with the dignity and grace that Alberoni knew would keep her safe in these dark and troubled times.

While Trogon Ophidian and Guillermo Vincolaré spoke of magic, dreams, and the higher purpose of the twelve ancient objects in the cottage on the grounds of his murdered stepfather's estate, Paulsgrave Williams busied himself at the wharf overseeing the four dozen members of his crew making needed repairs to the sloop *Marianne*. They would soon be leaving, and her filthy decks, separating seams, and storm-worn masts were in no condition to withstand the demands his continued mission would no doubt place upon her.

His time on Block Island, a closed community of eleven square miles a dozen miles from the mainland, where his mother and three sisters had lived since 1889, two years after the passing of his father—the former attorney general of Rhode Island—had been both healing and instructive.

His mother, Anne, a descendent of the Plantagenet kings of England, had stoically suffered the loss of two husbands. The second—the Scottish nationalist Robert Guthrie—most unnaturally and brutally, due to his beliefs. Guthrie had been a friend of Paulsgrave's father, serving as executor of his estate. As for Guthrie's ancestry, agents of William of Orange had murdered his preacher father in Scotland, forcing Robert and his family to watch.

It was Guthrie who had planted the seeds of rebellion in the fertile fields of Paulsgrave's mind—an effect he had on the young man's sisters as well. One of them, Mary, had married a smuggler and friend of Captain William Kidd. Indeed, prior to Kidd's hanging in London in 1701, her husband had helped Kidd to hide portions of his treasure— some of which had ties to treasures of the Templars—on Gardiner's Island off of New York and on Seaswan and her sister island in Mahone Bay near Nova Scotia.

His sister Elisabeth had married another smuggler, named Thomas Paine, a descendent of the pirate Thomas Paine, who had raided several Spanish settlements under a letter of marque from the governor of Jamaica before driving the French off the island the Williams family would make their home thanks to the graciousness of Robert Guthrie.

Guthrie was foremost in Paulsgrave's mind in the spring of 1716, when he and Samuel Bellamy had captured their first ship, in the Bay of Honduras—a Dutch vessel captained by John Cornelison. The damage the Dutch had done to the Jacobite cause through the reign of William of Orange and the War of Spanish Succession was great, and any strike against them served toward balancing the books.

Although Paulsgrave had not been involved in the collaborations of his brothers-in-law with pirates like William Kidd and Thomas Paine at the onset, fate had recently initiated him into the extended family's affairs. At the request of one of Guthrie's friends, a Scottish rebel named John Rathbon, Paulsgrave had sailed to see him on Gardiner's Island off of East Hampton, New York, in early May, where John Gardiner, Third Lord of the Manor, had hidden treasure for Captain Kidd two years prior to his hanging. Requested to turn over the treasure as evidence, John complied—mostly.

He kept a diamond for his daughter.

Paulsgrave's time with the fiery Rathbon and Lord John Gardiner had given him greater insight into the role William Kidd had played in the affairs of the Star Quorum. By the end of the first evening's feast, it was clear why it had been of utmost importance to the Crown that the short drop and sudden stop conspire to end the pirate's life.

What true treasures the Crown—and of course the Ravenskalds— had actually been after were still safely hidden, thanks to the agents provocateur linked to Block, Gardiner, Seaswan, and other islands off the Atlantic coast.

Placing his concentration on the knot of men fitting a new mainmast for the *Marianne*, Paulsgrave felt it pulled within seconds by a figure standing to his left, just within his peripheral vision.

"May I help ye?" he asked, not taking his eyes from the complex block and tackle rigging his sailing master had devised for stepping the brand new mast.

"I surely hope ye can, Captain Williams. I am Edward Low. Friends call me Ned. I am a rigger, sir. I hear ye are soon to leave the island, and I seek a placement on your crew. I have heard of your exploits, sir. Yours and Samuel Bellamy's, God rest his soul, and I could think of nothing more important than to lend my sweat and skill to the cause. I have spoken to your quartermaster and he directed me to ye."

Still not pulling his focus from the stepping of the mast, Paulsgrave answered, "He did, eh? Very well. Tell me Low—can ye read?"

"No sir, I cannot. As I said, I am but a rigger, but a skilled one. I could make that stepping go smoother, sir. I guarantee it. With just a few minor adjustments."

Paulsgrave stifled a smile. "Let us leave it to my sailing master, shall we? I know everyone on Block Island, Ned. Where do ye hail from?"

"Stepney, sir. Although I come to America—Boston specifically—seven years ago after my brother was hanged for thievin'. I was thievin' too, and wished to get away from it. Make a new start. An' I have."

"Good for ye to do so, Ned. All we can ask when we stray from the path is another chance. And, when it is granted, to seize upon it." Impressed by this honest, although clearly excitable, rigger, Paulsgrave then asked the two crucial questions he now asked of all potential crew. "Are ye married, Ned? And do ye have children?"

Paulsgrave could feel a change in the man's demeanor. Thus, he had his answer. "Look, Ned. I appreciate your commitment. I am sure your skills as a rigger are excellent. But we do not take husbands and fathers at present."

"That's the thing of it, Captain," Ned answered, his voice dropping to a whisper. "I *was* a father, but not no more. My son up and died and I cannot bear to be with my wife, nor her with me. The pain for us both is too great. Elizabeth supports my leavin', sir. Honest she does."

Satisfied the crew would complete the stepping of the mast without issue, Paulsgrave turned to look for the first time at the man with whom he had been speaking. Tall and too thin, and looking like he was badly in need of a sound night's sleep, Ned Low was in no shape to take part in the mission ahead of the crew of the *Marianne*.

"Elizabeth may not know it," he said, as kindly as he could manage, "but she needs ye, Ned. And ye her. Other children will bless ye, if it be God's will. The men of the *Marianne* face uncertain times and many coming hardships. Believe me—though ye may feel my words are a rejection, ye shall one day—"

"Be a captain! An' a damned fine one at that! Better than *ye*, sir! Better than the drowned Bellamy for sure! Ye have made a grave mistake, Captain Williams—mark my words!"

Such a change had come over the rigger Low that half a dozen of the crew had drawn their weapons and gathered at the rail, awaiting the slightest further move by the agitated man.

Seeing the situation stacked against him, Low stormed off, still spouting threats and predictions of the grandiose successes of his future as he disappeared into the early morning mist.

"Ye were right to reject him, my student. He is too full of anger and the need to escape his pain."

Paulsgrave turned to face his master, Trogon Ophidian. "Indeed. But how different than Sam or myself is he, I wonder…"

"Time will certainly tell. Now, to other matters. I heard the mast as they stepped it. Are your repairs near to completion?"

"They are. I sense a tension in your voice, Master Ophidian."

"You are listening closer, my student. That is well. There are three ships of war now in search of you, merely a day from here. I do not believe you can slip them as easily as you did the HMS *Rose* before you arrived. Make all haste to leave for the Caribbean. The situation on Nassau is unstable. They need a guiding hand, and you are the one to provide it."

"I assure ye, we shall leave on the morning tide."

"That is what I wish to hear. Please, Paulsgrave—stay sharp for news of de Fleury. He is yet to be found. I begin to fear the worst."

Assuring his master he would, Paulsgrave climbed the gangway, already making clear to the crew his revised and non-negotiable expectations before his boots had touched the deck.

PART FIVE

READ YOUR BOOKS AND DRINK YOUR TEA

"Really, Henry. Word in London is you are the *worst* triple agent in all of written history. Consider coming to work for me at the bookshop. The work is easy and the hours and pay are not ungenerous."

Stocking bookshelves, Bolingbroke thought. *That would indeed be my final circle of Hell.*

"Adolphus, my dear friend," the former lord, secretary of foreign affairs to Queen Anne, and earl to the court of the House of Stuart in exile said with a forced, transparent smile, "if only time allowed. I am quite busy now with... Well, I only wish I could say..."

Adolphus Vellum-Verlag, antiquities scholar and rare book and objects dealer, returned a disingenuous smile of his own. "No need for secrecy here. Remember to whom you are speaking. My family has been the arbiter of the most sought-after manuscripts and sacred objects in the war between the Templar-Masons and their allies and the Ravenskalds and the Mammon Lodge since the time of the Christ. We have held in our possession the most precious documents rescued from the Library of Alexandria. So do not say to me, 'I only wish I could say...' Say *what*? That you are here at my lecture to the Society of Antiquaries looking so bitter because, in addition to the many turns of fortune and humiliations you have weathered since the death of Anne and the shaming of James, you are now *assistant* to the warden of the Free Mason Grand Lodge? A warden, I need not add, that was, until recently, a minion of Mammon itself?"

"You are correct on all counts, Adolphus," Henry replied, wishing he had spent the afternoon in an inn trying to put on some of the weight he had lost during these years of endless trials. "But none more so than when you say 'I need not add.' I very much wish you had not. Insult to injury and all of that."

"What *injury*, Henry?" Adolphus turned away for a moment to wish a pair of scholars from Cambridge well as they were leaving, copies under their arms of the first several volumes of Antoine Gaillard's *One Thousand and One Nights* translation—based on the original 1548 Arabic version—that Vellum-Verlag was distributing *gratis*. The translation had been the subject of his lecture. "Your problem is that you *perceive* that you were injured when you were not. From where I sit—and my perch, being high, allows me to see for quite a distance— you have deserved everything that has befallen you, my friend. The question is, how to reverse course and climb again the heights."

This is why Henry had come. Although his manners were lacking and style all too direct, Adolphus Vellum-Verlag did indeed see far and with a practiced, discerning eye.

"Will you help me, then?" Henry asked, admonishing himself for the hint of pleading in his voice.

Looking down his nose at his much-maligned friend, Adolphus shrugged his sloped shoulders. "I of course would have to hear what you have in mind, Henry. After all, you can be a rather sizable liability… Between the ongoing Jacobite affair and the war between the forces of Light and Dark being waged with a ferocity that has been lacking since perhaps the darkest days of the Crusades, business is booming and I cannot afford to be questioned as to whom I am helping and why."

"Fair enough, Adolphus. I need your assistance in confirming that George Seton—whom, you will kindly remember, I was instrumental in freeing from the Tower of London—has received the Baptist Bowl as planned and will be delivering it to the Grand Lodge in the foreseeable future. Further, if such assurances can be made, it would be most helpful if George would give the object to *me* so that I may make the presentation of it to Sayer and Colson."

"Ah, Henry," Adolphus said, laughing, "is that all you ask of me?"

Not adept at the high art of sarcasm, Bolingbroke said, with all too much sincerity, "Any additional information you can provide on the whereabouts of the other eleven sacred objects over which there is endless fuss would obviously serve me well."

"Obviously." Handing Henry the several volumes of the Gaillard *One Thousand and One Nights*, Adolphus said, trying to appear sincere, "You should read these. There are magical lamps, flying carpets, all manner of mythical creatures and even the powerful *djinn* within its pages. Pay particular attention to them, if you sincerely wish to be useful. Some of the tales are metaphors for these objects that you seek, through the mystic visions of the Persians. After you have read them all, and come to appreciate fully the cautionary tales offered for those who wish to possess such objects and control such uncontrollable creatures, come and see me in my bookshop, a few doors down from here, and I shall see what I can do."

Nodding his head in agreement, Henry exited the tavern and made his way through the bustling crowds of Fleet Street.

Glancing through the first of the three weighty volumes, Henry wondered if another supposed friend had duped him yet again.

"**J**akey. *Jaaa-keeey*. Wake up now! Jee-sus *Christ*, you lazy fucker... *JAKEY!*"

Jake Givens sprang up in his bed, soaked in sweat, as were his sheets.

This was nothing new.

Ever since the two hooded thugs had worked him over, months ago, Jake had been dealing with reliving the assault nightly as he slept. Getting off the painkillers had only made the dreams more vivid and harder on his nerves.

Now, making it worse, which he had not thought possible, he was dreaming nightly of both the assault *and* the extraction of Kirstine MacGregor from Quarry Peak Psychiatric Hospital.

He and Kirstine spoke almost every day through a specially installed and secured DTEAU-administered video feed. She professed to be doing better. Keeping busy with "research," as she called it, although she never elaborated and Jake didn't push.

According to the psychiatrists and psychologists they were both required to see, pushing each other or themselves too hard could have serious consequences.

So they stayed put, as directed by the DTEAU team, making the best of it in different ways. For Kirstine, it was her "research." For Jake it was working on his body and his mind. He had bought some workout equipment, which he was up to using three times for an hour at a time each day. He could run to the beach and along the Atlantic shoreline on the days when DTEAU assigned him an officer. Those were the days that he would make the trip to Virginia to meet with Haxx, and if he was lucky, Kirstine would be there. But those days had gotten all too rare.

Besides the increasingly difficult workouts, Jake was doing research of his own, trying to learn all he could about multinational corporations and the military–industrial–intelligence complex that ran the United States and its satellite states under the guise of democracy.

Looking around his room in the pre-dawn dark, Jake saw a form propped against his doorframe.

"Dad? Why'd you wake me up?"

Randall Givens, CPO, USN (Ret.) let out a hot-breathed burp and stumbled into the room. "Makin' a racket with your wimperin' an' simperin', Jakey. Can't get any goddamned sleep."

Kicking off the covers to get the clammy linen away from him, Jake said, "I told you, Dad. *They* called me Jakey. So, if you could not, that'd be—"

Another belch. This time, Jake could smell the bourbon.

"Ungrateful. I gave up my very comfortable place to stay here with you, and this is the thanks that I get?"

Dilemma. Jake knew the truth. His father had been in VA housing for the past few years, although—after yet another altercation with a "fuckin' jarhead"—as Randall called Marines—and his near constant inebriation and belligerency—he had lost his room.

He was here because he had literally nowhere else to go.

The perception from those at DTEAU and from Randall himself that he was somehow *protecting* Jake was horseshit.

An oscillating fan on HIGH could knock the highly decorated ex–chief petty officer, and communications and cryptography specialist, easily on his ass.

"Not like I don't say thank you," Jake said, getting out of bed. "It's time for my morning workout. Don't suppose you'd care to join me?"

Randall laughed. "Liftin' weights is fer pussies. When I was in the Middle East during Gulf War One, we got *huge* by doin' our *duty*. You wouldn't have lasted—"

"A single day… I know." Jake pulled on a Coast Guard sweatshirt some girl on temporary assignment at the Manasquan station, a few blocks away, had left in his room before all this craziness began. It still smelled of her, which somehow he found comforting.

Plus, it pissed off his father.

"Your muscle beach bullshit can wait," Randall said, blocking the door. Although his belly had gotten soft with all the beer and bourbon, the rest of him was still as hard as the non-com who had been lead communications support for an elite SEAL unit during their operations in the Middle East. "I want to tell you somethin'. Somethin' serious, Jake—" He stopped himself before the second syllable left his lips.

Sitting back on his bed, where he put on ankle socks and sneakers, Jake said, "'K, Dad. Whatcha got?"

"I served with the guy who assisted you in the extraction. Known him for years. Ah… I see your eyes widenin' there in the dark. Spent a lot of time in the dark, Jake. Tunnels, caves, bunkers… We all did. It was what we were *there for*. Not sand worshippers. Not camel-kissers. Sure as shit not for protecting the fields a' black gold… *No…*

We were protecting our guys against somethin' that was pure, unadulterated... well... that's classified well above secret. Anyway... the guy... Commanding Officer Abel *Black*. Never knew if that last name was a real one or not. Suited the work. SEAL Team *D*. You won't find it in any tactical manual or organizational chart. No one makes movies about SEAL Team D, though Ridley Scott and James Cameron wanted to. Infinitely suited. But what we fought... what some of the guys in Iraq and Afghanistan *still* fight... was a darkness way worse than anything in the movies. Hybrids, demons, redheaded bohemoths like Goliath in the Bible... Those evil fuckers make the *Aliens* bitch seem a girl scout. You followin' me?" Not waiting for an answer—Jake knew well enough he didn't want one— Randall continued. "We can and will protect you, son. You and that doctor girl you're sweet on. Abel and I. Abel's out of the military now. Runs a private security firm—super hi-tech. I am doin' some consultin' in the realms of intelligence, communications, and surveillance for his company, the Kardax Corporation. Does most of his work for a multinational we need to keep close to... TRG."

The Ravenskald Group. Jake had been researching it after Kirstine and Haxx had both mentioned it. Aerospace, planned communities, hi-tech sci-fi weaponry, biomedicine, contained community development.

"Why you telling me this, Dad?" Jake asked, the question genuine.

Stumbling to the bed and dropping himself beside his son, Randall Givens whispered, "Because, Jake. These TRG bastards are the ones behind your Kirstine's kidnapping. They run the divisions of the DED—that's the Division of Eugenic Design. Bet your DTEAU pals didn't tell ya *that*. Again, you won't find it on any official website, so don't bother to look. If it's anywhere, it's strictly Dark Web... Don't be messin' with *that*... You leave it to *us*, Jake. Now... I know you think I'm a drunken fuck-up—and maybe I am—but I have seen some shit that would bring the strongest to their knees. And that shit will be comin' for you, son, if you ain't careful. Mark my words on *that*.

Sitting in silence for a few moments, Jake said, "I'm glad you're staying here, Dad."

"Me too, son. Me too."

An hour and a half had passed since a lookout upon the ramparts had cried, "A sloop has entered the harbor, and I swear to you all—she is shot to Hell!"

Standing on the wharf, only a few feet from where the port master had directed the sloop to anchor, Conall MacBlaquart could not help but agree with the lookout's assessment.

"What do ye make of it, Blackbeard?" he asked the former Edward Thache, who stroked the ribboned braids of his beard, deep in thought.

"A fine, fine ship she is. Will take a lot of patience and time to repair her. Whomever she encountered, they tried their best to sink her. Damned near succeeded. If that hole in the hull were just a few inches lower... Crew looks fit. Looks to be three dozen or more of 'em. Their clothes are not what one would expect from yer typical crew of scallywags. All ten guns appear to me new and well maintained. I am curious to meet her captain."

"As am I." Commodore Benjamin Hornigold had joined them, as had Captain Henry Jennings. "If I am not mistaken, we are about to get our wish."

Turning their eyes to where their commodore pointed, Conall and Blackbeard let out a gasp and a laugh, respectively, as a man emerged onto the deck of the sloop from belowdecks. Dressed in a robe and fancy pommeled cap, bloodied bandages visible on both of his wrists, his forehead, and his chest, he held in one hand a pair of books and in the other a cup of tea.

"I do say," he sang, in a high, squeaky voice that brought a chorus of laughs from the men assembled on the wharf. "Is this the fort of *Nassau*, of which I have heard so much?"

Stepping forward, Hornigold answered, "Yes it is. I am Benjamin Hornigold, commodore and nominal leader here. And ye are?"

Placing his porcelain teacup and saucer precariously upon the books, the oddly dressed captain of the sloop pulled a laced white handkerchief from a pocket of his robe and waved it in the air. "I come in peace, Commodore Hornigold. Ye are as famous as this fort. My name is Captain Stede Bonnet, out of Barbados, although, when I am out and on the account, I go by the name of *Ed*wards and fly several countries' flags."

"What a curious sort he is," Blackbeard said under his breath. "I think the man is mad."

"Aye," Conall answered. "Hae saems tae bae quite aff his haid."

Ignoring the pair, Hornigold continued his questioning, as he would with any new arrival. "What has befallen ye and your sloop, Captain Bonnet, that ye come to us in such a serious state?"

"Ooh," Bonnet squealed, using the handkerchief to fan his red, rounded face. "So glad ye asked! It is *quite* the adventurous tale! After a series of quick successes out of Bar*bados*—half a dozen in all—my crew and I came upon a Spanish *frig*ate. Although I thought it wise to *avoid* her—after all, we had only been *at it* since early summer—my brave crew of seventy, full of *vigor* and *verve* from our recent encounters, insisted we en*gage* her. If I had known it was the *Ave María y Las Ánimas* under the command of that Spanish rake, Amaro Pargo, I never would have *risked* it! Alas, by the time the ship and her captain were i*dent*ified, the fighting—and damage—were done."

Leaning into Blackbeard, Conall whispered, "Hae moost bae aff his haid... dancin' wit' the likes a' that Spanish privateer has gone poorly fer Vane on more than one occasion. Captain Bellamy was even impressed. Bonnet's lucky tae bae alive."

"Aye," Blackbeard replied, inching closer to the sloop.

"Well, Captain Bonnet, ye have certainly impressed us with your mettle," Commodore Hornigold said, tipping his tricorne and making a little bow. "Ye and your men—what is left of them—are welcome in New Providence. Let us talk tomorrow and see to your sloop soon after."

"Excellent, Commodore Hornigold!" Bonnet replied. "I so look forward to our *par-lay*."

Moments later, as Hornigold, Jennings, Blackbeard, and MacBlaquart sat themselves around a table in the commodore's quarters, Blackbeard said, "Why so welcoming, sir? The man is *aff his haid*, as Conall here keeps saying."

Pouring them each a mug of rum before firing up his pipe, Hornigold said, "'Tis simple, really. The man has money. 'Tis easy to see. But obviously little skill. And no respect from his crew! Imagine... them *insisting* he engage with the Spanish frigate! I cannot imagine why they did not simply vote him out. Their escape from Pargo was either dumb luck or a boon on the Spaniard's part. I hear he holds honor about all else, pious Catholic that he is.

"Point is, I see an opportunity. Ye should take him under your wing, Blackbeard. Put together a small crew to help him repair his ship— have them learn what they can. Both the sloop's recovery and his own shall take at least a few weeks. Use that time wisely. Get to know him. Bring him into your confidence. Share your knowledge of proper pirating and captaining of a ship with him. Then, when the time is right, I shall float the suggestion that, in order for his education to be complete, for him truly to be a proper pirate, that he allow ye to command his ship as captain while he learns from ye."

"A temporary situation, of course," Captain Jennings offered, understanding the plan.

"Of course," Hornigold answered, blowing a perfect circle of smoke. "That ship will only serve as a means of acquiring something better. When that blessed event occurs, ye shall return Captain Bonnet's sloop to his command, to serve as part of our fleet."

Pausing for a moment in thought, Blackbeard slammed his open hand upon the table, rattling the mugs and the onion bottle that held the rum. "Devilish brilliant!" he exclaimed.

Raising his mug in a toast, Hornigold said, "I thought ye would agree. Though there is an initial part to my plan that requires the particular services of our own Mister MacBlaquart."

"How caen I bae a' haelp tae ye, Gran'pa?" Conall asked, raising his mug and knocking back its contents.

"This evening, ye shall take the odd Captain Bonnet to dinner at Nassau's best tavern, the Fatted Calf. Here is ample coin to ply him with food and drink. The best the place can offer. Let him tell ye his story. It seems he is ready to tell it in all its rich, amusing detail, with little if any prompting. Note it all well, as we shall expect a full report at breakfast on the morrow."

Eagerly accepting the assignment, Conall excused himself to redo the braids in his now ample beard and change his shirt into one that was fresher and whiter.

As he exited, Blackbeard broke into a grin—an all too rare occurrence since the death of Bellamy and the news of his captured crew. "Ye remembered my evening with Sam, Gran'pa..."

Returning the grin, Hornigold answered, "I did indeed. As I recall, the information ye gathered was useful to us for a time. Perhaps, if Conall does his duty as well as I know he shall, we shall see this plan to fruition. The time is near to hand for us to call ye Captain once again."

Two hours later, as the sun began to set on the island of New Providence, Conall and Captain Bonnet—who had eagerly accepted his invitation—were sitting down to their first of many bottles of claret and Madeira and a steaming rack of boar's ribs.

Within moments, Captain Stede Bonnet began to tell his tale.

NEAR BRIDGETOWN, BARBADOS, 1694

Let me begin by saying, this claret is de-*lic*ious… truly *scrump*tious, although, and I am very sorry to say so, the boar could not be *rarer* if it was charging through the tavern!

Now, as to my life, my *origins*, as it were. You may not belief this, Master MacBlaquart—such a truly pi*rat*ical name!—but I was born from rather exclusive stock. *Hearty*, as it were… And, in truth, they *had* to be, my forebears, because *Bar*bados, before our family's arrival, was a truly messy mass of turpid, *tang*ly jungle and re*lent*less, horrid humidity.

Truth be told, much of it remains the seventh circle of Hell.

Not, however, *our* part.

So let us begin, in sixteen twenty-seven, when the Earl of Carlisle, James Hay—a favorite of your venerable House of Stuart—undertook the settlement of Barbados after the Portuguese had subdued the Arawaks and the Caribs, who were not doing a damned thing with it. Hay, a mighty specimen of a Scotsman with a disposition more than matching the climate, originally thought tobacco would be the crop to see the island successful, but it turned out to be—as you no doubt are aware—*sugar*!

War is good for a great many things, and the development of Barbados is near the top of the list. Cromwell—whom I count amongst my relations—sent teeming *boat*loads full of burly, banished Scots to the island between the years sixteen forty-eight and sixteen fifty-one, when battles were abundant and the pious Covenanters were making quite the fuss.

My ancestors arrived in Bridgetown not long after.

From then to the present, a matter of half a dozen decades, the Bonnets and our close relations, the Whetstones, have cleared more than four hundred acres of lowland jungle in proximity to the port.

I now shall speak to my lineage. My maternal great-grandfather was the celebrated privateer Sir Thomas Whetstone, who plied his trade most famously in sixteen fifty-eight and -nine. His son—my mother Sarah's father—was the deputy colonial secretary of Barbados, John Whetstone, nephew to Oliver Cromwell. *That* is my connection to that man of many faces, should you have had a doubt! John's wife, the loveliest soul I have ever known, was called Jennet.

I am sure you have heard of the *Whet*stones… No less than the famous circumnavigator of the globe, the dashing Woodes Rogers, *married* a *Whet*stone!

Let us talk now of the Bonnets. My grandfather, Thomas Bonnet the Elder, held a great estate—the lion's share of the four hundred acres already mentioned, most of it devoted to the growing and processing of sugar, worked by nearly a hundred slaves. He was a pio*neer* in the designing and running of plantations, a generation ahead of Jamaica and the Bahamas. Thomas had two sons— Thomas Junior and my father, Edward, from whom I derive my skills as a seaman. A cap*tain* he was, and a fine one at that! Unfortunately, as Fate would have it, he died in sixteen ninety-four, when my twin sister Frances and I were barely six years old. Do not *pity* me, Master MacBlaquart—such a rich*er*, point*ier* name than Captain *Ed*wards!— life is a foam-mouthed *mon*grel and we learn from it what we can.

My grandfather, the aforementioned deputy colonial secretary, undertook the task of looking after us, allotting my mother Sara one hundred and twenty acres and just shy of seventy slaves. Our property had two windmills and a cattle-operated mill to process sugarcane into syrup.

Five months later—for Fate is a jealous, mangy-anused *bitch*—my grandfather died. Grandmother Jennet soon followed, choosing Eternity with John over the welfare of her grandchildren. Or perhaps I am unkind…

Under the guidance—and *thumb*—of my ugly uncle Thomas, I was raised a *gent*leman, expected to take my place in high Barbadian society when I came of age. I enjoyed, as part of my training, a thorough, broad-based, and very *lib*eral education.

A few years later, my mother, who had never recovered from the death of my father and her parents, succumbed to Heaven's holy temptations, and, although my sister Frances thrived, I found myself thinking thoughts of getting away. My uncle did not like me, and I felt the same toward him.

Pursuant to those feelings, at the age of sixteen I received a commission in the Barbadian militia—happily purchased by my normally miserly uncle. After a cursory period of basic martial training, I was sent to the islands of the Caribbean and elsewhere where the uprisings of plantation slaves like the ones we fed and cared for on Barbados were causing a bit of a fuss. For the next five years, I served in the Lesser Antilles, Montserrat, Dominica, and St. Lucia, rising to the rank of major.

Now… open the Madeira, Conall, I beg of you, and order us bread with melted cheese, and I shall tell you of my return to the plantation in Barbados, and what horrors there befell me.

As I sighted Bridgetown, following five years of adventuring, and just having passed my twenty-first birthday, I knew that I could not go back to how my life had been beneath my uncle's thumb. I was at last a *man*—with a thick, oiled, and quite proper *beard* and a greater amount of *muscle*. Appearances, I prayed, would quite suffice to gain my Uncle Thomas's respect. You see, Conall, truth be told, his buying of my commission meant that my subordinates—who much preferred me to stay in my tent or some appropriated manor house, drinking my tea and reading my books—did the bulk of the exceedingly bloody work undertaken on the islands on which we served.

We must, of course, keep that between us. Let us drink upon that, yes?

As a wagon that my uncle had sent to fetch me from the docks entered the Bonnet–Whetstone acreage—what a gesture it would have been if he had come himself—I saw that he had prospered in the years I was away. Thomas had significantly extended the borders of the plantation and the grounds were positively *tee*ming with dark-skinned servants and slaves.

I immediately saw an opening and resolved that evening to take it.

After a meal that would have satisfied the biblical prodigal son, my uncle and I said our goodnights to the ladies still gathered at the table. My twin sister Frances was amongst them, looking as though life had finally shown her kindness after years of death and despair. Two years married to a successful sugar exporter on the other side of the island, she had graciously come to welcome her brother home—although the *hus*band, it seemed, could not be *bothered*.

A pair of long-stemmed pipes, a plug of imported tobacco, and a bottle of brandy selected as our silent evening companions, Thomas and I sat ourselves on the porch.

As I gathered my thoughts to make my proposition, my uncle, never one to let anyone else control the conversation, said, setting his pipe alight, "Look here, Stede. After the action and excitement you saw, I do have to wonder if life on a plantation will be something that will suit you. Let us be honest with each other... it never truly did. That is why I spent such a ridiculously high amount on your commission in the militia."

"Please, Uncle Thomas," I said, choosing a respectful tone that fell far short of pleading, "I am not the boy with the books I once was. Oh yes, I still have them... *read* them... *love* them... but I am capable of more. I am a Bonnet, same as you, with *Whet*stone blood in my veins, and I wish to help you build on the successes you have achieved. Father and grandfather would want me to. I know that in my heart."

Far from dismissing me out of hand, as he used to, my uncle, obscured in a cloud of thick grey smoke, leaned forward in his chair.

"Perhaps, Stede, you have made a serious point. There *is* something you can do... Something that would allow me to secure water rights from a neighboring plantation that the judge who owns it has for years refused to give."

How easy it had been! "*Any*thing you need, *dear*est *Uncle*, I can handle! I am proficient with paperwork and *all* manner of organization after my five *years* of service as an *officer*. I am adept at overseeing large numbers of subordinates and administering *disc*ipline when needed. At times, I shall tell you, it certainly was *needed*! If you put me in the field, overseeing the *slaves*, I think you will find me more than capa—"

A vicious, dismissive laugh brought my speech to a halt.

"Do not be ridiculous, Nephew! Mister Brocken, as you are well aware, having met him at the start of our dinner, is our overseer. He grew up in it. He is *good* at it. The slaves respect him. *Fear* him. Because of this, he rarely uses the whip. As for the daily keeping of the ledgers, paying of the bills, and other fiscal responsibilities, that is what *I* do..."

Taking a puff on my pipe and a sip of my brandy in order to steel my nerves for an answer I knew I did not want to hear, I asked, "Then what is it, Uncle, that you *do* need of me?"

"To marry Judge Allamby's daughter!"

Resisting the urge to push my uncle's hand from where he had placed it on my knee, I responded, "Marry Mary Allamby. Uncle Thomas... with all due respect... There is a *rea*son she is twenty-*five* and, although her father is one of the *weal*thiest men in Bridgetown, she has not secured a *suit*or. She is... well... first of all... she is not much at all to *look* at. I have my self-respect, my manly standards and *needs*..."

My uncle patted my knee. "Do not be shallow, Nephew. Besides... despite that beard hiding most of your face—you shall shave it tomorrow, you hear me?—I can clearly see that you are not much to look at as well. Let us hope Mary Allamby does not fool herself as you do with these stupid notions of *standards*."

Feeling these barbs entering my skin like the dart from a savage's blowpipe, I persisted in *spite of*–or rather, *because of*—the pain. "Fair enough. Although her *dispos*ition... She is not at all *friend*ly, Uncle.

Cannon and the Quill   184

On the contrary, she is quite the practiced *bully*. In a word, she is...
unmarriable!"

"Of course she is, Stede," my uncle replied, once more patting my knee before giving it a squeeze. "That is why my plan shall work. Judge Allamby wants nothing more than to marry her off and get her out of his house. He shall refuse me nothing when I make that happen, and that is fully my intention. Good to have you home, Major Bonnet. Speaking of... wear your uniform tomorrow. We are lunching with them at noon.

"And Stede. Be sure to shave that beard."

The next morning, I shaved as ordered, lunched as ordered—not half a fine a meal as this, though the Madeira *was* a good deal smoother—and, two days later proposed... as ordered. We were married that November, on the 21st, at St. Michael's Church. I remember that day, not out of fondness, but because it marked the start of the end of my life as a gentleman sugar-grower on Barbados.

What can I tell you about life with Mary Allamby? I mean, of course, Mary *Bonnet*. My *wife*. At least on paper and in name... Were most marriages like ours, and word was to spread of the agony that they caused, there should soon be very few fellows willing to forge the irons that their wives would use to enslave them. And I was very much a *slave*. Imagine... So well born, with *int*ellect and *pros*pects, with all the benefits of the *Whet*stones and *Bonnet*s and *Crom*wells behind me... though I might as well have been auctioned on the block after a grueling trip from Africa.

It is important you understand this, Conall... Mary was *horrific*. Pleasant enough at that first lunch—her father must have warned her to be bait and not a barra*cuda*—and during the weeks we... *she*... planned the upcoming nuptials. But, as soon as we were alone in the honeymoon suite as it were, she forcefully laid down the law. Asserting her dominance physically and with her scalding tongue, she prescribed a daily program of whipping me into some semblance of a *prop*er husband before there was any talk of *chil*dren.

And what was the substance of this daily program of training? I see your eyes are asking... To do *what* she said, *when* she said it. To listen to her drone on and on like a hive of agitated *bees* about her father, my uncle, and me.

Mary Allamby disliked men. She thought them best eradicated and she intended to start with me.

Things were no better at my uncle's prospering estate. He gave me very little to do. So, having little else to occupy my time when Admiral Allamby was not strapping me to the mast for another thirty-nine lashes from the vicious whip that was her mouth, I drank my tea and read my books and began increasingly to *bristle*.

I must admit, my mind was beginning to wander to the freedom of the sea. I had been happiest during my years in the militia upon the deck of a heavily cannoned frigate as we traveled from island to island. I gathered together from my father's library the books that chronicled the voyages and exploits of my grandfather. I re-read

Woodes Rogers's tome, *A Cruising Voyage around the World*, published four years earlier.

As the months piled upon themselves, mocking my misery as they marched so dismally on, I began to formulate the rudiments of a plan, which I would—in my increasingly rarer lucid moments—push aside like my untouched bowl of porridge each morning after dreaming on it all evening.

Two years later, deeming me finally fit to fill the role, Mary bestowed upon me the position of father. Although I heartily welcomed it, it was not to last. On seventeen May of seventeen hundred and twelve, my son, Allamby, merely an infant, ceased to live. Although the gods, in their devilish determinations, gave us three other children—my sons, Edward and Stede, and a beautiful daughter, Mary, who looks *nothing* like her mother—I never managed to get past the death of my precious little Allamby. His passing dredged up memories of my father and mother, of John and Jennet Whetstone... of how their deaths had put me in the path of my despicable uncle and his partner in crime, my father-in-law the *judge*.

Fitting occupation for an Allamby, I thought. He had taught his daughter well.

As the marriage marked its third year, I spent more and more of my time studying the books of grandfather and Rogers, and working up in greater detail my plan. The pull of the sea, the freedoms that it promised, increased throughout the winter, made all the stronger by what I was daily hearing from several plantation owners and their sons:

A pair of pirates, called Bellamy and Williams, were causing all manner of hell and havoc near the Leeward Islands and elsewhere with their roguish French companion, Levasseur the Vulture, and a Hell-spawned, tatooed *Chin*aman who was said to eat men's eyes.

Each night, as I balanced myself on the corner of the bed so as not to touch in any way my wife, I imagined their daring exploits and dreamed of joining their ranks.

One of the few *positives* of the life I was leading was that neither my wife nor my uncle paid much, if any, attention to how I spent my day. Mary kept herself occupied with the three children and running roughshod over the household servants, and my uncle was more than happy if he never saw my face or heard my high-pitched voice.

Come now, my dear Conall—don't pretend you have not noticed.

As the winter months gave way to the hellish humidity of spring, I felt I had accumulated enough knowledge between my time sailing as part of the militia and the enormous amount of reading I had been doing about the Caribbean pirates and their ships of choice to make a most momentous decision. I was going to leave behind my life on Barbados and take to the seas as a *pirate*.

The necessary means of my escape and desired profession—my sloop the *Revenge*, which now sits damaged and anchored in your harbor—was truly a labor of love in both the designing and the building, both of which I undertook with the utmost of secrecy.

Traveling to the Port of Bridgetown under the premise of meeting a tailor from whom I intended to purchase a new set of summer clothes—*pirating* clothes, although I kept that tidbit quiet—I met with a master shipbuilder with a solid reputation amongst the sea captains and other maritime workers in the bustling, deep-water harbor.

I have always found that attitudes change, no matter how you look, talk, or even act, once one knows that your pockets are deep, and mine unquestionably were. My years in the militia had paid for themselves. I had wanted for nothing and spent little of what I earned. I had considerable funds through the inheritances bestowed upon me at the passing of my parents and our wards. I had also managed to earn a considerable dowry from Judge Allamby for taking Mary off his hands.

I was shrewd enough to have hidden a sizable portion of my wealth with a handful of bankers throughout the island who were more than happy to earn a little extra each month for keeping our transactions private.

Although the shipbuilder initially dismissed me as insane when I requested of him to build a pirate-style sloop with ten guns and room enough for a brawny crew of seventy, a quick show of just how wealthy I was changed his position from dismissive skeptic to eager participant in my project.

Of course, I did not use my *real name*. Far too *dan*gerous. Talk about *in*sane! This was the first of many times that I would refer to myself as "Captain Edwards"—slave trader, former privateer, and son of a wealthy plantation owner in Jamaica who had traveled to Barbados because of the shipbuilder's un*para*lleled repu*ta*tion.

Such flattery is nearly as good as a big chest of silver and gold when it comes to winning over those you need to do your will.

An added benefit of the fictitious but admittedly impressive life story of the very successful Captain Edwards was that the shipbuilder, who had already laid the keel within a week of our signing the contracts, was more than willing to introduce me to a newly arrived seaman with an impressive amount of experience. He had served as a sailing master or quartermaster on several sloops, both during the War of Spanish Succession and after. His name is Daniel Herriot. Although he also hailed from Jamaica, as did my made-up captain, both men had spent enough time away from the island in the past decade for their never having been in the same place at the same time to be of zero consequence. Herriot was shocked but rather pleased to learn that, although we would be a proper pirate ship, I would pay the crew a weekly salary whether we captured prizes or not. This way, I was guaranteeing their pay without worrying about *percentages*. Although this was highly un*u*sual—"damned unprecedented!" according to Herriot—it also had its appeal, for no doubt obvious reasons.

As I watched my as-yet-unnamed sloop take its destined shape in Bridgetown, Herriot set about recruiting a crew. My offer made it easy, as did Herriot's impeccable reputation. Within a month, he brought to me a man called William Scott, whose skill as quartermaster Herriot sold to me as unsurpassed. We—meaning the two of *them*—therefore decided that Herriot would serve as sailing master, and the pair would be my chief advisors on all matters of where to sail and with whom we should engage. I readily agreed.

Not of great surprise, but surely of interest to *you*, Mister MacBlaquart—such a quality *nom de guerre*!—the addition of Mister *Scott* drew to the crew of the sloop many a *Scott*ish *Jacobite*, as loyal to the cause of the Stuarts as I am betting you yourself are. This made no nevermind to me... *why* they were motivated to go out on the account was less important to me than the fact that they *were*. And my brawny crew of seventy truly, truly were...

It was at the end of May, as the ship was nearing completion, that I heard tell of the tragedy that had befallen Black Sam Bellamy off the coast of Massachusetts. I must admit, it gave me pause. If such a powerful, able king of the pirates as the Robin Hood of the Seas could meet his doom in such a horrific way, what hope had *I* to survive? But, as they say, in for a penny, in for a *pound*, and the ship, still as yet unnamed, was nearly ready for sailing.

Assembling the crew, a bottle of the best rum in all of Bridgetown in my hand, I stood on the docks before the bow and christened the sloop the *Revenge*. This name appealed to the Jacobites amongst us—as I said, in the majority—and, for *me*, it represented a list that I had been mentally scribing for years. Revenge against my Uncle Thomas. Revenge against my mother and Jennet Whetstone for choosing Heaven and their husbands over me. Revenge against God for taking my firstborn son. Revenge against Judge Allamby and his horse-faced, shrewish monster of a daughter, Mary, simply for ex*ist*ing.

I passed the night before we were to sail upon our plantation, supping with my three children and doing my best to be kind to my wife.

I owed her a few hours of pleasantries and even physical overtures—although by now, she fully re*pulsed* me, same as I did her... After all, in the morning, I would quite literally be sailing away from the hell that had been my life for far too many years.

What an indescribable feeling it was, sailing out of Carlisle Bay, in view of St. Michael's Church, the site of my lowest moment outside the death of my son—my marriage ceremony with Mary. I am sure you know the feeling, Conall MacBlaquart—that feeling of *utter freedom*. I have assessed by listening carefully to your delightful, delicious brogue, that you are a Highlander. You may know some of my crew—certainly their *clans*. I have not a clue what brought you so far south—to this "short and merry life" as Scott and Herriot call it— but whatever you felt the day that you left home, it cannot be too far afield of what I felt that day! After all, I was the *captain*... of a *pirate* ship! This was not some bought com*mis*sion, foisted upon me by my *uncle*. This was *my* choice.

I was determined to make the most of it.

There is no question the crew were as well. They sang robustly the songs you must know from home as they worked the sails and rigging, testing out our fine sloop, the *Revenge*—which had been the envy of the port of Bridgetown, I tell you! In our first few days, we took two small ships. We were learning, after all. The cannons went unused, and the take was nearly nothing. But our confidence was up! Having read of the tactics of Bellamy and Williams, I encouraged the men to appear frightful... *wild*! They kept their clothes on, of course, for certain... *proprieties*... let us say... had to be upheld, at least at the start. Too much too soon while still so close to home and we were liable to have our necks stretched while my uncle looked on and laughed.

And I, in the role I had played for months—the experienced and cool-blooded Captain Edwards. What *fun* I was having! To de*mand* actions of others, the way so many others had *demanded* them of me!

I was more alive, more *me*, than I had felt in a very long time.

Scott and Herriot were so completely capable, I was able to be in my cabin as we sailed, reading my books and drinking my tea. I thought, early on, about what Mary and Uncle Thomas must have felt when they realized I had left. I had paid a handsome bonus to the shipbuilder to say nothing of our transaction, should they be wise enough to search for me in Bridgetown. I used the pretense that my family claimed I owed them a return of certain *fees* for slaves that had taken ill soon after we acquired them at *auction*. A spurious charge, I assured the shipbuilder, who was too engrossed in counting his considerable coin to embroil himself in some dispute over *savages*.

I may have mentioned as well that, if the pickings were ripe and the sloop performed as he promised, I might be back for another. Maybe even two.

Such were my thoughts, Conall, as we sliced through the Caribbean waters in search of prey.

The crew were starving for something substantial. I could hear it in their voices, see it in the set of their jaws and the glint in their mostly Scottish, Jacobite, eyes.

Two more ships we took, with disappointing results. Although the hunt was exhilarating and the boarding was fun, neither ship yielded either tradeables or spendables.

The men, whose songs of the sea they increasingly replaced with the caterwaul sounds of griping and bitching, whispered their frustrations in the ears of Herriot and Scott, who brought their gripes to me, along with every assurance that they were in complete agreement and, should the situation continue, changes would be made, through a mandatory vote.

Imagine! Only six weeks at sea and I was being *threatened*! I, the founder of their feast—the descendent of Thomas Whetstone and Oliver Cromwell!—the payer of their wages and the dreamer of the dreams that set them *free*!

Taking Herriot and Scott aside, I asked for an evening's respite, in order to consider my options. This, of course, brought back in vivid memory the evening my uncle laid before me the plan to marry Mary.

I had not spoken up. I had but *hint*ed at refusal, rather than introducing it as my partner, my ally in the cause—immovable and nonnegotiable.

As I tucked into my bed in my cabin, the sounds of a song of war wafting down from the deck above, I swore to myself that, come the morning, I would devise a better outcome than that long ago night in Barbados.

I would not marry failure.

I would see this through.

Ah, please… we need more Madeira over here! And what have you for cakes? Custards? Bring some of each… This lad is still growing and I simply *love* a sweet!

Now… to my decision. No suspense there, I know… It was a simple one, but as you are well aware, it cost me. Nearly, nearly my *life*…

Giving in to the crew's requests—I chose *not* to call them threats—I agreed to be more aggressive in our hunting and taking of prizes. I did have one condition—that we abandon Bahamian waters and venture farther out. I would simply rather *die* than be *cap*tured and forced to return to Barbados in shame to face my wife and uncle. To be accused of insanity and locked inside a room on one or the other of their estates to live out my days as a mockery.

Herriot and Scott requested an immediate vote and the crew to a man agreed.

Sailing north for the long coast of the American colonies, we captured within a few days a brigantine under a Captain Thomas Porter who came from Boston. Much to the crew's frustration, it had little of value, but I was keen on turning yet another perceived failure into a victory. Citing the need to be well prepared for weeks upon the seas, I order the vessel stripped, and the sheets, cordage, and provisions she yielded stowed within *Revenge*. Less than a day later, we took another ship, under a Captain Joseph Palmer. Searching her holds, Herriot and Scott—they had sug*gest*ed I remain aboard *Revenge* and I decided that was wise—found a worthy pirate haul! Sugar, rum, and *slaves*! Success! Oh the joy I felt as the bounty was hauled aboard.

Then, in the midst of my victory, as Palmer came over to complete our final negotiations, he recognized me!

Damnable luck! Unkind God laughing in derision from Heaven!

Threatening Palmer with an ugly demise if he told *anyone* of our encounter, I told him I had no choice but to send his ship to the bottom of the sea in a mighty conflagration. I had he and his crew put on Porter's ship, which, having no sails and cordage, would not be able to pursue us.

Watching the faces of my crew that night, their smiles lit by Palmer's burning vessel, I knew that I had come at last to my calling. A pirate captain was I, with a hold full of treasure!

As the hours went by, the men drank copious amounts of rum and sang songs in praise of *me*. It could have lasted forever, that memorable evening, though nothing ever does.

The next morning, Herriot and Scott, after conferring with those amongst the crew awake and sober enough to participate, informed me that we were going to undertake a siege of Charles Town harbor, a few days' sail away, which would afford us the opportunity to gather more plunder while staying well away from their guns.

This is what we did, taking several ships with additional booty, before heading out to open water and back toward the Caribbean, where we could sell what we could and consolidate our bounty into sacks of silver and gold.

We had made our decision not a moment too soon, for word reached us the following evening that no less than *Colonel William Rhett*, commanding a pair of formidable sloops, was hunting us!

Can you imagine? Hunted by the best! Captain Stede Bonnet, the scourge of Charles Town!

Why… what is this, young Conall? A group of musicians, warming up to play! Most excellent! A concertina, mandolin, fiddle, and pennywhistle. Per*fec*tion! Have I mentioned that I, on occasion, com*pose*? Nothing worthy of a concert hall, but some of my crew have taken to singing them while attending to their tasks.

*Gen*tlemen! Might I have a word? Lovely… I have a request. I have written a tune. I call it, "To Be a Proper Pyrate." Here are the words, with the music marked above. Can you…? Wonderful! *Won*derful!

Hello, happy denizens of this most remarkable tavern. I am Ste— , uh, Ste*ven* Edwards, captain of the stout sloop *Revenge*, and I would like to sing you a song.

Excellent, my musicians! Just like that. You really are too mar*vel*ous! Play low the opening chords, repeatedly, while I begin with a bit of talk… Ah… perfect… here is a mirror, hanging on the wall as if for just this use.

By the saints and angels! This Caribbean hu*mid*ity is enough to curl one's hairs! If only… Alas, as straight as ever… Well… My *hair* that is!

Oh, you *laughed*! Thank you… what a lovely audience.

People often ask me… Captain *Ed*wards—so *en*viably successful, *bon vivant* and yet *so* rough! What makes a proper pirate? Is it diet? Is it breeding? Tattoos or scars or earrings? Asking me, *expectant*ly… What makes a proper pirate?

Here we go, my fine musicians… Time for me to *sing*!

A fox-fur, quilted robe and a knitted, fitted cap
Books read by the crateful, bon-bons for a snack
Being delicate in diction—swearing makes unmannered minds!
For good measure, any treasure that is taken should be thine
Provide your crew a weekly wage, go *wisely* with the wine!

Here's the thing, me mates… I was born on a faraway island. Rich, bossy uncle… Bored, indifferent wife… *That* old sparkling gem!

After my militia man's commission, never drew my sword an inch
I was ready to inherit—to scratch a certain itch!
My uncle parried that I marry a haughty, horse-faced hag
So I wormed out through the window, built a boat,
and took a pass!

In truth, me mates, *others* built the boat. I mean, *honestly*—do these look like a *laborer's* hands?

I bought myself a crew, we took prizes left and right
Never once pulled out my rapier, until the dark of night
My men were growing cocky, I suppose that I was too!
Tried to score a man o' war, and got well and truly—

I am sure you know what I mean!

That's the time I first met Blackbeard, and that randy Hornigold
I bet that they could *teach* me, from the tales some *seamen* told!
One's all dressed in ribbons—God, I love those braids!
The other with his pipe… Oh, Edwards—you be*have*!

A fox-fur, quilted robe and a knitted, fitted cap
Books read by the crateful, bon-bons for a snack
Being delicate in diction—swearing makes unmannered minds!
For good measure, any treasure that is taken should be thine
Provide your crew a weekly wage, go *wisely* with the wine!

That's what makes a proper pirate… every time!

Oh… *thank* you! Thank you all *so much*! I am truly humbled. And these… my fabulous musicians! Drinks for them all, if you please, barkeep! I must return to business.

Now, Conall... It is time to tell you of our encounter with the Spanish man o' war, for it is truly *worthy* of this de*lecta*ble dessert.

FLORIDA STRAITS, AUGUST 26, 1717

The only thing worse, Master MacBlaquart, than a crew drunk on rum is a crew drunk on *power*. We had been in Caribbean waters for less than a week when a lookout spied a frigate on the horizon, flying the Spanish colors.

Within moments, Herriot and Scott were calling our men to the cannon and directing the sails to be set for battle.

Gazing through my spyglass, I saw the puckered lips of the Spanish captain as he glared back at us. I recognized him instantly by reputation—Amaro Rodríguez Felipe y Tejera Machado, captain of the *Ave María y Las Ánimas*! The infamous *fish*-face himself, Amaro *Pargo*! Although he had taken his lumps at the hands of Bellamy and that rat-like rascal Vane, he had lost his lieutenant and some say closest friend, Renaldo de Recalde, to a cannonball off Hispaniola six months prior and he has been the scourge of the seas ever since. Tales were being told of slaughters, burned ships, and a complete lack of mercy as Pargo sought redemption against the *pedazo de mierda cerdo*, the stinking piratical pig-swine, the spawn of *el Diablo!*, as he called us from the bow of his ship.

I called out to Herriot and Scott to retreat, though they would not have it. I explained to them the reasons why this was a mistake, who it was we were facing, and the fury the Spaniard was feeling. It did not a speck of *good*, although I called on their common cause, for, although they were the enemies of the Spanish, the Jacobites were also united with them in their being also Catholics.

As Pargo yelled first to his God and then for the cannon to be fired, I contemplated going below-decks. Herriot and Scott are skilled at what they do, but not against a capable captain such as Amaro Pargo, who had twice as many guns and three times the number of crew—a crew considerably more seasoned than was mine.

You know the outcome, my handsome Highlander pirate. I sit here before you unsure as to why I have survived, relying on the kindness of Benjamin Hornigold and not at all sure what it is my future holds. You have been kind these many hours to indulge me in my tale telling, my singing, my complaints about the food and the drink. I can see it in your face that your heart is as heavy as mine, although for different reasons. Oof... my stomach is too full! I have grown used to more modest fare through this long and hard-lessoned summer. There... there are Herriot and Scott, commiserating—nay, con*spiring*—in the corner. I doubt very much that, come morning, the *Revenge* will still be mine. Perhaps that is for the best. One thing though... Help me up, would you? I need to walk, to get away from the smug, accusing faces of the very pair that made such an inglorious decision to attack the frigate of Amaro Pargo… Where was I? Yes, yes… the one thing. The thing I can*not* do, which is return to Barbados, to my wife and uncle. I would, in a moment, undo the healing to my wounds and see myself deceased rather than that.

Ah… the fresh air. I do love the Bahamian breeze in the evening. Barbados is hotter than the armpits of Hell herself this time of year and so *un*relenting! Take me to my quarters, Conall. I am full and all talked out. One day, you shall tell me *your* tale. How you came to be here, yes? For I am most interested in a tale well told and I could listen to your brogue from sunset to sun-up. If my poor, dead Allamby would have grown to be half the delightful, polite, and patient young man you have proven yourself this evening to be, I would be immensely proud. He had that spark of promise, you know. Stede the Second and Edward do not. In their eyes, the set of their jaw, their stubborn, frustrated screams for immediate satisfaction, I see and hear the monster Mary Allamby.

Well… she can have them. Let her father and my uncle step in as they can. I shall have not a single moment more of it. Do not think me cruel. I could not bear it, Conall…

Ah, my rooms. Adequate, adequate indeed. Thank you again for your kindness. Sleep well, young pirate, as I know that I surely shall.

Tomorrow I shall face whatever it shall bring.

"An entire evenin' an' an achin' haid an' stomach, an' I caen tael ye both. Hae saems tae bae without a doubt completely aff his haid!"

Blackbeard, pushing a mug of the hair of the hound Angus's way the following morning, shook his head. "I have heard the same from at least a dozen others who dined at the Fatted Calf last night. Tell me they are lying when they say he was singing about my ribbons and braids. And Commodore Hornigold's *pipe*..."

Despite his blurred vision and ringing ears, Angus could tell that Blackbeard was making a threat rather than a request.

"Sorry tae say, all ye have haird is true."

Turning to Benjamin Hornigold, who seemed delighted by the details Angus had shared with the pair over the past almost hour—with the exception of the bit about his pipe—Blackbeard deepened his grimace. "With all due respect, sir. I do not see how we can manage him. For all we know, his wife and uncle have the wealth and connections necessary to bring the Barbadian militia or perhaps the Royal Navy to our shores. Is his sloop worth the risk of keeping him here?"

Lighting his pipe (a bit self-consciously), Hornigold nodded. "Absolutely, old friend. The ship is formidable and, with ye as captain and William Howard as quartermaster, utilizing Bonnet's two men—Herriot and Scott, is it?—as sailing master and boatswain, ye will soon take many a worthy prize."

"Howard?" Blackbeard asked, equally confused and intrigued.

"It is time for him to serve another captain," Hornigold replied. William Howard had been his quartermaster since January 1716. "There is no one better or more loyal in the Caribbean. I want the strongest crew possible sailing that ship. Bonnet's Jacobites, although clearly overanxious at times to prove their mettle, will no doubt serve ye well. They certainly will not question ye. In the week or so it will take to complete the repairs on the *Revenge*, ye and Mister Howard will get to know this Herriot and Scott. I shall look after Captain Bonnet, who shall revert to his former militia rank of major once ye are ready to sail."

Blackbeard tipped his tricorne. "I appreciate your trust in me, sir. It will be good to be in command again. There is much that I must do..."

"And ye shall. All in good time. There is more to my plan than just your well-deserved captaincy. Ye shall take our own Mister

MacBlaquart onto your crew. Give him responsibility commensurate with his experience and loyalty, both of which have become considerable. Ye shall take Caesar with ye as well. Conall, he shall be under both your care and charge. Agreeable?"

"Aye, Gran'pa Hornigold. I shall make ye proud."

As Hornigold and Blackbeard finished their breakfasts, Conall leaned forward, lowering his voice. "Thair is one thing… An' I donnae wish tae make even a wee bit a' trouble, boot it moost bae said…"

"Very well, then," Hornigold said around a mouthful of eggs. "Tell us."

Conall took a breath and began. "Wael… Cap'n Bonnet was a slaveholder an' damned proud tae bae. I donnae care for the way hae speaks a' oother maen. Nae matter the color a' their skin, Captains Bellamy an' Williams said each an' ev'ry one of oos are princes a' the world."

Pushing away his plate and letting forth a belch, Blackbeard laughed. "Poetry at the expense of power! I told Sam as much, on many an occasion. A man becomes a prince by dint of his own hard effort and not by the proclamation of the Robin Hood of the Seas, God rest his soul. In truth, some men are naturally more equal than others. My family could not have run our plantation without its dozens of slaves. Do not be naïve, Conall. Sam and Paulsgrave made trouble for us all by not only freeing but *recruiting* those that are destined to be slaves. We shall pay the price for their seizure of the *Whydah* before all of this is done. Mark well my words on the matter."

Unsure of how to respond in any other way but from his heart, Conall smacked his hand upon the table. "Remaember, sir, that many of oos are hair because of oppression an' imposed servitude nae different than that put upon the Africans. An' thair are plenty a' Africans amongst oos noow. Donnae forgaet Caesar, who shall bae sailin' with oos. An' Joseph Stanton was destined for a life a' slavery baefore I—"

"And look what *he* has become! Ye should have left him to his fate, Conall! Do not confuse men like him and men like us. My God… I thought I was done with this insufferable righteousness when we lost poor Sam!"

Seeing the look on Conall's face at this affront and wishing to spare him the no doubt physical response Blackbeard would give him for anything the frustrated Scotsman was about to say, Hornigold put a hand on each of their arms.

"Enough of this. Conall. I hear your words. Captain Bonnet is no longer a slaveholder, and it seems clear he wishes nothing more than to leave that life behind. Should he show any disrespect to Caesar, ye report the same to Blackbeard and he shall see the insult answered. As for ye, Blackbeard. Not all men grew up on a sugar plantation. Ye, Bonnet, and Jennings share that commonality. The great majority are men like Samuel Bellamy, Charles Vane, and myself who came from less than nothing. I know ye meant him nor me no ill will with your ill-considered words, and Conall, upon reflection when his temper has cooled, shall see it as well. Mister MacBlaquart, I suggest ye speak with Captain Jennings for insight into handling Bonnet on the subject of slavery."

Blackbeard, obviously embarrassed and regretting at least some of what he said, nodded. "I meant no offense to the memory of Samuel Bellamy. Nor to ye, Mister MacBlaquart. I know the sacrifices ye have made. Joseph Stanton was damned lucky to have ye by his side on that day in Boston. He will one day come to see it."

"Thank ye both," Hornigold said, obviously relieved. "Look sharp now. Here comes our bonny Major Bonnet."

Looking all the worse for wear, and dressed in a quilted robe trimmed with fox fur and a purple knitted cap with an ornate ball of yarn sewn onto the tip, Stede Bonnet, fresh bandages applied to his wounds, sat with a yawn between Hornigold and Blackbeard. "What an *interesting* evening, gents! Conall here is quite the dinner companion. Even saw me into my bed."

"Is that right?" Blackbeard enquired, arching a brow and stifling a smile.

"Laeft right baefore that, actually," Conall replied, his cheeks turning the same bright red as the largest squares on his Stuart plaid headscarf.

"I am glad ye have joined us, Major Bonnet," Hornigold said, relighting his pipe. "I have a proposal. In a week's time, the *Revenge* will be ready to sail. We shall add another pair of cannon to her ten and another hundred crew. My own quartermaster, William Howard, will ensure that no further mistakes or threats to your leadership occur."

"I see," Bonnet said, waving over a wench to order his breakfast. "Mister Herriot will not be pleased."

"Leave Herriot and Scott to me," Blackbeard replied. "If they are going to serve aboard our ship—"

"*Our* ship?" Stede asked, his eyes going wide. "Then ye shall *also* be aboard?"

"Indeed he shall," Hornigold replied, glancing over at Blackbeard to indicate that he should refrain for the moment from speaking. "I believe it best that he serve as temporary captain—at least until such a time as another sloop as worthy as *Revenge* can be taken—and to further undertake your training as a... well... *proper* pirate, might I say."

"Hmm," Bonnet replied, placing his chin on his fist to show that he was considering the proposal. "I suppose I would be a fool to turn down such an offer of tutelage by such a brute as Blackbeard himself... no offense meant. Brutality is more than proper for a pirate..."

"None taken," Hornigold said, again glancing at Blackbeard to keep him from speaking. "So ye agree?"

Thrusting his arms into the air, Bonnet shouted, "I do indeed!"

Taking the odd Barbadian's response as his cue, Blackbeard put his long, muscled arm around Bonnet's shoulders. "I would be honored to teach ye, Major! I can tell we will be the best of mates. Conall tells me ye are related to the Whetstones. I served under Rear Admiral William Whetstone on his flagship, the HMS *Windsor*, in 1706. We are practically family, Stede! So here is what I suggest. Ye will keep the captain's cabin. I am happy to sleep with the crew in the fo'c'sle. Drink your tea, read your fancy books, and stay the hell out of my way and perhaps, by the time we seize another suitable ship, ye will learn something about being a proper pirate."

Looking upon Blackbeard with a mix of fascination and fear, Bonnet blurted out, "*Prac*tically family indeed! Splendid. *Jolly* splendid. And, in our ex*ten*ded family, Blackbeard, is the famous circumnavigator and slaver, Woodes Rogers himself, through his marriage to William Whetstone's daughter. He is a *fa*scinating specimen. I have a first edition of his *A Cruising Voyage around the World* in my cabin, if you care to read it. I have already, several times..."

Giving a glance at Conall, who had visibly tensed at the mention of yet another slaver, Blackbeard gave Bonnet's shoulder a squeeze. "I know quite well the exploits of Captain Rogers. As for his book... Read it two more times, then pass it on to Conall. As for me... I shall be far too busy to read."

PART SIX

TRIALS, TRIALS, TRIALS

Powerful men, when shamed, cuckolded, or otherwise humiliated, will strike back with a force double that of the fierce nor'easter that laid to rest Samuel Bellamy and his prize ship, the *Whydah*, at the bottom of the Atlantic.

Such a man was Sir Humphry Morice, a leading Member of Parliament and director of the Bank of England. It was he who had owned the foremost slaver on the seas, the *Whydah*, built just two years prior, and the vast loss of not only the treasure the ship was carrying as its investors' payment for delivered slaves but the audacity of the act by a band of venomous rogues and villains had him in a fury.

Sitting in the offices of the Royal African Company, with whom he had partnered his businesses, Sir Humphry drummed impatiently on the long oak table as he awaited the arrival of the solution to the growing problem of the pirates. At the other end, smelling like the perfumed cock of the walk he fancied himself to be, Lord John Carteret, the RAC's governor, who had returned from the Isle of Skye—where he had been strengthening his alliances with both Adonijah Ravenskald and Malcolm MacCleod—stared into the space beyond Morice's head with his jaw set and fists clenched.

"Something bothers ye, John," Sir Humphry said, finding the silence too much for his already agitated nerves. "Something beyond the matter at hand."

"Yes. Quite. Although nothing that concerns ye, Humphry. At least, not directly. I wish to possess a certain object—I expected to have it in my collection months ago—and my lack of success galls me. A temporary setback, however. I take failure as a temporary condition, same as do ye, which is why we are partners."

The way Carteret said 'partners' recalled to Sir Humphry a time he saw an anaconda a ship of his had brought back from Trinidad flicking its tongue at the walls of the barrel the captain had used to contain it.

There were whispers that Carteret was the master of a secret lodge that sacrificed slave girls to a winged, demonic monster.

Watched the RAC's governor clench and unclench his fist in unconscious time with the clenching and unclenching of his jaw as they awaited their guest, Sir Humphry actually began to believe the whispered rumors were true.

Contemplating a new route of questioning to help relieve the painful silence and push the images of Carteret as half man, half snake from his mind, Sir Humphry looked up with relief as the door swung open and he saw the scarred, once-handsome face of the man he saw as the savior of the slave trade.

Captain Woodes Rogers, circumnavigator of the globe and many a man's hero, had finally arrived.

"Apologies, Sir Humphry, Lord Carteret. I was detained by a group of newly commissioned officers at the Admiralty who wished nothing more than a few minutes chat and to have me place my signature in ink in the copies of my book they are all required to read." Due to a missing piece of his lower jawbone and an absence of teeth on the left side of his face where he had taken a musket ball during a sea battle in the Pacific during his privateering days, Rogers was at times hard to understand, though no one dared to tell him so.

"No need for apologies," Sir Humphry said with a smile, pointing to the chair beside him. "Your popularity with both elements of the Royal Navy and the population in general is exactly why we know ye are the man for the job."

Lightly running his nails along the surface of the table, Lord Carteret forced a smile of his own. "Let us talk about this 'job.' Your qualifications as a sea captain, slaver, and privateer are beyond question, but these *pirates*"—again he was the anaconda, complete with an accompanying flick of the tongue—"these are rogues of an unprecedented sort. They feed on the fuel of the sick lie that is the Jacobite uprising. We quell them, although, like a hydra, they return with additional heads. A so-called Robin Hood drowns and in his place rises up some screaming idiot calling himself Blackbeard, threatening to burn the whole of Boston if the colonial governor does not release a handful of his pox-addled brethren! It is no less than anarchy. Killing them piecemeal in ship-to-ship engagements or hanging them half a dozen at a time is no longer feasible. Prior to Sir Humphry's recent and insistent call for action against these outlaws, the Royal Navy has not been sufficiently motivated to aid us. Economic losses mount at alarming rates. The very idea of these *hostis humani generis* turning slaves not only free but *arming* them and indoctrinating their feeble savage minds into their *cause*"—another flick of the tongue after he overemphasized the ess—"is vomitous to me. To *us*."

It seemed he held the ess forever.

"Quite right, Lord John," Sir Humphry said, needing a break from the snake-like sounds. "Our version of the Spanish *pieza* system for determining the asking price of a slave has served to stabilize the empire by allowing our colonies to prosper. Safe sailing lanes for our merchant ships are paramount. We have fought years-long wars over less. The taking of a ship such as the *Whydah* must not go unanswered a moment more. Your thoughts, Captain Rogers?"

The glimmer of unsatisfied vengeance in his eyes pulling attention from the spiderlike scars and missing bone of the lower half of his face—rumor was that he only realized he had swallowed the damned thing when visiting a doctor for intestinal discomfort—Woodes Rogers pulled a sheaf of papers from the inside pocket of his finely tailored coat. "Lord Carteret wishes to speak specifically of the 'job' as ye term it. Very well... the 'job' is the eradication of the pirates, starting with their comical representation of a republic in the Bahamas. I have experience in recent years with doing just this in Madagascar. Similar to what ye are experiencing from the nest of vipers in Nassau, the pirates plying the waters between Madagascar and Mozambique in eastern Africa were disrupting the agreements I had with the East India Company in Sumatra."

Lord Carteret growled under his breath. "Captain Rogers, if you wish to thrive in our employ, ye must *never* mentioned our Leadenhall neighbors ever again, do ye understand me?"

Rogers nodded casually, as he was used to dealing with ruthless, territorial men such as Lord Carteret. After all, he counted himself amongst their number. "As ye know, sir, my financial difficulties began with the broken promises and deceitful dealings of that not-to-be-named horde of scoundrels. The air of fairness in *this* building is refreshing to my nose. As to the requirements of the 'job'... We could not match the pirates of Madagascar—spurred on as they were by the myths of their hero, Henry Every—ship for ship, sword by sword, so I devised a plan. We offered them a pardon."

Lord Carteret laughed. "A pardon? Forgive them, you mean? Let them go unpunished, you suggest? Morice, my friend, I am beginning to think you have chosen our potential jobber rather poorly..."

"The facts and figures demonstrating the success of my decision are all here in these records." Rogers folded his sheaf of papers and placed them back in his pocket. "However, if ye are willing to dismiss the idea so completely out of hand, I have business elsewhere. I am due to meet with Daniel Defoe in a tavern a few streets away."

"Just a moment."

Lord Carteret was no longer laughing. "I do not need to see your facts and figures, Captain Rogers. I shall ponder your idea. It might just be bold and brash enough to work—at least in part. I am curious, though... What business have you with the spy and agitator Defoe?"

Skilled with the pen applied to political purposes in additional to fictional ones, Daniel Defoe had first run afoul of the Crown when he backed the Monmouth Rebellion—a plot to place the illegitimate son of Charles the Second—a Protestant—on the throne in place of the Catholic James the Second. Finding himself on the run—a more preferable fate than execution, which befell the bastard Duke of Monmouth—Defoe soon found himself in debt, resulting in his arrest, trial, and incarceration in Fleet Gaol, a stinking hellhole of a prison. Upon his release, Defoe returned to his work as an agitator and satirist—his target this time being the Tories, who charged him with seditious libel. After his enemies locked him in the pillory, where the always enthusiastic for a little vengeful cruelty masses pummeled him with rotten vegetables, Defoe spent time in Newgate Prison. Taking advantage of a relationship with the rising star that was Robert Harley, Earl of Oxford and Mortimer who soon became Lord High Treasurer—although he fell out of favor after the coronation of George, who blamed him for negotiating the Treaty of Utrecht—Defoe went to Scotland as a spy and agitator. His efforts contributed in some measure to the Treaty of Union and dissolution of the Scottish Parliament.

"A spy and agitator perhaps," Captain Rogers replied, his voice civil and controlled, "but he did his part for God and country as well. He certainly has no love for the Jacobites—something he has in common with all of us. As to his alliance with the former Lord High Treasurer, King George recently had Harley released from the Tower of London. As to why we are meeting, Defoe is working on a new novel about a castaway and wishes to interview me about my rescue of Alexander Selkirk from Más a Tierra in 1709 while William Dampier and I were privateering with the frigates *Duke* and *Duchess*."

Carteret once again growled, followed by a fresh flick of his blood-red tongue. "Selkirk... a Scotsman! And marooned for criticizing his captain! Better ye should have left him to rot on his island, Rogers. As for Harley... he may have been released, but he is banished from court. Sometimes our dear Hanoverian king is too kind. It would have been better to let him rot away. He and Bolingbroke carry the Stuart stench! I have no love for spies and agents... not to be trusted. I tried to turn Bolingbroke to our cause... He shall have his yet."

"Are ye finished with your criticisms of my friend Defoe, sir?" Rogers asked, causing Sir Humphry to cough several times in his worry that the two men were about to come to blows.

"Nearly," Lord Carteret answered, enjoying the mettle of this man. "I hear that Defoe is working on another piece... some celebration of the bastard rogue, Rob Roy Campbell. What is at the root of his unconscionable love of the Scots?"

Rogers rose and headed for the door. "I have not a notion. Although, I shall ask him at our meeting, for which I am perilously close to being late. When ye have made a decision as to my suitability for this 'job,' do let me know, would ye?"

Moving to close and lock the door as Rogers's footsteps echoed down the hall, Sir Humphry turned to his peer. "Before ye dismiss him out of hand, John..."

"You misunderstand me, Humphry. I find him delightfully arrogant and willing to stand his ground. If he is nearly a match for *me*, imagine what a formidable foe he shall be to the pirates. This notion of offering a pardon... I shall take it up with the king at the earliest opportunity. As to his friend Defoe... I believe we may have use of his political skill with the pen." Rising and stretching his black velvet–clad arms in the air, Carteret appeared to Sir Humphry Morice as though he was master of a pair of venomous snakes. "Now, if ye shall excuse me, I have developed an appetite quite voracious and must return to my home."

As Lord Carteret unlocked the door and exited, Sir Humphry knew the food of the civilized man could not satisfy his appetite.

Only slave blood could.

Xavier Hearst, head of the array of advanced projects in development by the Division for Eugenic Design in tandem with the multinational juggernaut The Ravenskald Group, parked his vintage Mercedes sedan where the facility security guards had directed him and removed his sunglasses, allowing his lizard-like yellow eyes to transform into a hypnotic shade of almost translucent blue.

Since the launch of the planned, high-tech community of Storm Haven in New Jersey nearly four years earlier, Hearst—who had always preferred to stick close to home—rarely left TRG headquarters, also known as Solomon's Temple, a nod to the first name of TRG's CEO and chairman of the board. If the situation was truly serious, those involved came to face his wrath in his suite of secure offices in Storm Haven. Otherwise, the holographic communication technology he had developed with the Defense Advanced Research Projects Agency—known inside the Beltway and elsewhere as DARPA—and the trio of DED divisions under the supervision of the Navy admiral he had traveled to eastern Ohio to meet was almost as good as being there.

Just ask anyone who had spent any virtual time with the diminutive yet frightening chief technology officer. Especially if he chose to let them see his cold, lizard-like eyes.

"Xavier. Thanks for making the trek. I promise it's worth your while."

As Hearst placed his hand on the biosensor pad that granted access to the most heavily guarded and secret of the U.S. Navy's Research Labs—designated U5-AIE—he glanced up at the speaker implanted in the wall, from where the voice had come.

"It had better be," Hearst replied, placing his arms horizontally out from his body and slightly spreading his legs as a nervous MP moved a security wand around the contours of his body.

"All clean, Admiral," the MP said, obvious relief in his voice.

"Protocols, Xavier. I am sure you understand. This way, my friend."

Admiral Christopher Adler, his silver-grey hair buzzed nearly to the scalp on the sides and back, pointed his guest into a dimly lit room containing a bank of quantum computers and a dozen large-screen 5K monitors split between two walls.

"All seven divisions of the DED at a glance," he said. "We'll have the feed fully operational for you at TRG Tower within forty-eight hours."

"Excellent." Moving his eyes rapidly from monitor to monitor, Hearst felt as close to joy as his mostly for show heart would allow. Within the workspaces of the various divisions he saw sound and EM weapons, psychological experiments, reverse engineering of alien craft, psy-ops experiments, wounded warrior rehabilitation/alteration/enhancement, and interspecies hybridization.

All made possible because of him.

"So... what is so secret I had to travel to this refuse can of maggots its governor calls a state? I am already feeling in need of a chemical bath to cleanse me..."

Unaccustomed to being spoken to in such a way—the admiral called the current U.S. president by his college nickname—Adler removed a key from around his neck, punched a series of coded symbols into a keypad lit by a foreboding red light, and pointed to a monitor that was emerging from a niche in the wall behind them.

"This is a live feed from one of our SSN-774 Virginia-class attack subs. It is currently off the coast of North Korea. Forgive me if I don't tell you her name."

"If I wanted to find and fuck her, Admiral, I would find it out on my own. And send you pictures of what I did to her, as I did it."

How many years until retirement and outrageous speaking fees? Adler thought, keeping his eyes on the screen. "She isn't running on her nuclear plant. Not since about a week ago."

Adler could hear what sounded like a series of clicks and hisses from beside him as Hearst began to smile.

"The Ezekiel Wheel?"

"Per your request. Once our extraction team delivered it, our best and brightest—along with some former Skunkers we spirited away—made the necessary modifications. The output of that device is—"

"You did your part, Admiral," Hearst said, turning for the door. "Leave it at that. How soon can you have it delivered to my office?"

"I'm confused," Adler said, feeling a headache starting just behind his left eye. "I thought we would reverse engineer it and make enough for the six dozen Virginia-class subs. Their enhanced logistical and weapons capabilities would change the tactical game in every sector of the world..."

"I asked *when*."

"Seventy-two hours, tops."

"Is that all, Admiral?"

The headache was now behind both of Adler's eyes. "Unfortunately not. The former XO of SEAL Team D, Ishmael Ramsay, has gone missing from DED 67. He was there for debriefing and because he is an excellent candidate for Project RUS."

"Yes..." Hearst whispered, sounding like a bushmaster before it bites. "Rehabilitate, Utilize, Specialize... Ramsay has spent time at Quarry Peak, in our psychological enhancement program, has he not? What resources have you mobilized?"

"His former XO, Abel Black—head of the Kardax Corporation, as you know... Mister Ravenskald cleared it. Black's reputation is beyond reproach."

Again came the hiss of the ready-to-bite bushmaster. "Black *shall* find Ramsay and, as long as we can track Black, all will be well. Another of our 'projects' is an open asset at present. CPO Givens is working on his son for us. With the correct amount of adjustment to his medications and neural chip—some further *conditioning*—he should succeed in having his son lead us to what we want from Kirstine MacGregor, despite Reinhardt's stupidity..."

Remind me never to be in an unmonitored environment with this psychopath, Adler thought, turning on his best commencement-at-the-Academy smile. "Givens will live up, Xavier. As will Abel Black. I assure you. These entities they fought in the Middle East..."

"Careful, Admiral. Speak their name and they appear."

Then Xavier Hearst was gone, and Adler, the pain in his eyes now so severe he could barely see, collapsed into a chair and wept.

Not since his days of sailing with Bellamy, Williams, and Levasseur had Conall MacBlaquart felt so full to the brim with purpose, strength, and hope.

Blackbeard had assigned him to the sloop *Revenge* as his representative, overseeing the repairs to the ship and, more important, gauging—and reporting on nightly—the mood, disposition, and overall qualifications of Major Bonnet's crew. As for Bonnet himself, although his wounds were healing rapidly, he spent most of his time drinking, eating, singing, and telling tales in the taverns rather than onboard *Revenge*.

Blackbeard could not have been more pleased.

On this particular morning, Conall was taking inventory of cordage, sheets, and supplies in the hold while trading stories with Caesar, whose growing fondness for and proximity to Conall both Blackbeard and Benjamin Hornigold were encouraging.

"I have feen-ished counting all of the candles, Capee-tano Conall MacBlaquart!" Caesar yelled out, slapping his hands together just as Conall was finishing the story about falling into the cattle pen one month less than three years ago in Balquidder in the Scottish Highlands when he was still Angus MacGregor, nephew of Rob Roy and victim of his cousins' relentless bullying.

How very long ago that seemed. How unthinkable that he would allow himself to be spoken to and handled in that way.

"Ad-meer-al Beard-Black will be very proud of Caesar. Caesar who is me!"

"Wael doon, Caesar!" Conall replied, banishing the past from his mind and putting a thick black line through *candles* on his task list.

"Who calls heemself Caesar on thees vessel?"

Looking behind him, Conall saw a recent arrival on the island, a Spaniard who had defected from a fort in Florida to try his luck with the pirates of Nassau. He was the kind of gruff, always tensed-up sort that Conall had no interest in being around, but Blackbeard had assigned him to *Revenge* within a few hours of his disembarking and asking around for a new situation.

Before Conall could stop him, Caesar, always friendly and energetic, moved past, halting himself a few feet from the Spaniard. "Cae-sar is me! Ask any-one and they will tell you this thing!"

Crouching so he could look the boy in the eyes, the Spaniard said, "They may call you thees, *mijo*, but thees ees not your name... Me think that someone ees fooling you... Someone *muy loco, si?* Slaves are never named for kings."

Taking Caesar gently by the shoulders and moving him back a few feet, Conall said to the Spaniard, "I nae mean tae bae sair, boot ye should bae tarrin' the riggin' as ye haev baen assigned. *Si?*"

Rising to his full, considerable height, the Spaniard took a step toward Caesar and Conall. "I know my duty, *besador des cerdos*! You hold no authority over me! And thees... *esclavo sucio* thinking he ees a king because of a joking name..."

Sending Caesar on deck to fetch him a fresh pair of quills, Conall stepped in close to the Spaniard. "I cannae recall yer name, big yin..."

"I am Alvarado César, descended from Capitan Francisco César, the great leader of *conquistadores*, who fearlessly led hees men through the perilous jungles of Peru two hundred years ago to find the fabled *Ciudad de los Césares*, the city of the Caesars, under the orders of the Venetian Sebastian Cabot. A city between two mountains in the Andes, overflowing weeth gold and vast fields of tobacco. A city by a lake, a true *paraíso, si?*"

"Did he find it?" Conall asked, knowing in his heart what the answer must be.

The Spaniard spit on the ground between his adversary's boots. "*Cuida tu boca*! Your mouth ees making for you trouble. Do not play with me, *usted amante de las ovejas—sin*ful lover of sheep—I warn you! Thees brave journey of exploration was just the start of my great family's contributions to the world and to *España*! Césars were weeth the hero Francisco Pizarro when he conquered the Incas! They were by hees side when he first converted the Incan emperor Atahualpa to save hees soul before sending him on to collect hees *recompensa eterna*! So do not make me suffer to hear that *esclavo sucio* calling heemself a Caesar! Not in the presence of a descendent of the mighty *conquistadores*! And one who ees named for Pedro de Alvarado y Contreras, governor of Guatemala, subduer of Cuba, and conqueror of Mexico alongside Cortés!"

Although he did not understand much of the Spanish language, Conall knew that, in the span of a few minutes, Alvarado César had called Conall—in addition to a lover of sheep—a kisser of pigs. Further, he had twice called Caesar a dirty slave.

Such insults could not stand. Conall's days of suffering at the words of bullies were done.

"Ack! I cannae ken this pride ye haev aboot the *conquistadores*, big yin. Mae bae baecause I knoo them bae anoother name— *carniceros*. Butchers. And *bastard* butchers at that!"

In response—and Conall had now been around enough to know exactly where their conversation had been heading—Alvarado César pulled a blade from his boot and swung it with deadly intent at Conall's midsection.

Anticipating the move, Conall arched his back, escaping disembowelment but losing his balance. As he fell into a barrier of barrels and crates, the Spaniard was upon him, pulling his arm back to deliver a powerful thrust to the center of Conall's chest, a move against which the Scot could not defend himself.

So Conall closed his eyes, and prayed the end would come to him quick, knowing it was better to die fighting for justice than silently prolonging one's life.

Instead of the insertion of the knife, Conall heard the sound of dry twigs breaking, followed by the Spaniard screaming words the Scotsman did not understand but could tell were both blasphemous and cruel.

"Leave alone my Capee-tano Conall MacBlaquart!" Caesar was yelling as Conall opened his eyes. As the African boy stood at the entrance to the hold, some fifteen feet away, he held his arm out straight in front of him, his fingers curled as if they were holding a length of wood.

Before him on the ground, his face a mask of pain, his knife sticking straight up from the decking, Alvarado César was cradling his arm, which hung at an unnatural, grotesque angle.

It was not the sound of snapping twigs, but of bones, that Conall had heard.

"Crawl away and attend to your arm, you vay-ree bad man, or I shall snap the other one," Caesar warned, his teeth clenched and eyes ablaze with focused concentration. "But first, apologize to the Capee-tano for your rude language and ill intents!"

"*Lo siento*, Capitan," the Spaniard whispered. "I lost my head and I am sorry. Forgive me."

Conall nodded. "Haev that arm attended tae. Blackbeard weel bae sair as hell aboot the trouble ye haev caused."

Once the Spaniard had gone, Caesar's powerful, unnatural eyes following him all the way, Conall stood and brushed himself off. "I cannae ken hoo ye managed tae break a man's arm from so far away, boot I am grateful tae ye, mate."

Dropping his arm, Caesar quickly returned to the jovial boy everyone knew and cared for. "Obeah is vay-ree powerful for the Ashanti, Capee-tano. To be used though wisely but when needed. My grandfather Kwasi, who I miss so, so, so, so much, taught me this when I was only just barely walking. I could not have you dying... I love you too much!"

Conall smiled. "I care fer ye as weel, mae fraend. Ye bae careful with that Obeah, ken? The less who knoo what ye caen doo with it, the baetter."

"Cae-sar shall do as you say, beeg yeen Capee-tano! Unless the trouble is mighty... then it is Jumbee and what happened to Devon Ross..."

Before Conall could ask what Caesar knew about Joseph Stanton's murderous mentor, Blackbeard had descended the stairs, an unpleasant look in his eyes. "What has happened?" he asked, his tone a clear indication of his anger. "Alvarado César's arm is broken in two places! He will be next to worthless when we sail in a handful of days. He claims it was an accident, but I see his knife there in the decking. I want answers, Mister MacBlaquart. *Now.*"

Pulling the knife from the deck and handing it handle first to his captain, Conall said, "Difference of opinion. Hae nae cares fer Caesar's name. Nae fitting fer a slave..."

Slipping the knife into his belt, Blackbeard clenched his hands into a pair of menacing fists. "Again ye are on about slavery! I have had with ye, Conall! I have recruited one hundred more men for the crew, added another brace of cannon, and I am determined to make sail for the Florida Straits within the week. Ye are to study the crew, not provoke them! If they do not trust ye, they shall dissemble in your presence! Protect and look after Caesar as we have tasked ye with— at least until we run into that scoundrel Abriendo—but enough with the antislavery palaver, *ken*?"

"Aye," Conall said, cursing himself for sounding afraid. "Though I haev tae ask—meanin' nae disraespect—why is this Spaniard soo important?"

Stepping in close and lowering his voice, Blackbeard answered, "I have recruited César to be a spy... To help Major Bonnet get his revenge on Amaro Pargo. His knowledge of the Florida Staits shall prove an advantage to us as well." Though his tone remained hard as an anvil, Blackbeard's words now softened. "Do not displease me further, Conall. I need ye. The quill to my cannon, yes?"

"Aye," Conall said, though he was only now beginning to understand the true implications of what this partnership might one day require him to do.

L t. Robert Maynard, second in command of the Royal Navy forty-two-gun Fourth-Rate HMS *Pearl*, had been searching for a diversion for the better part of the afternoon, and it seemed he had finally found it.

Enduring another tongue-lashing about his *outsized* ambitions from his captain, George Gordon, Maynard had informed the junior officers after the captain had departed that he was going ashore for the evening as well, and that they should handle the watch until morning.

Descending the gangway and stepping onto the dock, Maynard took a moment to get his land legs while considering his options for the night. First, a decent cigar and bottle of claret at a comfortable inn—perhaps the Bull and Bowl. Then a bit of companionship—and not from a tavern owner's daughter—followed by a good meal and more of his yet-to-be-identified companion's companionship.

Then, near a fish-hawker's cart, sea bag held too tightly to be a local and draped in an oversized green cloak tailored for someone two times her size, there she was—the answer to his dilemma.

"New to Hampton, miss?" He asked, glad that he had left the ship in full lieutenant's regalia, complete with his cleanest shirt and new length of jet-black ribbon securing his long blond hair. "I would be pleased to get you acquainted—with coastal Virginia as well as with myself."

Grasping her sea bag tighter, the target of Maynard's interest blew a lock of bright red hair from her freckled forehead. "I am nae hair fer long," she replied, her thick brogue agitating his ears, but not to the point of abandoning his plan. After all, her form was fine and her porcelain shine complimented his own lightly tanned skin. "I seek passage tae Nassau as soon as—"

"Nassau?" Maynard interrupted, a bit too harshly, judging by the widening and then squinting of his target's glass-green eyes. "A den of rats and vipers if ever there was one, m'lady. A very dangerous place. Full of beggars, whores, and the worst sort of degenerates—*pirates*. If I had my druthers, we would wipe them out, hanging twenty or thirty at a go, instead of wasting time guarding these merchantmen in the harbor."

"I thank ye fer yer warnin'," the girl replied, an edge to her voice that Maynard found intriguing. He had experience with Highland lasses, as they called themselves, and they never disappointed.

"Boot I nae haev a choice. I haev traveled froom Glasgow, Loondon, an' Boston since March."

"Your reason must be important," Maynard said, resisting the urge to stroke her porcelain hand with his fingertips. She was not even nibbling at the little bit of bait he had cast into the creek, so he knew he was far from landing her. The tease was half the sport and Maynard could be patient.

Hell, he had made a career of it, watching other men make captain while the curmudgeonly rule-stickler Gordon held him down with the heel of his high-shine boot.

"Aye," the girl replied, her tone softening just enough to signal to Maynard progress. "Important business indeed. I am goin' tae aid mae, ah... *broother*, at the request a' mae da. Hae roons a tavern thair..."

"I see," Maynard said, not certain he believed her and not caring either way. He suddenly had his angle. "I am about to dine at a very top-notch tavern, the Bull and Bowl, not far from here at all. I think, if ye join me, ye shall learn a great deal that would be helpful to your... *brother*, was it?"

"I nae knoo what tae say," the girl replied, an uncertainty in her eyes that Maynard would have to navigate with care. "I nae knoo yer name..."

"Of course... How ungentlemanly of me. I am Lieutenant Robert Maynard, of His Majesty's Royal Navy. See that specimen of a warship, just anchored there? She is the *Pearl*, and more often than not, she is under my command, as our captain is rarely aboard. And ye are?"

The girl curtsied and said, "I am Ailish MacDonald. I thank ye fer yer offer, Lietenant, boot I am tired. Mae ship only raecently arrived an' I haev mooch tae doo tae make mae arrangements in Hampton. I wish you—"

"Now, now," Maynard said, grasping her by the shoulders as she began to turn away, "Ye must not be hasty. It is just a meal. Some pleasant conversation. Although, if ye are in need of a bed, I am sure I can arrange it. After all, how often have ye had the opportunity to dine with a Royal Navy man, and one at the top of the staff of a celebrated Man o' War?"

"I couldnae say... Boot if ye weel oon-hand mae, I weel bae on mae way..."

"Unhand ye? No need to be unkind. We are just having a conversation, which shall flow all the easier after a glass of claret..." Maynard bent his head to her neck to take in her scent.

"Ock! Yer hurtin' mae arms! Please… let mae—"

"Damn ye to Hell, Maynard! Let that child go! Have ye no manners at all?"

Maynard clenched his teeth at the voice of Captain Gordon.

"I meant no offense to Miss MacDonald," Maynard said, squeezing Ailish's arms in his pincer-like hands before letting her go. "Just trying to help a poor, lost lamb navigate the weeds."

"I very much doubt that," Gordon replied, his demeanor laced with disdain. "Come away from him, my girl. On behalf of His Majesty's fleet, I apologize for my subordinate's behavior. Let me make it up to ye." Handing her several coins, the captain pointed to a two-story building just up the thoroughfare. "I highly recommend the King's Arms Inn. Mention my name, Captain George Gordon of the *Pearl*. It is where I am staying. The owner, Missus Clark, will see ye well set up."

"Thank ye," Ailish whispered, accepting the coins and departing.

"Unbelievable," Gordon said with disgust. "I swear to God, Lieutenant… If ye do not shape yourself up, I shall be forced—"

"To transfer me to Ellis Brand's command on the *Lyme*?" Maynard asked, too thoroughly frustrated physically and mentally to temper his tongue.

"That shall never happen," Gordon answered, "although ye and your co-conspirator will be in each other's company on the morrow. Brand arrives on the evening tide with Governor Spotswood. They have been touring the forts and batteries along the coast. These damned pirates are having their way along the Carolinas, and we shall not have it in Virginia."

"Finally some sensible talk," Maynard said, retreating a step. "If ye will excuse me, Captain… all is in hand on the *Pearl*. I am spending the evening at the Bull and Bowl. Most likely alone, thanks to your intervention…"

Gordon shook his head. "Whatever privileges ye may think ye have earned have been erased by your treatment of that girl and your vile tone with me. Ye shall report back to the *Pearl* with all haste until I summon ye for our meeting with the governor in the morning."

Finding his best—and only—option to consult with Captain Brand at the earliest opportunity, Maynard saluted his captain and turned for the gangway.

He would find a way out of Gordon's grasp no matter what it cost.

As for Ailish MacDonald, he would see her paid for her slight.

Charles Vane, captain of the pirate sloop *Ranger*, pulled his frockcoat tighter around him as he sat behind his desk in his cabin. *I have grown too used to the high temperatures and oppressive humidity of the islands*, he thought, pulling the cork from the neck of an onion bottle nearly devoid of rum with his teeth and taking the remainder of its contents into his throat.

With the hand not holding the now empty bottle, Vane held the collection of Shakespeare's plays that had occupied the bulk of his waking hours ever since they had anchored off the coast of Rhode Island, on orders of Absalom Ravenskald, to lie in wait for Olivier Levasseur five days earlier. Pushing his way past the comedies, for which he had no use, and the histories—which he had lived long enough under the thumb and boot of Empire to know were the same story of subjugation and lack of soul of the supposed aristocracy merely told in different decades—Vane turned to his favorite of the thirty-seven scripts.

Perhaps it was the opening storm and shipwreck—and their implications for the conflict between the ruling and servant classes—or the fact that *The Tempest* took place on an island. Then again, it might be that Vane had his very own Caliban in *Faccia del Diavolo*, his quartermaster Devon Ross. No matter the reason, the *Ranger*'s captain knew what it *wasn't*. The play dealt far too much with magic, and if Vane knew anything, it was that magic was utter bullshit.

Or, he *had*, until recently. After all, was he not here, off the coast of Rhode Island, a veritable nothing of a colony, waiting to intercept a ship carrying a pair of magical items that Ravenskald had told him were older than the stories of the Bible and more powerful than he could possibly imagine?

Turning the water-stained tome's thin, easily tearable pages, Vane reached for a full bottle of rum from the shelf to his left, as his eyes fell upon the words, "Hell is empty and all the devils are here."

This was certainly true. But Hell was not a place of magic, nor were devils its practitioners. How could they be? Devils like Ravenskald and Ross did not traffic in magic... they trafficked in power and the blade, same as Vane himself.

An' there ain't a thing magical about me, he thought, again using his teeth to release a cork and the liquid relief beneath it. *I just knows how ta harness the natural anger a' those who 'ave also been undah the thumb an' boot...* Then, after another long drink, he said aloud, quoting from the book, "This thing of darkness I acknowledge mine," before flipping more pages and settling his pointer finger on his favorite passage of all:

"Full fathom five thy father lies;
Of his bones are coral made;
Those are pearls that were his eyes:
Nothing of him that doth fade,
But doth suffer a sea-change
Into something rich and strange.
Sea-nymphs hourly ring his knell: Ding-dong
Hark! now I hear them,—Ding-dong, bell."

He read it once aloud and, dissatisfied with how his clumsy reading sounded, Vane cleared his throat, took another swig of rum, and standing, repeated it again, slowly and more loudly.

"...Hark! now I hear them,—Ding-dong, bell."

As if in answer, though Vane knew better, he heard the clang of the *Ranger*'s bell and a voice from high in the rigging: "Sail ho!"

"An' so the Frenchie bastahd fin'lly arrives," Vane said, slamming the book closed so it resounded like a pistol shot and the cork back into the now half-empty bottle with the flat of his hand.

"Permission ta enter, Cap'n."

Hell is empty and all the devils are here.

"Entah, Mistah Ross, if ya please."

This thing of darkness I acknowledge mine.

There he stood, in the doorway, like a spectre.

"We 'ave spotted the Frenchman's flag. I 'ave called fer the assemblage of a boardin' party."

Slinging his baldric over his shoulder, Vane sent his sword home into its scabbard with enough force to make it sound like a pistol shot, as he had with the book. Then, checking a pair of actual pistols to be sure they were charged and ready to fire, he stuck them into his sash.

"Very good, Mistah Ross. I shall be joinin' ye, a' course."

"As I anticipated, Cap'n."

Half an hour later, despite the copious amount of rum he had consumed, Vane stood near the quarterdeck of the ship they had just boarded, stone cold sober due to the anger that was welling up inside him like the lava from a soon-to-erupt volcano on some distant, unnamed island.

The bastard Frenchman had duped him, and now he played the Fool.

Although the ship had bore the flag of La Bouche, it bore no sign of Olivier Levasseur. Upon closer examination, despite its cannon and the dress of the men who lined its gunnals, the vessel was merely a merchantman packed with worthless items.

It was not even worth burning, although Vane might do so just for spite.

Questioning the captain—a frail old Dutchman who pissed his pants and vacated his bowels simultaneously as Vane drew a pistol and his sword—he and Ross soon learned that Levasseur had paid the captain to fly the Frenchman's flag. Being that the Dutchman's voyage had been full of bad luck and his return home was sure to see him retired, he took the payment in gratitude, without question, and sailed for the spot to which Levasseur had directed him.

The deeper he looked into the old man's eyes and the more the smell of his urine and feces filled his nose, the less inclined Vane was to spend the time it would take to properly burn the vessel.

Instead, after ordering Levasseur's flag lowered and brought to him, he used it to have the captain mop up most of his fetid mess, directing Ross to fetch a sack in which to store the soiled cloth until Vane had an opportunity to suffocate the crafty fucking Frenchman with it.

Back on board the *Ranger*, Vane lit a pipe and watched the Dutchman sail away.

"I request permission ta speak freely, Cap'n."

Once again, the devil was at his door.

"If ye feel the need, Ross..."

Entering the cabin and closing the door behind him, *Faccia del Diavolo* nodded. "I do. I owe ya, Cap'n. I truly do. Ya took me into yer crew, made me quartermaster, an' 'ave been all too forgivin' a' my mistakes."

Vane, taking off his baldric and putting up his pistols, fell heavily into his chair. "Maybe 'tis the crushin' disappointment a' the evenin's events, but I feel a but comin' on... So out wit' it, Mistah Ross, so's I can return ta my readin' an' a little bit a' sleep before figurin' out 'ow ta save yer 'ide an' mine..."

Remaining near the door, the middle finger of his left hand in contact with the hilt of his knife—Vane doubted he was even aware of it—Ross said, making every effort to sound respectful, "'Tis jus' this... Why the 'ell are we fightin' as pirates when we are now yoked like oxen ta Ravenskald's cart? Defeats the fuckin' purpose, seems ta me. Sure, we 'ave taken our lumps—ye an' me both—but the men believes in ya, Cap'n. Even that surly misfit Stanton. They would follow ye ta the gates a' 'Ades 'erself. Alls ya 'ave ta do is order the settin' a' the course. But ta sit here, bein' made fools a' yet again… That will not track, Cap'n. Not fer a moment, an' sure as 'ell not 'til mornin'.'"

Vane nearly smiled, so impressed was he by the size of the balls on this half-faceless Caliban before him.

"Ta another cap'n, that might all sound like a threat, Ross. But I know bettah. Fact is, yer right. But do not think fer a second I 'ave gone soft. Far from. So 'ere it is, all laid out fer ya… Tomorrow mornin' before dawn, we sail south off the Atlantic coast, toward where I 'ear on good authority Edward Thache—who now goes 'clusively by the nom de guerre a' Blackbeard—is sailin' fer. That bein' Delaware or Jersey. Been ravagin' 'round Virginia, my sources say, despite a 'eavy naval presence. Once we rendezvous, I intend ta convince 'im 'tis time ta take the Bahamas an' make 'em what they oughta be— the centahpiece of a pirate fleet that can strike at will, an' wit' fiercesome power an' numbahs, anywhere it wishes. I am guessin' after the death a' that damned idealist Bellamy, 'e 'as finally come ta 'is senses. We can practice on this ex slavah Rhett off a' South Carolina on our way… sharpen our mutual swords on the whetstone of 'is face, if ya will… No offense, Ross… Some big-balled bastard like yerself blockaded Charles Town not one month ago. Time is now." Then, taking a sizable puff on his pipe and exhaling it through his nose, Vane asked, "Satified, Ross?"

"Fully, Cap'n. An' I appreciate the indulgence. Although, just one more thing… What about the Ravenskalds an' their guard dog Carteret?"

Placing his hand on the collection of Shakespeare, Vane said, "Remember what is said in *The Tempest*, my wicked, twisted Caliban… 'What is past is prologue.' Them bastahds are pure prologue. Our story is the one about ta start up propah, an', like the magician Prospero, I shall ring it in wit' a devastatin' storm."

As Vane quoted Shakespeare off the Rhode Island coast, Edward Thache—(the soon to be infamous) Blackbeard—was seven days into what would be a highly successful trio of weeks. Captaining Major Stede Bonnet's custom sloop *Revenge* while its former captain read his books and drank his tea in an embroidered, fur-trimmed robe and cap in his quarters as agreed, Blackbeard captured eighteen ships. The latest prize was the merchant vessel *Betty*, which its captain readily revealed to have its holds full of Madeira—always highly in demand and easily converted to coin.

Thus far, the ill-tempered Spaniard, Alvarado César, had proven himself as useful as Blackbeard had hoped he would be. It was his knowledge of the waters off Florida—and the habits of those who sailed them—that had gotten their voyage off to a successful start. César also had the ability to build a new type of hand grenade that was less likely to explode prematurely, which burned hotter and longer than did its more primitive predecessors.

Blackbeard was not the only one who found himself increasingly impressed by the crafty Spanish spy. William Howard, newly appointed quartermaster of *Revenge*, with the help of César, had drilled a series of perfectly placed holes in the *Betty*'s hull to sink it. Stede had come up from his cabin after the boarding parties had returned and tried to offer his help in the matter of the disposal of the *Betty*, but Blackbeard, and in no way kindly, quickly reminded the bought-and-sold major of their agreement, causing Bonnet to retreat with no further comment.

To all that he encountered, Blackbeard presented himself with full commitment and vigor as the daunting, half-crazed figure history (often inaccurately) remembers. Two slow fuses to a side burned beneath the rim of his tricorne, reddening his face and not only reflecting but *magnifying* the ill intent in his eyes. Upon his long, broad torso he wore three braces of pistols, always primed and ready to fire. His beard, which hung to the hammer of his topmost pistol, he kept braided and adorned with bright red ribbons, the color of the blood he hoped his presentation and appearance would prevent him from ever having to spill.

In the quiet moments between the chasing, capturing, and boarding of ships, Blackbeard thought of Samuel Bellamy. What was Black Sam thinking as he looked down upon his former friend from the firmament?

Blackbeard hoped that he was pleased. After all, although its most promising days were certainly behind it, the Republic of Pirates was not dead. To the contrary, the previous day, as the sun rose, the *Revenge* had rendezvoused with Benjamin Hornigold's latest sloop, the *Runner*, with its twenty-six guns and dozens of seasoned, loyal crew. Together they had most efficiently tracked, chased, and captured a merchant ship from Liverpool under the command of the agreeable and accommodating Captain Codd. A handful of hours later they had taken another merchantman, from a Captain Pritchard from St. Lucie, whose initial bravado as William Howard made their demands came to an abrupt, embarrassing end as Pritchard caught sight of Blackbeard coming over the gunnal, after which he promptly pissed his britches and assisted Howard any way he could.

Sitting in the cabin of the *Runner* twenty-four hours after their reunion, Blackbeard pushed his empty breakfast plate away and slapped the table at which he and Hornigold sat. "I do not understand ye, Benjamin! The prey is easy. We have met with a level of success neither of us anticipated. Samuel was right… the *pretense* of violence *prevents* it! If we keep the prizes small and spread out, we will not be worth the Royal Navy's trouble… sail with me, as we always planned! Jennings is capable, yes, but he is not destined to be the commodore of New Providence. *Ye* are! In his heart, Sam always knew it. That bastard Levasseur poisoned his mind… But he came to his senses, as I knew he would. Do not sit there in silence, Benjamin! Explain to me your decision to go south when we are only just beginning our conquest."

Pulling his pipe from the pocket of his coat, Hornigold took his time packing and lighting it. "As ye say, Edward, Jennings is capable but no commodore. He still grieves his falling out with his former pupil Vane and I do not think he believes any more in our vision of a proper republic of pirates. Perhaps he never did."

Blackbeard slammed the table again, this time hard enough to make the plates rattle. "All the more reason to return only when ye have more ships and men to support your authority and your coffers are full to overflowing!"

"We do not have the time for such a plan, my overly excitable friend." Hornigold's voice was soft. He was playing his role as Gran'pa to the hilt. "I spoke at length to Captain Codd. Prior to his leaving Liverpool, he heard a bit of scuttlebutt from the owners of his ship that Humphry Morice had convinced other slave traders that the solution to their problems was installing their own man in the Bahamas to deal with cold, extreme violence against us."

"Is that so?"Blackbeard whispered, leaning in and raising an eyebrow. "And who might this man be?"

Leaning in to meet him, Hornigold responded, "Captain Woodes Rogers. Have ye heard of him?"

Gritting his teeth, Blackbeard growled, "Rogers… I have heard of him indeed. Our own Major Bonnet talks as though he is God. Reads his book as though it were the Bible. Ambitious, Rogers is. Tough as a blacksmith's anvil. Not much to look at after taking a musketball to the face, but certainly one worth navigating with a certain amount of caution. Just like that bastard Rhett down in Carolina. Both equally able to work with and against the authorities, as it suits their needs and plans. We would do well to learn from them, sir. Their ways will eventually become ours, if we wish to survive."

Puffing his pipe, Hornigold slowly nodded. "Mayhap so. Come with me, Edward. The Bahamas can be saved, but I cannot do it alone. Perhaps, together, we can light a fire under Jennings. Whether or not the rumors of Rogers are true, Morice and his murder of crows will surely send *someone* to do their bidding. They are taking far too great a loss at our hands to ignore us any longer."

Rising from his chair, Blackbeard placed his hands upon the butts of his middle brace of pistols. "I cannot do as ye ask. I am sailing tomorrow for Delaware, and then on to Philadelphia. I have some experience and allies there from my early days as a privateer, and the pickings are even easier than they are here. It shall also put me closer to Boston, where I may yet have my revenge, depending on the outcome of the upcoming trials. I promise to return to New Providence when my plans for the present have run their course. I hope that shall suffice."

Extending his hand as he stood, Hornigold said, as Blackbeard took his hand in his own, "Indeed, my friend, it shall."

Sitting low in the stern of the longboat carrying him to the shores of the Isle of Man—above which rose the formidable towers of the stronghold Castle Rushen—George Seton, former Fifth Earl of Winston, urepentent Jacobite, and aided escapee from the Tower of London—clutched the burlap bag that contained the Baptist Bowl and said a prayer to God.

Not that God would venture anywhere near such a place as this.

Seton had studied the history of the Ravenskalds, including this house of war, in the months since his release from the Tower, hoping to find some clue as to how he could manage to retain his soul in the aftermath of what he was about to do.

The Kings of Mann built Castle Rushen in the late twelfth century. They only ruled from the comfort of its keep, however, until 1265, when, after the death of Magnús Óláfsson, the Ravenskalds had adopted it as their own. Consult the historical record, and you will see that Robert the Bruce and Edward Longshanks each held it for periods of time in the early 1300s, and Queen Elizabeth had ordered the building of the clock tower in 1597. This is a tiny matter. Although they may have been the castle's inhabitants, or controlled the island on which it sat, they answered to the Ravenskalds, or a more pliable tenant was enthroned.

Over time, the Ravenskalds had added to the fortress, protecting its entrance with a drawbridge, gatehouse, and porticullises designed to allow death to rain down upon all those who might try to take it.

None ever did. The mission would be suicide, even for the most highly trained of men.

The custodians of record at present were the Stanleys, who had worked with the Ravenskalds during their engineering of the English Civil War, playing the enthusiastic Royalists against the actors chosen to play the allies of Oliver Cromwell. One Stanley in particular had tickled the Ravenskalds' fancy— Ferdinando, known as Baron Straunge, who was not only at one time in the line of succession of Elizabeth the First, but found himself poisoned for the privilege.

History points its finger at the anti-Papists, who were convinced that Baron Straunge was a secret Catholic, despite the fact that he turned over a potential co-conspirator, Richard Hesketh, to the authorities. In truth, a steward in the employ of the Ravenskalds poured a vial of arsenic into Straunge's wine. Whether or not a Papist held the throne was in itself of zero interest to the Ravenskalds. Ferdinando's death centered on what he did or did not know about the coded manuscripts of Marlowe, Kidd, and Shakespeare—all of whom he supported in their careers. Some thought that Shakespeare had even been a member of Ferdinando's theatre troupe, Lord Strange's Men, before he went out on his own. What a struggling young writer–Rosicrucian might say to such a powerful man, one could only guess, and the Ravenskalds preferred to conduct their affairs by erring always on the side of prevention.

Would such be the case this evening, George Seton thought, as he stepped past the main gates and into the castle proper, *even though I turn over the Baptist Bowl and swear my allegiance to their cause?*

He was soon to find out.

Before a roaring fire in the central fireplace on the far side of the keep stood Adonijah Ravenskald, wearing a set of expensive-looking floor-length robes. In his right hand, he held a long wooden staff.

"George! Welcome to Castle Rushen. We have waited *ages* for you to come!"

Flinching as the doors were slammed closed and locked behind him, Seton thought it best to explain the delay without waiting a moment longer.

"I had every intention of coming to ye sooner, Lord Ravenskald," he stuttered, taking a few steps forward before stopping himself. His knees were shaking with such ferocity he was worried he would fall and damage the skull on the rough stone floor. "But there were complications when I reached the north of Orkney."

"Do tell me more," Adonijah said, his voice reverberating off the six-hundred-year-old walls of the keep.

"I met the Templar agents sent by Archibald Sinclair as planned, who gave to me the skull of the Baptist to deliver to the Freemasons in London... I have it here in this bag... but before I could depart I was forced to hide for a time on the Isle of Rousay due to the feeling of being... *watched*."

"Watched by *whom*?"

Seton felt sweat begin to drip from under his arms although the keep was cold and damp. "I assume it was the Freemasons... That in truth they do not trust me. Perhaps because they do not trust Colson and Bolingbroke, who made possible my escape after turning traitors to Lord Carteret. I swore an oath to the Masons, My Lord... an oath that all of us take seriously. An oath that, should it be broken, will invite all manner of unpleasant harms."

Adonijah made a sound that resembled a fox at work in the hen house. "I solemnly promise to be as the Sphinx. That I will not write nor share these, our sacred secrets. Nor print, carve, nor engrave, nor otherwise delineate them. Nor cause or suffer them to be so done by others, if in my power to prevent it. *Blah, blah, blah…* I do so freely, under no less a penalty, on the violation of any of them, than to have my throat cut across, my tongue torn out by the root and buried in the sand of the sea at low water mark, or a cable's length from the shore, where the tides regularly ebb and flow twice in twenty-four hours."

"How do you—"

"Because a Ravenskald wrote them, you fool. Well… did you, Seton?"

"Did I what, My Lord?"

"Do so freely?"

"I did."

Adonijah shook his head. "Then you are, my friend, well and truly fucked. So let us have dinner at least, before we decide whom it is that shall kill you in this most delightful manner."

Twenty minutes later, at a long table piled high with an array of edible delights, Seton was actually managing to eat despite the churning of his stomach.

Adonijah had insisted upon it.

"What did you think of Rousay?" he asked, tearing a hunk of pheasant with his sharp, perfectly straight teeth.

"Beautiful, My Lord," Seton answered. "One can feel the history."

Chasing the meat with a long swallow of mead, Adonijah smiled. "You have done your reading, George. Well done. History indeed. It was our Viking ancestor, Jórkell, who made a shrewd alliance with the Orkney jarls Sigurd Eysteinsson and his son Sigurd the Mighty that made possible what the Ravenskalds presently are. All that we have acquired in terms of wealth, land, and influence over the centuries we owe to him. He was brave, he was wise, and, most important of all, when the time came, Jórkell chose to die a warrior's death rather than betray his ideals. Ever since his own death and burial, the patriarch of our family receives a Viking funeral, exact to his in every detail. Provided he shows the same bravery, wisdom, and honor as did Jórkell. Would your—rather, *will your*—family do the same for you, George Seton? Or, more accurately, what is *left* of you?"

From somewhere below them, Seton heard the ringing of a bell, saving him from having to speak or force down any more food. Standing and waving at Seton to join him, Adonijah grasped his staff from where it leaned on the edge of the table and headed for a door in the rear of the keep.

Handing a torch to Seton and keeping one for himself, Adonijah proceeded down a set of steep stairs, cautioning his guest to watch his step, which, given the subject of their ongoing conversation since his arrival, seemed all together absurd.

A broken neck due to a fall down these stairs seemed preferable to the consequences of breaking his oath to the Freemasons.

Exiting the staircase, Seton found himself staring at two men, their faces bloody and bodies emaciated and in places badly broken, chained to the damp, moss-covered walls.

One of them was partially clothed in the vestments of a Roman Catholic Cardinal. The other, far younger, was naked.

"George, I would like you to meet some other of our guests. Apologies that they did not have time to bathe and dress, or join us for our dinner. This is Marius Adenot who, until recently, was *frequently* enjoying the bed of the buxom niece of a very powerful— and, as you can imagine, very angry—viscount. That is, when he was not taking her from behind in the gardens of the Tuileries Palace, where he served the Duke of Orleans as tutor to the future king of France. His companion here is Cardinal André-Hercule de Fleury, *former tutor* of Louis the Fifth, and one of the men from whom you Jacobites receive your orders."

As Seton sought to process Adonijah's words and what he himself was seeing, a figure emerged from a shadow-hidden passageway deeper inside the torture chamber. In one of his bloodstained hands he held a carpenter's box, from which protruded all manner of bladed, pointed, and serrated implements. In the other was a cage full of rats.

"Ah, at last!" the master of horrors said, the joviality in his voice out of place in this subterranean aberration, which Seton now saw was full of a variety of infernal machinery. "I presume this is Seton. I am Absalom Ravenskald. Sorry I missed dinner... there is always so much to *do*."

As Absalom turned and set himself to work, George Seton, once renowned for his fortitude in the face of troubles, began to cry.

"Continue with your work, brother," Adonijah said, as though Absalom were building a birdhouse, "George and I are going back upstairs."

"Am I not to be tortured here?" Seton asked, embarrassed by the snot that was pouring from his nose.

"Whatever made you think that?" Adonijah asked. "You must get a good night's rest, for then it is on to Edinburgh to take a knee before the Masonic masters that hold the highest offices of the order before returning to London to deliver the Baptist Bowl as originally planned to Anthony Sayer and the traitors of Carteret."

"I do not understand," Seton whispered, falling to his knees in relief and confusion as the man called Marius Adenot began to scream just beyond his field of vision.

"That is why you shall never know the honor of a Viking burial, you traitorous, unworthy bastard," Adonijah hissed before heading up the stairs.

Olivier Levasseur looked upon the fort as the sun set behind it and was overcome with the deepest of grief and remorse, feeling neither the Mouth nor the Vulture, but a man suddenly tired to the very marrow of his bones.

It was near the spot where the *Postillion* had just anchored, on the same beach that he would soon be walking upon, that his fallen friend Bellamy had risen to commodore of the Republic of Pirates—leaving his post as soon as the crews—largely by way of Levasseur's campaigning and manipulation—voted him to it. Levasseur was not one for regret—he had left a life of wealth and privilege in Calais to become a privateer and had turned pirate in the Caribbean islands rather than heed Louis the Fourteenth's order to return to the French Royal Navy.

If the king knew of Levasseur's work with the Star Quorom it was never mentioned. Louis most likely thought the lure of adventure had been too much for a young hothead like him to ignore.

Perhaps, in part, that was true, though he knew where his heart belonged and how righteous was the cause.

"Odd to be back here, yes?" Abraxas Abriendo had snuck up behind him during his revery.

Damned old weezard.

"I wonder eef Sam ever truly believed een zee possibeelity of a *république des pirates* or eef he was only serving zee higher cause."

Abraxas placed his hand on the Frenchman's shoulder. "If you are asking if events of the past year were your fault—if you somehow coerced Samuel Bellamy into doing anything he did not wish to—then you are a lousy specimen of a friend. Bellamy may have been at times naïve, but he *was* a true believer."

"*Oui*, old man. He was truly as you say. Forgeev my doubt. I have much to consider and I mees his council. Eet was upon orders from zee Quorom that I parted company weeth heem in February and proceeded to zee Spaneesh Main. My meeshon there was—"

"Not my business, I know. If it was, I would have been told about it. The Quorom is not shy about ordering us about with a minimum of information. I understand your plight, Olivier. We narrowly missed a dangerous encounter with Captain Vane. What he would have done had he succeeded in surprising us I am loath to imagine. The mirror would now be in the hands of the Ravenskalds. We must never allow that to happen. Although I cannot help but pity that merchantman whom agreed to fly your flag off Block Island to lure him in."

239   To Be a Proper Pyrate

Levasseur turned to face the wizard, leaning against the gunwale. "It was zee mirror that saved us, yet again, Abraxas. Had you not seen Vane approach as we moved south out of Nova Scotia, we would have been hees prey. As for the sheep that pretended to be us, I do not fear for their lives. Vane is full of vinegar and wind, but he knows well enough not to slit zee throats of innocent merchant captains. Damn! How nakeed I feel without Xiang Yu and the might of zee *Oiseau de Proie* off our bow! I pray he has found Cardinal de Fleury, alive and unharmed. Zee time we wasted een coming here... and I do not see Capitaine Thache's flag in zee harbor! Ees he 'out on zee account', as thees cocky Eengleesh say?"

Scanning the harbor, Abraxas said, "It appears so. I tried to tell you as much. Now that he has transformed into this devilish rogue who calls himself Blackbeard, it does his mission no good to lie anchored in New Providence. The same applies to us. Did you believe you could strike an accord with him, after your history?"

"*Oui!*" Levasseur replied, striking his fist upon the gunwale. "Bellamy's death shall unite us. Zee stakes in thees game are now very high. For us all. The navies of our respective empires weel soon come for thees place and anywhere else a pirate calls home. Ah... what ees thees? The flag of *Grand-père* Horneegold approaches on thees longboat here. Ahoy!"

Moments later, Benjamin Hornigold and Henry Jennings were standing upon the deck of the *Postillion*, listening to all Levasseur and Abriendo had to share.

"Edward is in the north Atlantic," Hornigold said, puffing thoughtfully on his pipe, "somewhere near Philadelphia by now, I should think. Had ye not had to take such a circuitous route to come here, ye may have crossed paths. That is likely for the best. I am not sure he would have agreed to a parlay... he might very well have answered with a full complement of cannon!"

"Such a strutting *coq* with hees *rubans rouges* and sparkly hat ropes!" Levasseur said, conjuring a much-needed laugh.

Sharing the laugh to be polite, Hornigold asked, "Will ye be staying with us on New Providence for any length of time?"

"*Oui,*" Levasseur answered. "I am unsure as to how to proceed. I must await word from Xiang Yu. Your hospitaleety ees much appreciated."

"As for me," Abraxas said, "I must seek passage to London. My masters have tasked me with meeting a bookseller and antiquities dealer there. I have put it off for far too long. I will be taking the obsidian mirror with me, after I lock it with a spell. As we have learned, no one can be trusted."

"We shall find a trustworthy captain to take ye to London at the first opportunity," Jennings said. "In the meantime, we invite ye to join us for dinner."

"We graciously accept," Levasseur said, enjoying the look of disagreement on Abraxas Abriendo's face. "I have much to tell thee of our near avoidance of a bloody encounter weeth your former *bon ami* Vane."

Simon Van Vorst, one of the nine survivors of the April nor'easter, looked around the crowded courtroom and knew that he was doomed.

Following seven months living on the absolute minimum of food and drink required to keep them alive, their gaolers had brought the men of the *Whydah* and *Mary Anne* to the bar four days earlier to make their statements of guilt or innocence. There were seven of them, just like today. John Julian, the Miskito Indian, was facing a life of slavery—*and may it be a short life at that*, Van Vorst thought—on the farm of a minister named "Deacon John" Adams.

History would know his son and grandson—John and John Quincey—as the second and sixth US presidents and, respectively, very private and very public abolitionists. The roles they would play, however, were a revolution and eighty years away and did poor John Julian no damned good at all. He attempted to escape several times and once killed a bounty hunter. He met his death on the gallows in 1733.

The other missing man was Thomas Davis, sitting at this moment in gaol, awaiting a separate trial on October 28. The court-appointed lawyer for the accused pirates, a Mister Auchmuty, had asked permission—*damned meekly*, Van Vorst thought—from the thirteen judges to have Davis testify on behalf of his former shipmates. Being that he was himself accused—and no doubt guilty—the judges had refused.

Simon Van Vorst, although a simple man of the sea, was no moron. Of all of them, Davis was most likely to succeed in convincing the judges that Captain Samuel Bellamy forced him into a life of piracy and therefore he would be found not guilty and set free.

Although all of the accused had agreed to declare the same—that they were forced—Davis had one distinct advantage.

He was the only one telling the truth.

In December of the previous year, their former ship, the *Sultana*, accompanied by the *Marianne* under Paulsgrave Williams, had chased down the cargo ship *St. Michael* out of Cork, Ireland. Sorely in need of a carpenter, and learning that Davis possessed those self-same skills, Bellamy had force him to board the *Sultana* and serve its captain and crew, promising to release him at the first opportunity, as forced service was well below the righteous captain's moral standards. However, he proved to be exceptionally good with the mallet, gimplet, and axe, and the crew had stated, with no exaggeration, that they would kill Davis before letting him go.

Under the articles, Bellamy had no choice but to relent.

There the seven of them were, four days ago, trying not to piss themselves as they stood at the bar. Van Vorst led off with a resounding "Not guilty!" followed by five others, a pause, and a heavily accented "*Geel-tee!*" from John Shuan, who spoke not a word of English.

Motioning for the laughing crowd to still themselves, Mister Auchmuty motioned for the court's Sworn Interpreter, a merchant called Peter Lucy, to translate for John Shuan, who could tell he had erred but did not understand how. After a few moments' whispers between he and Lucy, during which the Frenchman's eyes went wide and his head swiveled vigorously back and forth on his veiny, overlong neck, he exclaimed, "*Non geel-tee! Non geel-tee! Non!*"

With the confusion cleared up and the seven pleas recorded, the seven accused went back to the gaol in their heavy chains to await the start of the trial.

Now here they were. Van Vorst stifled the urge to spit as he spied the damned Saver of Souls, Cotton Mathers, sitting in the second row with his Bible pressed to his chest like a newborn on a tit.

As they called the session to order, Van Vorst gazed upon the thirteen judges who held the unnatural right to decide his fate. Eight of them were on His Majesty's Council—that German bastard, George. He was the whole reason they were out on the account! Damn all inbred nobles! Then there was Governor Samuel Shute and his lieutenant, Elisha Hutchinson. Next to them sat William Dunner and John Meinzies from the Vice Admiralty, Collector of Plantation Duties John Jekyll, and Captain Thomas Smart of the ship of war *Squirrel*.

A ridiculous name for such a deadly vessel!

Next came the reading of the indictment by His Majesty's Advocate, a Mister Smith, who droned on in an overly officious and offal-tinged voice about the seven accused "piratically and feloniously... engaging in sundry acts of Piracy, Robbery, and Felony committed as though they were wild, savage beasts!"

In summation, they were villainous all, and God damn their rights and reasons! *Hostis Humani Generis*: enemies of all mankind! It was the very same dung served up daily in ink by the local libel-rag, the *Boston Newsletter*.

As the testimony unfolded, Van Vorst made note of the court recorders scratching busily away... whenever the prosecution or judges spoke. As for the defense put forth by the feeble Mister Auchmuty—who looked as though he would rather be elsewhere—and the pirates' own attempts to convince the judges that they were pirating against their will—barely a word of it was recorded.

Even the Swedish Peter Cornelius Hoof's detailed description of Bellamy ordering him flogged for trying to leave the island of St. Croix after impressment to the crew in February 1716 seemed not to move the crowd.

As the shadows of the setting sun began to fall upon the accused, Van Vorst knew the cause was lost. One by one their names were read: first, his own, followed by John Brown, Thomas Baker, Peter Cornelius Hoof, Hendrick Quintor, and John Shuan. The Frenchman began to cry as the merchant Peter Lucy translated what they all heard loud and clear:

On November 15—the court having found each of them guilty of piracy—they would hang by the neck until dead (dead, dead).

As their gaolers led them from the courtroom, Van Vorst glared at the one man whose name the judges had not called.

Thomas South, the smiling bastard, had apparently convinced them Bellamy had forced him into piracy. They were releasing him from his chains as Van Vorst exited the room.

Better it would have been, he thought, *if the sea had taken us all.*

As Baron William Craven descended the steps that led to the Mammon Lodge deep beneath Lord Carteret's mansion, he felt his stomach clench as thoughts of all that he had endured in the dungeon and nearby replica of a Sultan's harem hall that sat just above his head flooded his system with revulsion and regret.

It was on New Year's Day 1716 that he had submitted to Mammon's leather-winged embrace, allowing the terrible demon to feast upon his blood. This after enduring the vile ritual of *blooding* during a foxhunt at Carteret's hands. The effects of either event were not what he and Carteret had hoped. Craven still lacked anyone's respect. The Ravenskalds and the Family still treated him as less than a man—no better than his idiot brother Charles, whom they had dispatched from his position as deputy governor of South Carolina a year ago April. Given that the Abermarle in North Carolina was William's domain as a Lord Proprietor, this was less than ideal.

To add to his distress, Carteret's summoning him in the middle of the night did not bode well. As Palatine—chief among the Lords Proprietors—and head of the Mammon Lodge, Carteret was no one with whom to trifle, and word amongst the board of the Royal African Company was that the Ravenskalds had failed to invite him to Castle Rushen as planned. They had further conspired to deprive the Palatine of the one object he most desired.

The Baptist Bowl.

Instead, they had sent it with the traitor George Seton back to Anthony Sayer, head of the Free Masonic Grand Lodge, also in London—a man whom Carteret, who never had any shortage of enemies, now considered to be one of his greatest.

In the torture chamber just above them, in which Craven had witnessed innumerable atrocities as part of his "training," he could hear the screams of the poor bastard who had delivered the news to Carteret two days earlier.

Not bothering with a greeting as Craven entered the altar room, Carteret, dressed in a hooded black robe with red trim Craven had never seen, growled, "When I find George Seton—and I shall, William—I shall make the Masonic payment for oath-breaking seem like a flogging with a water-logged noodle." As William played the elements of the "payment" in his head—including a slit throat and tongue torn out by the roots—Carteret continued his rant. "The failures of Devon Ross and his inept pirate captain and the betrayal of Andrew Colson and that worthless slug Bolingbroke have pushed me past the point of sanity. The taking of the *Whydah* by that bastard Bellamy could not burn me more than if I were the owner of the vessel rather than Humphry Morice. Mammon has failed us, William, and so we must look elsewhere for the power we require to coldly avenge these wrongs."

Dreading the answer, William asked, "And where have you decided to look, Lord Carteret?"

In answer, the master of the lodge clapped his hands three times, and a door behind him opened. Twelve robed and hooded members of the lodge entered, each pair escorting a naked child. The children's blank stares indicated to William that their captors had drugged them.

Gasping as he turned away, William prayed that he might have a great draught of whatever it was the children had imbibed so that he would not have to witness what was no doubt coming next.

"Man up, damn you!" Carteret yelled, grasping Craven's face and turning it toward the procession. "Take note, William, that these are not savages. Five of them are the fetid offspring of Jacobites. One is the granddaughter of George Seton. I will enjoy most deliciously feeling her life ebbing out beneath the Abraham Blade."

Defocusing his eyes, which he kept open lest Carteret try to pry them open, Craven whispered, "And the sixth?"

"Most regrettably, time was short. He is a scabby urchin. A climbing boy, they call them—making stale bread and weak coin for cleaning out chimneys. It ends unwell for them, William. Blindness, black blood from the lungs, some half-pissed nobleman having the fireplace lit while one of them is up inside… I am giving him a gift. For that matter, since the destruction of the Jacobites is nigh, I am giving a gift to them all. It is an honor to have one's throat opened by the Abraham Blade. Especially on this newly installed altar I had brought from Avebury. Its dimensions are perfect for our purposes." Carteret looked at his reflection in the gleaming Abraham Blade. "They will come for this, you know. The Ravenskalds. They are ever more emboldened by the fruits of *my* efforts… Do you know the story of this blade, my friend? I believe you need to, for our ritual to work!"

Gesturing for Craven to sit upon the floor, as though he was a child in need of a bedtime story rather than a baron and Lord Proprietor, Carteret threw his arms wide, his eyes now agleam in the torchlight like the blade he held white-knuckle-tight in his hand.

"Abraham, seized by a righteous need to prove himself to God— what a pair of imbeciles, William!, both the old man and his *Abba*— bound Isaac to a large, flat boulder in the Land of Moriah, at the future site of Solomon's Temple. The Ravenskald ties to that site are deep and awash in blood... a tale for another time. A great many Jews believe that Abraham knew it was all a show... that his God would never ask him to *actually* murder his son, but consider the abominations detailed in the Old Testament, William... their ancient, bearded Papa is exactly the type to demand such a sacrifice! Consider the destruction of the Nephilim and the horrors visited upon Job by some minor demon with God's encouragement and approval! Better to worship in Hell than kneel to such a bitter old bastard. No, no... I can assure you that Abraham would have gone through with it if some voice—perhaps not God's—had not told him to stop. *Mock* rites of passage are reserved for cowards like the Masons."

"I have read that the Muslims believed that Isaac would have gladly sacrificed himself," Craven muttered, needing to hear the sound of his own voice simply to prove that this was not some terrible nightmare.

Carteret raised his brows. "Perhaps. Likely, even. Some day, William—perhaps this very day—I may ask you to play the willing Isaac to my eager Abraham. Would you, William? I need to know. Abonijah Ravenskald did not give me a choice when he set the venomous *tanin* that lives in the Aaron Staff upon me. It is important, acquiescence... I believe that..."

Not able to offer an answer, Craven posed a question. "How did the knife come to the Mammon Lodge, and to you, my Lord?"

"Ah... yes. Let the sedatives work upon the children a little longer. Quite clever, William. Compassion, even in the face of abject evil. I grant you a boon because the answer is important. Isaac, from that day, jealously possessed the knife. Perhaps it was better not to give his father the means, should their blood-lusting God ask a second time. Marrying Rebecca, Isaac had two sons—Jacob and Esau. Jacob, born mere minutes after his older brother, steals Esau's birthright and secures his blind father's blessing. An embarrassment of a family, William! Lack of loyalty leads to all manner of misery. Mark that well.

"Now we come to core of it. Jacob, found out by Esau, who vowed to murder him, fled Beer-sheba to seek sanctuary with an uncle in Haran. It was in the middle of the night that a ladder came down from Heaven, which Jacob climbed. He was given by the Archangel Uriel a set of codes and their secret formulas—forget this drivel about him speaking to God. Uriel told him that he would have a son with the ability to decipher dreams... it was to this son that he was to give these gifts."

"Joseph," William whispered, "of the coat of many colors. The message from Uriel… Is that why Joseph was favored by his father above his many brothers…. Why they sold him into slavery?"

Carteret nodded. "For twenty pieces of silver. Betrayal after betrayal, William. The bible is full of them, testaments old and new. Joseph endured almost as much as I have… Falsely accused of rape by Potiphar's wife, Zuleikha, after he rejected her, he was imprisoned. It was there that Uriel appeared to him and dictated a very special scroll, which bears his name. A scroll encoded by the ciphers given to Jacob by that same sulfur-tongued archangel."

"What of the Abraham blade?" William asked, now fully invested in the story.

"Jacob took it as part of his stolen birthright. *Just what Abonijah wishes to do to* me… His son Reuben hid it, upon his death and burial, in the Cave of Machpelah—on land purchased by Abraham three and a half millennia ago. There it remained for many generations. The land eventually became the city of Hebron. Herod, King of Judea, built a structure there so that the people could worship their patriarchs.

"Still, the Abraham Blade remained hidden in the cave, until the coming of the Crusaders. It was the ninth Grand Master of the Knights Templar and a knight of the Crown of Aragon, Arnau de Torroja, who found it in 1182." Pulling himself from his reverie as he stood staring into the sparkling blade, Carteret said, all trace of the storyteller's mesmerizing tone gone, "How it was taken from the Templars by the Ravenskalds is a tale for another time. The moment has come to summon our new master, Moloch… his meal grows cold and tired."

Raising the hood of his robe over his head, Carteret nodded to the dark priests of the lodge, who brought the children forth, one by one, as they began to chant, *"Wa hay-nah sa ma ka Dominus. Mu-kah do hay-nah ka. Tach ma, tach mu, sa mu sa Dominus. Co-mama sa. Co-mama sa Dominus…"*

As they laid them upon the altar, Carteret slit their throats with the Abraham Blade. As their blood flowed into a large gold bowl, he intoned, "Master Moloch, oh great and mighty *melekh*, we offer you these children, soon to be passed through the fire—*le-ha'avir ba-esh*—in the way prescribed by the servants of Baal and the idols of Canaan and Baal. In the way of your servants in Carthage and Assyria. Accept our sacrifice and welcome us into your service!"

Craven put his hands to his ears as the chanting of the twelve priests rose to its unnatural crescendo: *"Wa hay-nah sa ma ka Dominus. Mu-kah do hay-nah ka. Tach ma, tach mu, sa mu sa*

Dominus. CO-MAMA SA. CO-MAMA SA DOMINUS! MOLOCH! MOLOCH! MOLOCH! DOMINUS MOLOCH!"

As the very stones of the lodge began to crack, William heard a roar, as the beast appeared through a portal of red and yellow fire.

Bull-faced, with strands of tangled beard that resembled seaweed, Moloch towered above the tallest of the priests. William squealed in fright as Moloch turned his head toward the last of the sacrifices—Seton's granddaughter—as Carteret, his eyes rolled up white in his head, dragged the Abraham Blade ever so slowly across her pale, delicate throat. Stretching his neck at the sight and smell of her bright, running blood, Moloch dragged his two short horns, which protruded from either side of his head at right angles, on the ceiling. Although they were blunt, Craven knew they were deadly. His eyes glowing like coals in the hottest part of the fire in the dead of night, their new king and master snorted and stomped the ground with his ebony, cloven hoof. Craven, despite himself, marveled at the demon's smooth skin, bronzed from millennia within the flames. Barrel-chested, with long, unnaturally tapered fingers with sharp nails at their ends, Moloch took the limp body of the porcelain-skinned corpse in his thickly muscled arms and spread his short, fanned wings as he licked the last of the blood from the gaping wound in the neck. Craven shivered at the sight of the open wings, which were nothing like the leathery bat wings of Mammon, but similar to those of the Assyrians, Sumerians, Babylonians, and Mesopotamians depicted in art and books of magic.

One by one, the priests handed the corpses to Moloch, who threw them through the portal of fire and into whatever hellish realms those six damned children would walk for all of their spectral lives.

As the bull-demon and infernal king turned back toward those assembled around the altar, Craven began to vomit a thick green bile.

It would be hours before he stopped.

Pulling upon his oar as the *Ranger*'s longboat neared a spot on the shore between two docked merchant vessels as a heavy rain began to fall, Joseph Stanton wondered how much more he would have to endure.

During the past five weeks, Charles Vane and Devon Ross had been damned near insufferable. Although they had ceased arguing with one another, each had taken cruel—at times brutal—liberties with the crew. Joseph most of all. Neither one had forgiven him for disrupting the planned rendezvous in Boston by seeking out his sisters, nor for each domino that had fallen since. While quoting Shakespeare's *Tempest* like a pair of mad actors, they would punch or kick him to emphasis a word or phrase.

Ross, aptly cast as the creature Caliban, had pulled a fistful of Joseph's hair while he was using the absurdly named holystone to whiten the *Ranger*'s planks, saying, "As wicked dew as e'er my mother brushed/With raven's feature from unwholesome fen/Drop on you both! A southwest *blow* on ye/And *blister* ye all o'er!" as he smashed his fist into the side of Joseph's head before pressing a lit fuse to his cheek.

Joseph had taken that, and all the other beatings, in silence.

Their time would come, same as anyone's, if he was patient.

Patient he continued to be. They had taken their time sailing to Philadelphia, boarding a number of merchant ships along the way, at times torturing their captains for information on the whereabouts of Levasseur and Edward Thache, and causing far more havoc than was prudent in such well-protected waters. There were days at a time when they beached on some tiny island off Massachusetts, gazing toward the shore and celebrating the demise of Bellamy and his crew.

Joseph hoped with all his heart that counted among the corpses the riotous sea had claimed was that sheep-shagging bastard Angus MacGregor.

"Quit yer daydreamin' an' get us tied up, Stanton!" Ross was yelling, stepping out of the longboat and guiding it into the soft sand just ahead. "An' be quick about it. We ain't lettin' ya out a' our sight, an' we need outta this rain an' into the arms a' some large-breasted lovelies wit'out no furthah delay."

Charles Vane only nodded in agreement, checking the charges in his pistols and sliding an extra dagger into his belt.

"Aye, Mister Ross," Joseph said, doing as he was told with all due haste and efficiency.

As he tied the final knot, he imagined it affixed around Devon Ross's neck, while pitying any unfortunate forced to lay under covers with such a sordid son of a whore as *Faccia del Diavolo*.

"Damn this rain, Conall! Will it never cease? How do these Philadelphians endure it?"

Blackbeard was in a rare mood—helped no doubt by generous draughts of rum and ale—and Conall MacBlaquart was enjoying it as they sat beneath an overhang outside a tavern called the Rusty Mallet and Twice Bent Nail.

As focused upon vengeance for Bellamy's men as Blackbeard was, their abundant success in the waters off Delaware and New Jersey in the previous weeks had softened his visage and his way with the crew. Although routines and expectations were far from lax, the trio of officers—William Howard, quartermaster; Daniel Herriot, sailing master; and William Scott, boatswain—were instructed to shorten watches and lengthen rations when appropriate and safe to do so.

An outpouring of hearty welcomes and offers of lodging, free meals, and free women had met Blackbeard upon their arrival in Philadelphia three days prior, starting with the pilot and harbor master and extending with every step Edward Thache took. Never one to divulge much at all about his past, Angus surmised that sometime after leaving the employ of the Royal Navy, Blackbeard had spent considerable time in the place called the "City of Brotherly Love."

"Another ale, Angus? This is rather fine... Scottish methinks," Blackbeard said, wiping the remains of his most recent emptied mug from his lips and whiskers, although the dark spots on the ribbons in his beard betrayed his messy intoxication. "Or, if ye would rather, I know a lovely little thing named Mara that might enjoy a change of scenery, if ye take my meanin'."

Shaking his head, Conall replied, quietly, "I am fain at present, Cap'n. An' raemember tae call mae Conall, noot Angus. Who knoos what pryin' ears mae bae aboot?"

"What pryin' ears indeed, ye black-hearted bastard!"

Conall felt a pair of hands entwine themselves in the collar of his shirt and in the tails of his House of Stuart–patterned plaid headscarf and hot breath raise the hairs on his neck as his unknown assailant pulled him up from his stool, dragging him into the rain-soaked mud of the thoroughfare.

Kicking out behind him with both of his boots and connecting with his attacker's groin, Conall felt the pair of hands slacken enough for him to twist away. As he rolled through the thickening mud, nearly avoiding being crushed by the rear wheel of a passing wagon, he turned around to identify whom it was who had assaulted him.

As Conall took in the pained, angry face of Joseph Stanton, he tried to lift himself from the mud as his committed enemy charged him. Before he could rise to his knees, Joseph crashed into his midsection, driving his back into three inches of black, sucking mud.

For the next several minutes, they traded blows to one another's faces and bodies, bringing blood and cries of pain as a growing circle of onlookers created a fighting ring twelve feet wide around them.

Conall could hear, although just barely—his ears were ringing and caked with mud—the harsh voices of Charles Vane and Devon Ross cheering Joseph on in his bloodlust. Several voices, including Stede Bonnet's high-pitched singsong, called out for Conall as well.

The one voice he could not hear, but wished to, was Blackbeard's.

As Joseph's knee connected with his groin, Conall's midday meal of roast capon and potatoes bubbled up in his throat, causing him to turn and retch into the mud.

Joseph again tangled his hand in the tails of Conall's headscarf. As the man who hated him more than even his cousin James hissed into his ear about his being better blessed to have died in the storm that took Sam Bellamy, Conall felt the cold steel of a knife press against his arm.

Then Joseph was yelling as someone pulled him away. Conall felt his headscarf take a few hunks of hair in its knot as his assailant held fast to its ends.

Feeling himself pulled to his feet, Conall looked into the eyes of a widely smiling Blackbeard. "Did ye think I had abandoned ye, my lad? Bastard pulled a knife from his boot. That ain't hardly fair now, is it? Ye make me proud, Conall... shot by yer cousin at the order of yer uncle... if not by our African boy's magic almost certainly killed by Alvarado César—who now respects ye no end... and currently near-to pig-stuck by Mister Stanton... rather impressive fer a lad who not three years ago could barely swim or tie a proper knot! Yer a real scallywag now, with so many wanting to kill ye. And I am willin' to wager yer uncle would, upon hearin' this list, now welcome ye home with open arms. All ye need is a good, long scar on yer face and it looks like Stanton's fixin' to grant it to ye. Look sharp now. This is yer rite of passage."

As Blackbeard stepped out of the way, Joseph stepped toward Conall, a wicked-looking blade in his hand.

Looking around for a plank, barrelhead, or something else with which to defend himself, Conall snapped his head toward the sound of a sharp, shrill whistle.

Alvarado César, his arm in a sling after Caesar's obeah had snapped it like kindling in two places, was holding out his knife with his working hand. "Take this *cuchillo*, *mi hermano valiente*, and finish this *hijo de puta de cerdo despiadado* so that we all may dance in a mix of the rain, his *sangre*, and the mud!"

Catching the knife and turning toward Joseph, Conall said, "If this is how it has tae bae, thaen it is time wae finish it."

As the two bloody, mud-soaked men moved inward toward each other, they both heard a voice that stopped them cold in their tracks.

"Angus MacGraegor! Are ye off yer haid? What in God's name are ye doon?"

There in front of him, like a vision come from Heaven, stood Ailish MacDonald, her face a mask of anger and disbelief Angus wanted nothing more than to kiss a thousand times in some faraway, peaceful place.

Then Joseph let out a roar, and Conall felt himself fall.

Finis (fer noo…)

ABOUT THE AUTHOR

Joey Madia is a novelist, screenwriter, historical educator, playwright, actor, and director. He also writes narratives and designs the puzzles for Escape Rooms, based on literature and historical events. He is founding editor of www.newmystics.com, a literary site created in 2002 that houses the work of more than 130 writers and artists from around the world. His website is newmystics.com/joey. He also has profiles at Stage 32, Instagram, Amazon, Facebook, Goodreads, Film Freeway, Reedsy, and IMDb.

Made in the USA
Middletown, DE
15 October 2021